HOME TO INDIA

by
Jacquelin Singh

THE PERMANENT PRESS
SAG HARBOR, NEW YORK

Copyright © 1997 by Jacquelin Singh

Library of Congress Cataloging-in-Publication Data

Singh, Jacquelin.
  Home to India / by Jacquelin Singh.
    p. cm.
  ISBN 1-877946-85-0
  1. Americans—Travel—India—Fiction. 2. Married women—
India—
  Fiction. I. Title.
  PR9499.3.S528H6   1997
  823—dc20   96-21746
                                                                    CIP

First Edition, June, 1997

Manufactured in the United States of America

THE PERMANENT PRESS
Noyac Road
Sag Harbor, NY 11963

For
Ranjit

Author's Note

Before 1952, when the Hindu Code Bill was passed in the Indian Parliament, it was legal for a Hindu (or Sikh) to have more than one wife at the same time, while divorce was virtually impossible.

Jacquelin Singh
New Delhi
April 1997

Contents

Carol, Now   7
Summer   21
Monsoon   59
Fall   101
Winter   117
Spring   151
Carol, Again   189
Summer, Again   195

". . . the author of every book is a fictitious character whom the existent author invents to make him the author of his fictions."

—Italo Calvino in *If on a Winter's Night a Traveler*

Carol, Now

1

I have been saving Helen for later. I have spent an adult lifetime doing it. All these years, stray memories of her have been hovering like uninvited guests, ready to step nimbly across the threshold. And I have made polite excuses. I knew coming to grips with her—the *idea* of her—would take more time and energy than I could allow. Once in, she would take up too much of my attention. I had to think about a career (which I eventually had, and am now retired from). I had to think about renting apartments, buying houses, moving into condominiums. I had to plan vacations and sabbaticals, engineer judicious moves from college to college, university to university, committee to committee, consultancy to consultancy, until the carousel stopped, and I had to get off. Now, attention is all I have. And time. It occurs to me today, as I go through old letters and papers, that this is the "later" I have been saving Helen for.

I have to deal with her once and for all, so that I can make my final move unencumbered. They have said I can take only one or two possessions with me to the new place—a few photographs, my favorite books, a souvenir or two—whatever will fit into one room. And I know Helen isn't one of these. There won't be space for what she was and what she might have finally become.

There is, in fact, so much uncertainty in the accounts which various friends gave of her over the years that scarcely one of them is reliable. Helen was, to be sure, an ordinary girl, or so she appeared. At the same time she was a bundle of conflicting loyalties and contradictions. She remains for me, after so many years, an enigma.

Was she carried off like that by her own whims and im-

9

pulses against her sense of survival? Or was it the logical outcome of all that went before? None of her letters ever helped me decide. And she wrote to me often, in the beginning, when she first went out there. They were long letters of mundane detail. It is possible she was trying to prove that I had been wrong that day when I declared she was going on an adventure. The idea appeared to quietly infuriate her.

"I don't know why you keep hugging that idea, Carol," she had said to me. "Why don't you let it go?"

"But what you're considering doing *is* unusual," I remember saying.

We were sitting in the coffee shop in the International House at Berkeley, she looking out through the big plate glass windows onto Bancroft Avenue and I facing her and the door that led into the Great Hall.

"Unusual?" she took up. "That's what everybody seems to think, even if they don't say it," she said, studying the irrelevance of the spoon in the cup of sugarless, black coffee on the table before her.

And so when she wrote to me afterwards, her letters dwelt on the ordinary, the externals: what the weather was like, how the food tasted, how the relentless throb and hum of insect life filled the days and nights. Sometimes she enclosed snapshots, not her own excellent pictorial compositions, but ordinary, grainy prints of herself and Tej against blurred backgrounds or amongst a host of smiling, foreign faces. They seemed part of her compulsion to prove us all wrong, to let us know she was *not* having an adventure, but simply living life.

I searched in vain between the lines of her letters for an indication of what it meant to her to go so far away. What it was like to go back in time by centuries. Surely there would have been the initial thrill, followed by a seizure of panic at the realities of life lived without technology.

There she was, becoming a part of, or at any rate living intimately with, the fixtures of another culture, knowing that she was not like someone on a guided tour, but locked into a process that offered no end in sight. The language factor, daunting enough in itself, would have been just one dimension. And what was it like to be taken in like that, into the household of strangers ten thousand miles away, not as a guest or casual visitor, but as a *bride*? Tej's bride?

Helen attached no comments to her accounts of the externals, so I will have to make wild guesses (not knowing the place, never having been there) and some calculated surmises, based on my knowledge of her—at least as she was before she went out there. The one impression she was bent on conveying was that there were everywhere and in every situation correspondences, similarities in degree or kind, to life as she'd always lived it. But what these were remained unexplained in her accounts, and in any case, after all this time—forty years—it is beyond me to recall what actually these correspondences were.

Everyone predicted she would be back in Berkeley by year's end. But by then I had completed my master's degree and had got my first job, in Michigan, dogsbody to a classics professor, working on a translation of Dante. I scarcely noticed that Helen's letters, at first getting more infrequent, had almost stopped coming altogether. She might have lost my new address, or indeed might never have received it. Or was back in Berkeley and didn't want to disclose the fact to any of the old crowd, who were in any case scattered to the four corners by that time. I knew she would not want me in particular to know she had come back, at least until she had pulled herself together, because I had been set against her going in the first place. I suppose as I was her best friend, she would have expected me to understand her, or anyway not *try* to understand her, but simply and unconditionally accept what appeared to me to be her own special brand of lunacy, a peculiarly self-destructive kind. Her return would have signaled a kind of defeat. And Helen didn't like defeats any more than anyone else did. I will never know for certain whether that is what it turned out to be, because I lost track of her for a while about the time my own life got complicated.

First, there was the dismaying fact that the Dante professor, with whom I was hopelessly and abjectly—now as I recall it—in love, was nearly twice my age and besides was married. Then, because he was in the Army Reserve and the Korean War had started that summer, he was called up. He went off to attend a crash course in Korean for intelligence personnel,

11

half a continent away, and I had to face my first abortion alone. Instead of stepping out onto the Dali landscape of the postwar scene, holding his hand for reassurance and waiting for him to reveal the future to me with one parting of the curtain, I sat alone on the treeless plain amongst the soft watches, the crutches, and the bemused, burning giraffes, dealing with the scene as best I could. I sat there, a young woman of the time, with a shoulder-length pageboy bob (achieved by the nightly application of pin curlers, unaided by sprays, foams, and mousses) in my uniform of cardigan, pleated plaid skirt, navy blue blazer, white buck saddle ox-fords and lots of red lipstick. The demure exterior concealed a person inside more at home in the Dali landscape than an observer would have dreamed.

I wondered if Helen had had to discard all her cardigans and white blouses with round, lace-edged collars for some pastel-colored sari as soon as she got there. This trivial idea occurred to me as I read through a letter of hers (I have it in front of me even now) which reached me at a time when I was obsessed with the growing swell separating the pleats of my plaid skirt, too big now for my navy blue blazer to hide. I teetered somewhere between panic and hysteria while contemplating that very real, small being I would have to say goodbye to even before it took a breath. And yet, the look of sweet complacency that distinguished the faces of my female contemporaries was, as I recall, still quite intact on my own features, even if nothing else in my life was.

After my double loss, the father and the child, there was always Dante. Besides, I drew comfort from the fact that my predicament (if not I myself, Carol Thorpe) had been celebrated in lofty lines of iambic hexameter in many an epic scene and my tears dissipated in the sorrows of other, nobler spirits. They dwelt in other places, other times far grander than my own, simply for being mythical, remote. And so it was at infrequent intervals, while lighting a cigarette after dinner (in a new student housing complex now, in a different city) or walking back from another, distant university library in the cold night, that I remembered Helen Graziani, the way one seizes on an idea at such times, like a hand grasping a live electrical appliance it can't let go of.

12

"It's as if everybody thinks I'm some kind of fool, doing something different just to escape being mediocre," I remembered Helen saying. The corners of her mouth turned up in a short smile, but her green eyes weren't laughing. "You imagine I'm out for adventure or something?" she said. "Some kind of lark?"

"If not for adventure, then for what?" I asked.

I don't believe she heard my question and I don't believe she was interested in it, because just then her attention became riveted on something outside, beyond the window, in the middle distance. Her hand replaced the spoon in the saucer, but she didn't let go of the handle. For a moment that stretched too far, there was nothing to give evidence that she was even breathing.

I turned around to see what had changed her to stone, and as I did so, the scene outside fell into focus. In the distance, fog came swirling in through the Golden Gate, skimming the bridge cables, crowning the city. The middle distance was designed only to support the Campanile, now striking . . . twelve? The foreground swarmed with students heading up the hill to lunch. An unextraordinary sight to my eyes. By the time I turned around again, Helen was looking at me. "You're dead wrong," she said, "like everybody else." There was an odd moment when I thought she was going to laugh outright. But she didn't. She had a joke she did not want to share.

The scene rearranges itself. The philosophy major (no one knows his name) is sitting alone at his usual table by a pillar in the middle of the coffee shop reading a paperback novel and ripping out the pages, crumpling them up, and throwing them away as he finishes reading each one. Four Hungarian refugees, the burden of life lived on the run still upon them years after their escape and deliverance, argue furiously over a bid at bridge. Streams of other residents shoulder their way into the crowded space that is blue with cigarette smoke and fluorescent lights. "Erotica," she of the elegant profile, dangling earrings, and ivory Florentine skin, makes her entrance like a mascot in the midst of a pack of intellectuals. She is complacently unconcerned about their arguments over Proust, not bothering even to pretend to understand, and meeting their profoundest insights with dimwitted silence. The conversation has been in progress for more than a week now. She is their Muse, her mere presence working its magic on their brains when creative thought has given out. Behind her cool gaze may lie an insight or two, who knows? Besides, she is decorative.

This noon, as usual, the place is noisy and disordered. Hamburgers and french fries are being passed along, and cherry cokes; mugs of coffee are being handed over the counter. An Indian girl, all sari and black hair, is balancing one in either hand, trying to get through the jam to her companion at a far table, a Pakistani who owns a car.

Was it before or after Helen had looked out the plate glass window so intently that the subject came up of her plans, much speculated about and mystifying. It might have been before. Perhaps it *had* been a peculiar way to put it, an *adventure*. Was it my word choice that offended her? Did it suggest something exploitive, some disgraceful motive that denied someone their humanity?

"I don't know why you keep harping on that," she said. Or had she said, "I don't know why you keep *insisting* on that?" *Harping* was probably her word; *insisting* mine.

"Forget I said it," I replied. Or I think I did. Or perhaps going over this scene so many times in my remembering imagination I am adding some things that might have been good or helpful to say at the time, but hadn't actually been said. I'm quite certain, however, that I went on to suggest that she was very brave.

"That's another strange word," Helen took up immediately. "That and *adventure*. I'm not going tiger shooting." Her manner, usually so straightforward, struck me as mocking and inexplicably unpleasant. "I'm not even going to go live amongst wild elephants. Just people. Like you and me."

"You know and I know there are many kinds of bravery," I said. Or perhaps I just sat there noticing the way she fumbled with her lighter as she took out a cigarette. Perhaps I just sat there, without even saying that, because surely she knew, and was merely pretending not to know, not to acknowledge, the other kinds of bravery that would present their demands when the time came.

14

I'm trying to remember what precisely was said (it has become important to me now that I'm putting all my things away). I'm also trying to discover why this particular occasion and not others comes to mind in relentless detail. Why I keep recalling the way the coffee shop felt that morning (like a too-warm garment), the sound of friends' voices at nearby tables, the rattle of plates and silverware, even the scraping of chairs and the shuffling of feet on the tile floor. It was an ordinary day, a working day. I had already gone to my Greek seminar, and the effort of sitting through the presentation by a Viennese refugee bent on trotting out trivia had made me hungry. I ordered a Spanish omelette and toast and sat waiting at the counter for it to be ready so I could move on to a table by the window. When I turned around, I saw Helen. She was already there, saving me a place.

"I overslept," she said when I sat down opposite her, as if some explanation were due. "Missed my Goethe seminar." She was halfway through a cigarette and black coffee. As always, she had her twin lens Rolleicord along. It sat in its shabby case amongst the notebooks on the table beside her.

"This is by way of breakfast," she said. "I don't feel like having anything else."

She sat with her elbows on the table, circling the white mug of black coffee with her white hands, her fingers still holding the cigarette and her wrists emerging white and stark from the pushed-up sleeves of her black cardigan. Like most tall women, she had, as if by design, arranged herself in the act of sitting down so that legs, arms, torso—all were composed, as it were, into an agreeable whole. She hadn't bothered to do her hair in a coronet of braids that day, but had simply left it loose to frame her face. The flat lighting of the room illumined her features and made them animated. No shadows settled there. Only her eyes, restless and bright with impatience, looked as though she had had no sleep. And then I remembered seeing her and Tej, in the midst of the ritual coffee break at eleven the night before, rush, laughing, through the swinging doors out into the lobby and down the stairs.

Someone at our table (labeled the "intellectual table" perhaps because it was frequented by Englishmen whose Oxbridge accents lent "tone" to the hot discussions) had said something at the time about Helen "crossing over." I suppose what he meant by that was that she was nowadays more to be seen at the Indo-Pakistani table than at ours. She often sat enthralled by the company and the conversation, overheard tables away. It was as if these Punjabis, with their shared heritage, language, and culture, were surprised to suddenly find themselves on opposite sides of an international border and needed to talk about it . . . loudly. This proved more gripping to Helen than our prolonged arguments over the virtues of hypocrisy (it's better to believe and betray than not to believe at all), or the vice of mediocrity and ways to avoid it at all costs. Not even the presence amongst us of a couple of ex-Resistance fighters, recently arrived from France and high on the new existentialist writers whose books and articles they had brought with them, was enough to hold her interest.

As we sat there in the coffee shop that morning, it was obvious Helen didn't want to talk about herself and Tej. "*Tej* rhymes with *rage*, not *wedge*," I remembered her saying once, correcting my pronunciation of his name. "You could also say it rhymes with *sage*, which is more like it," she added with a laugh. "He's more wise than angry." Now she didn't even want to mention him. For a moment his image came to mind. It was easy to picture him. He had a way, though slight of build, of filling up a space, enclosing everything around him in his aura. It had something to do with his musicianship, with the affair with his sitar that he celebrated, inviting all who listened to share his passion. But I'm making him larger than life. In any case I guessed from the way Helen looked around the crowded room searching for something else to talk about that she did not want to discuss him. We sat there without saying anything, I attending to my Spanish omelette and noting that the onions in the sauce were underdone; Helen lighting another cigarette.

"Are you really going away forever with your Sikh friend?" I asked, bringing up the subject again. If Tej had been just another enthusiasm in her store of enthusiasms, she would have been open and frank and amusing. As it was, mention of him caused her to withdraw behind a show of vagueness and inattention.

16

"Is that what people are saying?" she said without answering me.

"What about your folks?" I went on. If she had been someone else I would have said "family"; but Helen's people (like mine) were definitely folks. I hoped mention of them would provoke some response beyond her evasive counterquestions. I knew her mother, especially, was bound to lie at the bottom of a coil of any uncertainties she might have.

My remembering this now, after so many years have passed, is hard to explain. Why in such detail? Why this occasion? Why, even in those early days in Michigan did I keep going over it in my mind, at all odd hours, in strange places, amidst my own crises? She was, it is true, a good friend, and like a sister, even taken for granted. But what did her fate have to do with mine, or mine with hers, to make me obsessed with it? What happened to her? Why did she suddenly go silent after that last puzzling letter?

In particular, I need to know why this brief scene in the International House coffee shop that late morning has so taken hold. Sometimes I think the details I claim to remember are only my elaborations, variations on a theme recalled in old age. I wonder, for example, if I actually did ask her about her family on that occasion or if it was later, when it appeared she was determined to go away after all.

I can hear her voice now, the way it went faint as though she had wilfully turned down the volume: "What about my folks?" she said.

I had her at last! It was, then, not the first time she had considered her mother, her father, her three sisters, and all those Italian relatives. The fact was not lost on me that she had parried yet another question of mine with a question of hers.

"How do they feel about your going away?" I persisted.

When she understood I was not going to stop until I had an answer, she said, "They don't know anything about it."

I tried not to look surprised. "I see," I said, as I let this sink in. "Well, I guess you can look upon it as a kind of elopement then? But the distance is so great between here and . . ." I hesitated again.

"Now it's an *elopement*. Not an adventure any more, but an

17

elopement," she said. "Why do you insist on dramatizing it?" She smiled. I knew her well enough to realize that beneath her offhand dismissal lay a fierce reluctance to say anything further about Tej, about going away with him, about leaving everything here—family, country, years of study, all kinds of human investments that had nothing to do with money or time.

"If it's not an elopement," I said, "then what will it be?"

I don't think she heard my question. And it is always here that I stop (as she did, to look out the plate glass window) and try to go on with what happened next. I shall try to conjure it up once more. She's looking out the window. I follow her gaze out toward the fog-wrapped city across the Bay, with the streets of Berkeley spilling away down the hills onto the waterfront, the day sunny this side, the Campanile striking the hour, unreal blue sky, theatrical clouds.

It's almost fall, and I know without seeing it that Faculty Glade it still all green grass, minus the pink-and-white daisies now, and that Strawberry Creek still cuts its way, as it has to, through the verdure. The air is chilly outside, but not cold, and I know without feeling it that a smart breeze is whipping the foliage of the eucalyptus trees down by the Forestry Building. Somewhere outside Sather Gate undergraduates are waiting to meet friends between classes or stopping to read the posters, sharing space on the steps of Wheeler Hall with the Great Danes from the fraternity houses, or just sitting in the sun.

None of these everyday sights could be the cause of Helen's sudden and complete attention. Whom or what had she seen outside? Under the force of her concentration, all else hung suspended. When I turned around again, she was already standing up, gathering her things, slinging the strap of her camera bag over her shoulder, ready to go. For an instant, I had the irrational notion that she had been appropriated, taken over, possessed, so that, although the young woman in front of me *looked* like Helen, she was really somebody else. The illusion passed as quickly as it came.

"What will it be?" I asked again.

"Nothing. I don't know," she said. "In any case, you're dead

18

wrong, like everybody else." She got up. "I've got to go now," she said, and hurried away.

It might have been her final goodbye, but it wasn't. It doesn't seem to me that she has ever really taken her leave, even after years of my not hearing from her. I have one of her letters in front of me. It's one I picked up from the pile just now, and it happens to be one I got from her early on. It's dated June 26, 1950.

"Dear Carol," it says, in the timeless voice that memory confers on the writers of old letters rediscovered, "Here I am . . ."

Summer

2

" . . . halfway around the world from Berkeley, in a Punjab village called Majra, sitting in our garden with a glass of cooled buttermilk in one hand and the *New Yorker* in the other. Can you picture it? It arrived only three weeks late (the magazine, not the buttermilk). The bearer is our village postmaster, a youth with a B.A. and a black umbrella who doubles as a postman and comes on a bicycle from Ladopur, the town two miles away, to deliver it. For news we depend on a battery radio. Yesterday, North Korea invaded the South. American troops are to be sent! It all seems to be happening so far away, although it's going on in our backyard.

"I write this amongst gaudy green parrots scolding each other in the mango trees and a bereaved gander, recently widowed, forcing—for the fifth time this morning—his amorous attention on a puzzled, but not unwilling hen."

I interrupted my letter to Carol Thorpe long enough to take a swipe at a persistent fly. He had his small, compound lenses aimed at my buttermilk. I missed, he buzzed off, and I picked up my pen again from the unpainted wooden stand nearby, where I had set it down. I tried to imagine Carol over there, reading this letter. Good, dear Carol. The placid playmate from down the street whom I had grown up with. My frequent friend in high school. My college confidante in undergraduate days. And now the classics major. Carol had turned into a nag those last few months in Berkeley. But she was only doing what she did best—acting like my conscience, my Self in the sensible mode, me with an eye on what was in my own best interests. The older sister I never had.

What else would she like to hear, I wondered. I reread what I had written, all about the "cooled" buttermilk. How could I explain to Carol that what I was calling buttermilk was not the same stuff you got in cartons at the Safeway? And "cooled" was a turn of expression for "at-least-not-warm." Which was all you could ask for without a refrigerator. And we didn't have one. Nor even electricity to run one. As a matter of fact, we had no plumbing, either. No running water, no faucets, no showers, no toilets. In place of the latter were adult-sized potty chairs with lids that the British, with their genius for uncompromisingly adapting to all sorts of places and situations, had devised and called *commodes.*

The trouble was, once you tried to explain one thing, a whole bag of supplementaries would need emptying, and there would be no end of trying to deal with them. Better to let the "cooled" go undefined. And a lot of other things as well.

For instance, I couldn't have told Carol I was writing this letter at the exotic hour of six o'clock in the morning because, after a couple of hours, it was going to be too hot to do anything but shuffle around, exerting as little as possible, before having lunch and then lying down for a nap until tea time, and then going for a walk through the powdered dust of paths through the fields before sunset (after sunset there might be snakes), then having dinner and finally going to sleep to the whine of indignant mosquitoes mad to get inside the net festooned on bamboo poles crossed at either end of the cot.

I thought it might be possible to say something about the garden, but now that it was June, dry, yellow grass struggled through the hard, packed clay, and the supports which must have been put up for long-departed sweet peas sagged in the wind that was already starting up.

Sweat from the previous night's lovemaking had dried and caked on my skin. My hair was sticky. It would be too much for Carol to hear about. Better to get back to details that would reassure her that all was well. Now she was in Michigan, and the early summer would be making its gentle appearance. It was easy to picture Carol taking a job translating Dante, or helping somebody else translate him. I could see her, earnest and nearsighted, slogging through the library stacks armed with three-by-fives, chasing down references

24

and compiling a bibliography, while her boss had all the fun and got all the credit. In the midst of this, Carol would probably like to hear about the postman, the *New Yorker*, the gander, even. She liked comfortable, everyday, recognizable things.

I'm certain Carol would have found far too unusual the item of furniture I was sitting on as I wrote, had made love on a good deal of the previous night, and had sent Tej off from before dawn, in order to spare the rest of the family— Mataji and Pitaji, the girls, and Hari, Dilraj Kaur, and little Nikku, the cousins from Amritsar, neighbors on adjacent rooftops—the sight of us in bed together. Sleeping out of doors in summer was a way to keep tolerably cool, but it lacked privacy. The charpoy itself, a cot fashioned out of a bamboo frame mounted on wooden legs and strung with rope, sagged in the middle, so that whatever else was on it toppled into my space as I wrote.

Best not to burden Carol with the charpoy, but I could have written a treatise about its uses. As the setting for even the most extravagant of amorous encounters, for example, the charpoy provides the logical place for babies to be conceived, and later birthed, on. The sick and the elderly die on it and are carried, bound to it, to their funeral pyres. Tipped upright and leaned against a wall, it creates acceptable shade on a summer's day. Set it on its side, and you can drape wet clothes over it to dry. And of course you can simply sleep on it, with a thick woven dhurrie thrown over the ropes, and sheets on top of that. The foot end, where the ropes can be tightened from time to time, has gaps where your heels get entangled if you thrash around too much. Otherwise, it is serviceable and good, and lightweight for easy moving indoors out of dust storms or rain on summer nights. In winter, I was told, it makes a sofa to settle down on while one sits wrapped in a quilt. But how was I to get into all this with Carol? Carol would have fretted over the rough ropes, imagined my spine getting permanently curved from the sag, sent yet another letter urging me to say if I was all right and asking when I was coming back. All letters from the States were variations on this same theme.

"I don't know!" I heard myself say aloud. "I don't know!"

I looked around to see if anyone had heard me. Veera Bai, the Harijan woman who swept our yard every day, looked up from her work briefly and then went back to her sweeping. Mataji had already bathed and washed her hair. The curly grey strands amongst the black were highlighted by the sun. Her bedding was folded for the day, and she was sitting on one end of her charpoy on the roof reading her prayer book and reciting her morning prayers from the *Japji Sahib* while the maidservant Ram Piari stood over her, rubbing and pounding and slapping the thick, dark, orange-colored mustard oil into Mataji's scalp. The cot drooped with her weight. She didn't look up. Nor did the girls—Tej's sisters Goodi and Rano, sitting on low stools beside her. The two were crouched over some embroidery they had started together the evening before and were bent upon finishing before another sun went down. It was a bright length of muslin, a dupatta that when worn over their heads or draped over their shoulders would catch dozens of sunbeams in the tiny round mirrors they were stitching into it. Hari was bathing. I could hear him singing and splashing water from the pump at the back of the house.

Pitaji, Major Sant Singh Sandhu (Retd.), would be off on his rounds of the farm. It's what he did every morning, if he didn't go hunting with the cousins from Amritsar, three young men of indeterminate age who all looked alike. Middays he escaped to town on farm business. These trips often turned into social forays as he searched out friends to talk to. Life in the army had made him gregarious to the extent that Majra company fell short of his taste for talk. In the evening Pitaji made another round of the fields before dinner. Sometimes he would send for me to listen to him talk about world affairs, Indian politics, or the price of sugarcane. Today Tej had gone at dawn with the Amritsar cousins to oversee the loading of the last, drying stalks of sugarcane for market. Now that the juice that plumped up the weight (and the price) had largely dried up, it was hardly worth the effort and cost of hauling it off. Still, Pitaji had decided it must be done, and Tej was probably already waiting for the tractor driver to bring the trailer around and mad with impatience to finish the job so he could return to me. To his sitar. To his music, for the rest of the day.

I contemplated for a moment the surroundings. The compound of our house was closed off from the rest of the village by a mud wall two feet thick and seven feet high. In the six weeks I had been here, I had scarcely gone outside it. The photographs I had envisaged taking still lay curled up in the Rollei as unexposed film. Women of a landlord's household do not have the freedom of the village, and especially not for taking photographs. It would create excitement of the wrong kind; it would invite criticism from all sorts of people. I had, then, to rely on my imagination for the pictures I might have taken. From the roof where Mataji sat, there could be seen—and photographed through the widest of wide angle lenses—the whole expanse of fields, and in their midst, the mud houses clustered together. The horizon would be as flat as a table top and the sun a pale orange mask of a face behind a veil of dusty beige. The blindfolded camel was walking around in circles, powering the Persian wheel well outside our gate. I could hear the creak of the wheel and the slosh of the water from where I sat. And the circles would expand to include the whole village, those dwellings that rose up like natural extensions of the earth from which they were fashioned, the fields, and even the towns I had never seen, but felt must be there, endless copies of Ladopur as far as the imagination could take me. I had been told that in the monsoon season one could actually see the foothills of the Himalayas to the north. Now they had to be wondered about.

Inside our compound a series of rooms with thick mud walls leaned along the north side, shaded by a tamarind tree under which the vicious Moti had sat furious and chained since dawn. He had nothing to do but await his release at sundown, while Jim and Lal roamed the yard free, sniffing the morning air, marking their territories, and frightening the butterflies. Ram Piari had finished Mataji's massage now and was rolling up the beddings from the charpoys and stowing them inside the house for the day. Gian, a youth conscripted from the village for odd jobs around the house, was stacking the rope cots against the outside of the storeroom

27

wall. Something he whispered to Ram Piari as they went through their routine caused her to flash him a fierce look. As soon as he had turned his back, she pulled her dupatta more tightly over her head to hide a smile.

And *she* was already in the kitchen, up before everyone else, overseeing the work of Udmi Ram and Chotu and Ram Piari, keys jangling from her kameez pocket and her bare feet slapping the packed earth of the kitchen floor as she strode back and forth. She would have bathed, washed her hair, said her prayers, and seen to the servants' getting up and starting the wood-burning *chulas*. The kitchen would be all smoke and boiling water, steaming buffalo milk and tea things taken out. Six-year-old Nikku would be sitting on a low stool, drinking sweetened cow's milk from a big brass tumbler. I could hear the striking of brass utensils, one against the other. Soon it would be the groan and squeak of the wooden beater in the earthenware butter churn. *She* was seeing that everything got done. But how did she manage to shout without raising her voice?

Mataji was joining her now for the first of the day's series of ongoing conversations. The kitchen was the favored locale. It might have been that it offered the two women an excuse to sit together without seeming to waste time. No one could accuse them of idleness if they cut and peeled, stirred and ladled while they talked. I often caught bits about the flamboyant life of Mataji's younger brother, Uncle Gurnam Singh. It was obvious Mataji didn't approve of what he was doing with his life and to his family. There was something about another woman.

The kitchen, indeed the whole household, was a scene that would have done just as well without me in it; nor had it taken me long to arrive at this. Now, after all these weeks, I had almost got used to it. But not quite. Sometimes I wanted to stand up on the flattopped roof and shout to the village at large: "Hey! Look at me! I'm Helen! I can recite the Lord's Prayer in Gothic, tell you the difference between an Italian and Shakespearean sonnet. I can give a recitation of Goethe's lyrics from the Weimar period. I can take pictures and develop and print them myself. I saw the world premières of *Gone With the Wind* and *Citizen Kane*; the sneak preview of

28

Casablanca before it was released. Humphrey Bogart was in the audience! I can tell you who starred in the original version of *A Star is Born* and who Bette Davis' costar was in *All This and Heaven Too*. I can conjugate verbs in five Old High German dialects and recite the first twenty-five lines of Virgil's *Aeneid!*"

But I had no audience, and besides, knowing all this was about as practical in the present circumstances as being able to write all the four Gospels on a grain of rice.

There were clearly other skills to be cultivated here. So far I hadn't shone at any of them. Trying to light the wood stove had ended in blackened fingers and tears in my eyes from the smoke and frustration. Rolling out chapattis had provided a hilarious time for all as the wet, sticky dough slipped and slid beneath my rolling pin, producing a polygon of varied thickness, instead of the neat, perfect circle aimed at. Attempts at crochet had resulted in tight little masses of sweat-stained cotton thread with no shape, and holes everywhere.

She had always been there to smilingly take the offending rolling pin or crochet hook or metal tube blower for igniting the fire out of my awkward hands to finish the job perfectly herself.

"Marvelous," I thought, "how I have managed to keep Dilraj Kaur out of my letters back to the States all these weeks and out of my conversations before leaving. But I have. She is my secret from all those at home. An obsession here and now. A raging preoccupation."

An angry crow flew in from nowhere and began hopping sideways toward the glass of half-consumed buttermilk on the stand by my charpoy. His uniform of navy blue and grey feathers gave him a military look as his brisk, greedy eyes scanned the glass. I gulped down the last bit to spite him, picked up the unfinished letter to Carol, then set it down again. It was getting too hot to write. Thought, like something physical, melted away at high temperatures. I would finish the letter later, in the evening when it grew cooler.

"No," I said to myself, getting up to find a place in the kitchen scene. "it's too out of the ordinary. I couldn't tell Carol I have a co-wife, or will have one, as soon as Tej and I are married."

3

How had it happened? How had it come about that, of all the women I had ever known, I was the only one with a co-wife? It was like having some rare disease or a special talent, one that was interesting but not exploitable. It wasn't something I wanted to share with Carol. Besides, a whole lifetime's worth of will had been used up just getting to Majra, so that even a simple matter like finishing the letter to her that I had begun in the morning became a major undertaking. Now that it was evening, it should have been easy enough to take care of. But it meant sitting inside our clay oven of a room, writing by kerosene lamp, and missing the best part of the twenty-four hours out-of-doors.

Gian would already have set out the charpoys for the night. The tractor driver and the cousins from Amritsar would be getting instructions from Pitaji about what needed to be done in the fields the next day. Hari would be arguing forcefully for a bigger share of the profits, complaining, as he often did, that he was being overlooked in favor of "others" (meaning Tej) because he was the younger son. Chotu would be bringing tea for the unexpected guests from Ladopur, the Tehsildar, a petty official, who owned a horse-drawn carriage, and his powdered wife. With a rattle of plates and spoons, Chotu would set the brass tray, too big for him to carry comfortably, and polished to a high luster with ash from the fireplace, heavily down on a marble-topped table in the yard. Mataji and the Tehsildarni, their faces carefully concealed from each others' husbands, would be sharing information independently gathered on the scandals that had rocked that small town of shopkeepers and temple priests the past week: what elopements had taken place, which police official transferred for taking bribes, what the Christian Mission miss-sahibs had been up to. The sight of nurse-evangelist Ina Mae Scott, straight and stoical at the wheel of her jeep, with the cook sitting at the back as she drove out to faraway villages every morning, never failed to arouse the curiosity and awe of the citizens of Ladopur.

Dilraj Kaur would be seeing to dinner that wouldn't appear until just before bedtime, and Goodi and Rano would have put away their completed embroidery piece at last. Freshly bathed, hair oiled and braided, they would be silent but keen partakers of the gossip. Discreet drops of *ittar*, dabbed behind their ears, would have rendered them as fragrant as the jasmine blossoms that were releasing their sweetness on the summer night. The girls were not twins, but only looked as if they were, even though at eighteen Rano was three years older than Goodi and an inch taller. It was because they did everything together, dressed similarly, and chaperoned one another everywhere, like nuns. From the roof, where Tej sat exploring an early evening raga on the sitar, came the plaintive sounds of his improvisations. They suggested some nostalgic remembrances, some whispered longings, some half-uttered vows.

If I sat outside, instead of writing the letter, the Punjabi conversations would flow over me in a pleasant stream of sound, low and easy and unnecessary to deal with, and reminiscent of something in the life I had left behind. A chance reference to Uncle Gurnam Singh, Mataji's much-talked-about younger brother, a stray word or phrase, half understood, would be enough to carry me gently forward into the next hour, the next day. The sounds, which by day were shouted across yards and up to rooftops in competition with the overwhelming brightness of the sun and the white blankness of the landscape, became soft and blurred at nightfall in deference, perhaps, to the peace that comes with evening.

Yet I had to tear myself back in time and distance long enough to say something to Carol, to speak in the language she spoke, drawing from the bank of experiences that we shared. She would like to know, now that the life I had sought was indeed mine, what I was doing with it. It called for an explanation. I ran through recent memories for clues. Ran-

31

dom events, recollected now in more tranquility than I knew what to do with, lay strewn about like piles of snapshots waiting to be sorted and pasted into an album, an act that would surely provide some sense or sequence. They were glimpses of myself, of friends, saying goodbye to San Francisco and to each other. We're smiling, with arms linked self-consciously, and perhaps they're sensing as I do the recurring surprise one always experiences during snapshot taking: how another body feels—vulnerable, tentative, the nerves vibrating in the hollows of shoulders, the roundness of waists.

Here's one of me alone as I board the *Franconia* at New York, and another—a cartoon—drawn by my own anxieties and urgencies on a mind crowded with guilt and hope. I'm a lonely stick figure on a tightrope, swaying and dipping my way across a chasm between two cliffs, one with a big sign in block letters saying "California," the other, "India." I don't look right or left or backwards: I can't, because I'm blindfolded, going forward into the arms of Tej waiting at the end of the rope. I'm trusting to luck, to the right delicacy of balance, to chance, to a sixth survival sense and self-hypnotized out of my mind.

It was when I boarded the P. & O. liner, the *Corfu*, at Southampton that I met Edith Ritchie. Even before that, on the boat train from London, she had sat across from me, bosomy and sensible in a tweed suit and the no-nonsense shoes of a fifty-year-old British woman. Her coarse, steel grey hair was cut in a little-boy bob. I noticed her because she chain-smoked cigarettes through a carved ivory holder that had elegantly yellowed with age. It drove me wild, as I had recently given up smoking. She must have seen me watchin̪g her, or rather the cigarette, with unexpected interest, because later, when she introduced herself, she mentioned seeing me on the train.

"I'm going out to meet my brother in Penang," she said. "Haven't seen him for twenty years. But we always write."

That was the extent of information I got from her. But it was enough for me to take her on as a confidante, the kind possible to have on a ship because you know you will never see them again. Like a young, female Ancient Mariner, I grabbed her with my little plump hand and told her my story—as much as I wanted her to know, or needed to tell as we pitched and rolled through the Bay of Biscay, watched the dipping Portuguese fishing villages bob on the horizon, jammed the deck with everyone else to get photographs of Gibraltar, and discovered Algiers one Sunday morning rising out of the sea with its white concrete, red-roofed buildings balanced improbably on the African shore.

There was something about Edith Ritchie's Scottish, red-apple cheeks and half-closed eyes as she watched everything going on around us day after day in the upper lounge of the *Corfu* that made her seem safe and comfortable. In her low contralto voice and rolled *r*'s there was wisdom and understanding and without her needing to prod me, I poured out my stored-up impressions. I told her about the dreary flatness of the Nevada plains, cluttered with short-cropped tumbleweed and sagebrush as seen from the window of a Union Pacific train bound for Chicago; about negotiating the narrow, fog-drenched, neon-lit, early-morning streets of that city in a taxi in which was piled my big red steamer trunk, as I sped from one station to another to change trains; about the banks of the Erie, ice-jammed and lined with lonely houses and old fences and presided over by a mournful, grey sky on a late March afternoon; about New York City itself, mental images of which had been so fixed in my mind by Hollywood clichés that I felt I had seen it all before, close up.

"Except for the Indian restaurant," I told Edith. (She said I should not observe formalities, but call her by her first name.)

"Oh?" she said. As she spoke her half-closed eyes were not looking at me, but across the room at the gin-powered piano player with thinning blond hair who indefatigably tinkled out show tunes for a Noel Coward or a Gertrude Lawrence to sing to: "Tell me about it."

"Well," I went on, remembering it as it was and planning how I should present it to her. "It was on one of the picturesque little streets in the middle of Manhattan. I had turned off Fifth Avenue, west on Forty-Seventh Street. I was looking for this restaurant I had seen advertised in the *Times*. It's called The Maharajah."

"I see," she said.

33

"Anyway, there were all these restaurants and antique jewelry stores jammed tight together and a kosher delicatessen. It started to drizzle, and I had no umbrella. Once I found The Maharajah it took me a moment or two to realize it was up a flight of stairs."

"And then?" Edith said.

"I remember the sign outside said: 'East Indian Curries: Pakoras, Chapattis, Rice, Halwa.'"

"Did you enjoy your meal?" Edith asked.

"Oh yes," I said, recalling the place, the way it was. At two-thirty in the afternoon it was empty. I sat, damp-haired and chilled, at a table by the window, looking out through droopy lace curtains at the dismal scene. The service was vengefully slow: the Brooklyn waitress resented my coming so late for lunch, and was going to make me suffer. When the meal arrived, the curry was lukewarm and the rice cold, but the red chilies in the sauce more than compensated for this, and I ordered tea to neutralize their effect and the feeling, sharper than the chilies, that I was alone.

Halfway through the Mediterranean I said to Edith (we were standing together at the rail after lunch, watching dolphins plunge and play in the wake of the ship), "This is itself a kind of microcosm, isn't it? I got the same feeling on the ship crossing the Atlantic."

"I suppose it is," Edith agreed.

The idea did not appear to be original to her, but I went on in my own mind, seeing us as on a Flash Gordon spaceship. It was a place neither here nor there, a place where time had its own meaning, or no meaning at all. But above everything I had the sense of myself as going back the way my Italian grandfathers Graziani and Colombo had come just a generation ago, back across the sea to the Old World, and beyond. I thought about my bewildered, obedient grandmothers, traveling in steerage with all those children. Not understanding where they were going. Already homesick for their villages. Wondering what awaited them in the new place. Was the urge that drove me against their tide the same that drove the Crusaders, the Venetian traders, Marco Polo, beyond the Old World, back to where everything began? Had religion and trade merely been excuses for finding out what the

34

source was really like? There was no end to my ability to trivialize history as I tried to make sense out of my own urges to discover a real home. At that moment, and by that ship's rail, watching the dolphins play in the receding Mediterranean, I felt I had left my Western birthplace and yet was going home where yesterday and tomorrow met. Tej would be waiting for me there.

Before long, we were ready to enter the Suez Canal. I still had not told Edith about the two weeks in London between sea journeys, the shows I went to, the sightseeing I did, about the ham sandwich, cut up into nine neat squares and served by an Australian boy who had come to London to be an opera star and was waiting counter at the Silver Cross in Whitehall until that happened. I hadn't told her about the things I had bought in London with money saved from what Tej had left for me there at the American Express: a pair of slacks and a blue negligé with ruffles at the neck. In fact, I hadn't mentioned Tej so far. Instead, I said, "I saw Anton Walbrook one night, at an Uday Shankar show in Swiss Cottage."

"I see," she answered, as if she had not really heard of the famous Hungarian movie star before, nor of Uday Shankar either, nor felt she ought to have, for she went on in quite another direction. "No matter how long you stay away from your home and family, my girl," she said, making *girl* a two-syllable word, "always keep in touch. Always write to them. That's very important. Don't forget it." She punctuated her words of advice with stacatto jabs of the cigarette holder and warmly patted my arm with her free hand.

I thought of the letters that had already arrived from California and that had begun reaching me even when I was still in Berkeley those last few days. They were messages that I would have to answer sooner or later. My mother saying, "Hurry back to the U.S. and give yourself time to decide on marriage. Don't be swayed too much by Mr. Singh. Your Papa says I'm taking it too hard and Gloria and Julia and Nicoletta are disgusted with me. Still, I hope that you meet a handsome *American* on your way over who will be more convincing than I have been. Dreaming again!"

35

Papa wrote to me in London and said he hoped I had enjoyed my trip and that everyone spoke of me a lot.

I went back to my cabin and read the letter from Tej, the only one I had received from him since I left Berkeley: "Aren't you glad we shall be together in no time now?" It began. "Seven months is a long, long time. Do you know what I am doing now: I am sitting in a mango grove, keeping watch over the house being built and the material lying about. You will be surprised to know, there are no serious musicians for miles around. Not even a tabla player I can practice with. And, yes. I must tell you this. My revered Guruji, Pandit Shankar Dayal, is no more. He died after a long illness a week ago in Jullundur. I have no heart to go on with the sitar." I read the last few lines again, as well as the spaces between them: Tej had left a lot of pain unexpressed. The old sitar maestro had been his mentor and his inspiration.

At Suez I got my first taste of what the future was going to be like. The time of pretty picture postcards was over. The white sky of Egypt settled over the white sands, and hot winds blew through the ship's lounge. The British rubber planters on their way to Malaya, in obedience to some unwritten edict, came down to lunch in knee-length, white cotton drill shorts and white stockings between which peeped pale, bony knees. The piano player had tied a white handkerchief around his neck, inside the open collar of his sweat-soaked shirt. Moreover, ship romances were getting out of hand, now that we were well out of European waters. It could have had something to do with the heat. Passengers and crew met on intimate terms as stewards became favorites with the British girls going out to seek their fortunes in Kuala Lumpur and points east. They could be seen after lunch in the lounge, reclining on divans in attitudes of amorous lassitude, oblivious to the music from the piano, to the occasional partnerless onlooker, to Edith who sat watching them through her after-lunch gin and cigarette, deeply inhaling smoke through the carved ivory holder.

"I have a portable record player," Edith said. "We could listen to some music out on deck after dinner tonight."

I took her up on the offer. "I have some records of 'Scheherezade'," I said.

After all, it was the Red Sea: Ali Baba country. It would be something to remember, those violin cadenzas weaving an arabesque of sound as smooth as the waveless water that the ship glided over, as oriental as a silken cushion thrown on a Persian carpet.

And it *was* memorable in its own way. The stars that were supposed to enhance the scene were absent, as was the cool breeze that should have brought relief from the heat of the day. In their stead, a pall of dust hung suspended in the air. The first cadenza was hardly over when Edith remarked that, judging from my abstinence from the goings-on after lunch in the lounge, I didn't seem to fancy the young men on board as much as one would imagine a young girl might.

"No," I said.

"Smart girl," she remarked. She smiled the smile of a conspirator.

Something veered me off from taking the conversation any further in this direction, but Edith continued.

"You seemed to be different from the others," she said, "even on the boat train."

"I'm a very ordinary person," I replied, not knowing what else to say, and feeling there was something not quite right about the way she squeezed my hand as she made a point and failed to release it afterward: it was casual but not uncalculated.

"My dear, you are not ordinary at all, going out by yourself, halfway around the world, traveling all this distance . . . a beautiful girl, really. . . ." She squeezed my hand again.

"I have a very ordinary purpose," I said, withdrawing my hand from hers. "I'm going to get married."

"Oh," she said.

"To the most marvelous man in the world," I added foolishly. I knew Tejbir Singh was not the most marvelous man in the world, except in the only sense that mattered to me. Yet I needed something extravagant to say, something to turn off the scene so that I could retrieve my "Scheherezade" records and get back to my cabin. Bombay was still three more days away.

4

As the *Corfu* approached Ballard Pier, the Gateway of India became a constant on the skyline of Bombay. The closer we got, the larger it loomed as it floated midway on the waves of an opalescent horizon. Even close up, after the *Corfu* had dropped anchor, the Gateway wouldn't stand still, but bobbed and tilted in the foreground.

I leaned over the rail of the upper deck and looked down. Tej was standing on the dock as I knew he would be, looking up and waving, while I must have waved back. Out of habit, I reached for the Rollei and caught him there. I got it so that he looks far away in his turban and Nehru jacket, and crowded out by the confusion on the pier—cargo waiting to be loaded, coolies pushing past each other and shouting, hundreds of dock workers milling about, relatives come to greet disembarking passengers with marigold garlands, and others I could imagine no reason for the presence of. The shot is a Cecil B. De Mille spectacular with fresh details. Tej is not smiling exactly. And he's not serious. It's his expression with the hundred questions. Wondering what to make of me in my black moiré silk skirt, nylons, and spike heels, endured, heat and all, especially for the occasion? Wondering if this is indeed the woman he has been waiting for? With the gold leather belt, and with hair braided and drawn up like a coronet on top of her head? Behind Tej was a host of spectators and participants crowding the scene: the whole of Bombay? And behind them, peering over their shoulders, curious and unseen, was Tej's family and friends and relatives hundreds of miles away to the north.

When I lowered my camera again, Tej gestured for me to stay where I was, that he'd come on board. Was he trying, as

I was, to see him and me in Berkeley again and at the same time to adjust to us here, as through a different lens, now in this alien scene? I could feel him hurrying up the gangplank and rushing up the stairs. There was so little time left for me to prepare myself.

All at once his arms were around me in an embrace circumspectly achieved in the Indian setting, where everything is permissible in public, except affection displayed between a man and a woman. Just at that moment I caught the eye of Edith Ritchie as she disembarked for a day of sightseeing in Bombay before sailing on to Penang. She looked quickly away.

The intimate moment I had long looked forward to dribbled away in a multitude of complexities. There was nothing beyond the stamp of the immigration officer on my passport that I could hold up as proof that I had truly arrived.

Tej was hurrying me along to the customs shed, walking faster than I could keep up, looking back from time to time to see if I was still there, helping me over potholes in the pavement, guiding me along. Would the family accept me, I wondered. Would they like me? Would I like them? What would we have to say to one another when we met at last? Tej had told me that Mataji was the only one in his family who would not be able to talk to me in English. Where and when would that meeting take place, finally? There were other questions I dared not even ask, as we went through one formality of arrival after another: questions that began and ended with Dilraj Kaur. It was a name that was impossible to utter; an idea that was hard to ignore.

There was a moment when coming out of the customs shed Tej stopped short and took a long look at me. "Helen," he said, "you've become thinner."

"So have you."

"I haven't felt like eating," he said, his voice uttering the words, but his eyes expressing quite another message.

"Neither have I," I said.

About the time we got on a tonga to go to the hotel, I'd started to take in the surroundings. My hand baggage and the red steamer trunk occupied the driver's seat, so that he, light as a bird, had to perch on one of the traces that attached the trap to the harness on either side. He delivered a stream of comments to which Tej replied in monosyllables.

"Have you brought your sitar?" I asked Tej during a pause in the tongawalla's monologue.

"It's in the room," he said. "But you weren't supposed to know. I was going to surprise you with a serenade."

By then the tonga was lurching along the broad streets of Bombay drawn by a skinny horse that alternately swayed and bolted through the heavy traffic. So far I hadn't dared to look at Tej too long or too searchingly. I couldn't have endured finding a stranger beside me in that tonga, in that city.

"About the house," Tej was saying, "it's got the roof on, and the floors are almost finished. We just need the polishers to come. We can move in soon. After the rains, if all goes well."

"Oh?" I said. I tried to create for myself an idea of the dwelling going up in a Punjab village that would, for all I knew, house me for the rest of my existence.

"You'll like it. There'll be a fireplace in the sitting-room, and a kitchen, and a terrace on the roof," he went on.

Meanwhile, Bombay slid by haphazardly. I wanted to put it all together but couldn't. Finally, not knowing one street from another, but assuming Tej did, I gave myself up to the ride. Getting to the hotel had become yet another stage in the journey which had not yet ended.

Tej was still talking as we checked in. "You know, before Mataji's mother died last month, she became delirious—was shouting that you had arrived and asked the girl attending her to make tea at once." Then, as we walked up the two flights of stairs to our room, he said, "It's a good hotel," and unlocked the door and showed the bearers where to set the suitcases down. "There's a big bathtub, and . . ." (after the bearers had got their tips and left, and the door locked again) ". . . a view of the street. From the end of the hall . . . there's a window. You can see . . . the sea . . . from there, and . . ."

Delight set in before he could finish. Remembered faces and gestures and voice sounds and touches—different from before—assembled themselves into a fresh reality behind the locked door. We seized the moment and squeezed from it

40

the last measure of seven months' worth of minutes, hours, and days ticking slowly away in waiting. Our first fight came later. For the present, this reality was all I could be sure of, this and Tej's music. The sweet, explosive notes burst like bubbles from the sitar. And for as long as they lasted, we were in Berkeley again. Bombay itself was sliding into the sea in a great pre-monsoon blur. Rain was supposed to sweep in from the Arabian Sea any day. The busy streets looked like no busy streets I had ever seen. People were living on them, sleeping on them. They never emptied. Sidewalks, buildings, sky, pedestrians, all registered as dazzling, shifting images by day. By night, shadows masked the sleeping forms on pavements in front of offices and shops and apartments, with only the random light from a hawker's stand or a fruit seller's kiosk to reveal their identities as human. At one point, a car's headlights caught like a camera flash the fleeting vision of a mother sitting, as in a living room, with her wide-eyed infant in her lap, under the arch of a bridge.

At six o'clock in the morning it was already hot. I had no sense of things: how the city was laid out, where we were staying. I only knew the room was high-ceilinged and cavernous and furnished simply. Perhaps this is what all the hotel rooms in Bombay looked like. Light slammed in at dawn through the half-open wooden shutters, and with it a tired breeze from the sea. I looked down into the street below, where I would presently be joining the throng, escorted by Tej, and wearing my newly-bought sari. Old men in white dhotis, white shirts, and black pillbox hats walked purposefully past. Hawkers selling furious green parrots in cages and others, flowery neckties, found their spaces on the pavement for the day. A seller of garlands sat surrounded by heaps of marigolds outside a temple across the street. A panwalla stacked fresh betel leaves and small tins of condiments on his stand that was covered with a wet red cloth. Street urchins pushed and elbowed their way through the crowd as if toward some grim goal. There was excitement out there, but it lay beyond an invisible bubble that held me in. Is this what being foreign feels like, I wondered.

I closed the shutters again; the hot, humid air had made

41

its way in. The sitar lay where Tej had set it down the night before. He hadn't given up his music, in spite of his declaration in the letter. If anything, he played better than ever before. Halfway through an improvisation, matters of more urgency claimed our time, and he left the alap, the slow opening movement to the raga, before he had finished. Now he still lay asleep under the ceiling fan. Sweat trickled down his forehead and into the strands of hair at his temples. He turned over, then, and sleepily pulled me to him. "I missed you so much, *missi-bawa*," he whispered.

From Bombay to Delhi by the Frontier Mail, it was a matter of hurrying slowly. The individual shots are frantic, but put together, they become a sequence in slow motion, composed of long waits at railway stations along the way, alternating with headlong hurtlings through the Rajasthan desert. There are takes of exhausted, sweating passengers staring through the open windows of third-class carriages with wooden seats. They are packed as tightly as the belongings they have stuffed into big, square tin cans with close-fitting lids and padlocks. They sit clutching the lunches they have tied up in squares of cloth and supporting themselves against the bedding they have rolled up and tied with rope.

The sequence includes a sudden, disoriented awakening at night in our first-class compartment, shared with a Gujarati couple and their two teenage daughters, when lights from a station flooded my bunk. My watch said two o'clock. A glass of steaming hot tea was handed in to me through the open window by Tej who had, it appeared, leapt out onto the platform as soon as the train stopped. "Here, this will do you good. It's authentic 'stationwalla' *chai*," he said, and went off to stretch his legs and have a look around.

I sat and stared out the window, half asleep. There was something on the platform I kept looking at without seeing as I sipped the hot tea. It was composed of movement, precise and continuous, and carried out in a box of a space underneath the tea-stall counter. Gradually it gathered itself into focus with stunning force: a child about six years old, crouching in a little world too small for him even to sit upright in, was washing plates and tea-cups and spoons. I set the half-empty glass of tea on the stand beside my seat and lay down again.

When day came, Tej and I played canasta and talked, aware that every word was being listened to by our inquisitive fellow passengers. During the odd moments when both Tej and the Gujarati man were absent, the woman questioned me in heavily accented Gujarati-English about what my husband did for a living, what his salary was, who my in-laws were, and where I came from. She mistook me for a Kashmiri, and I let it go at that.

"We'll get a first-class coupé, a carriage all to ourselves," Tej announced the next morning as we left Delhi for Abdullapur, the railhead for Majra. It was seven o'clock, and the dry heat of Delhi was already rising from the rails, a heat in which there was no more moisture than in a furnace.

Once the red steamer trunk was checked into the baggage car and we installed in our coupé, Tej set his sitar carefully on an overhead rack, stowed our hand luggage under the seat, and proceeded to pull down the seat back to form a bed. Even as the train pulled out of Delhi's main station, we were hurriedly undoing the leather straps of the khaki-colored canvas holdall that contained our bedding, spreading the cotton dhurrie, arranging the sheet, taking out the pillows. We fastened the wooden shutters tight against the dust, the hot winds, and the blistering landscape that spun dizzily past outside; flung off our clothes and lay down on the improvised bed.

The big supply of still-unanswered questions which I had carried around with me was, like hand baggage, getting heavier with every stop. It was about to burst the lock and spill out.

"Where is *she*?" I asked Tej as we lay together in the darkened compartment.

"Who?"

"Dilraj Kaur," I said, pronouncing her name aloud for the first time and nearly choking on it.

"Oh," he said, turning on his back, "what does it matter where she is?"

"It matters to me and you know it!"

"She's in Majra."

"Will she still be there when we arrive?"

43

"Why shouldn't she be? It's where she lives."

"I know, but . . ."

"But what?"

"It will be awkward," I said. "For me and for her too."

"Don't worry about her. She can take care of herself," Tej said.

"Then what about *me?*" I cried. "What am *I* supposed to do? Pretend she's not there? Pretend she's not your wife?"

We both sat up, facing each other.

"I don't even know what the sleeping arrangements are," I went on. I could hear my own voice as though it belonged to somebody else. "Will all three of us sleep in the same room? The same bed? Will you sleep in the middle? Will we take turns?"

"Shut up!" he shouted. I thought he was going to hit me.

The clickety-clack of the wheels on the rails poured in and filled the silence between us that followed his momentary outburst. We stared at each other, my heart racing with rage. I began to cry. Miles went by. I could not have imagined a train could make so much noise. At last, Tej reached out his hand to take mine, and I grasped it. It was almost impossible to carry on a fight with no clothes on.

"I am no good at saying 'I'm sorry'," he said. "I'll probably never say it again, no matter how at fault I feel, no matter how miserable. It's my nature."

We spent the rest of the journey to Abdullapur that morning alternately making love and coming up for air, drenched with sweat and euphoria. I realized only later that my questions (even the reasonable ones) remained unanswered.

We had to be quick at Abdullapur station. The train halted there for a bare five minutes. We grabbed our baggage which we'd already lined up beside the entrance and opened the door of our coupé. We stepped down into the white heat of noon. There at the bottom of the steps to the platform stood a twenty-year-old with smiling lips and eyes and black, curly beard: Hari come to meet us. It had to be Tej's younger brother. Three other young men were also there to receive us. I discovered later that they were the cousins from Amritsar: Prem, Sukhdev, and Jeet, although who was who I would have been hard put to say.

44

"*Sat Sri Akal*, Bhaji," Hari greeted Tej as he reached out to help us with the suitcases, and then looking over Tej's shoulder, he paused an instant. The look he gave me was shy and straightforward at the same time. He wanted to see what I was like, but he had no one to compare me to. "Bhabi, *Sat Sri Akal*," he said, looking me straight in the eye and smiling. The other three, like bearded musketeers, stepped up to greet us then, their sharp, black eyes taking me in with one brief, curious glance.

The time for meeting the rest of the family was not to be quite yet. I remember writing to Carol about how it was too hot at that time of day to walk the two miles into Majra from where the paved road of Ladopur left off and beyond which our tonga-driver refused to go. Instead, I told her, we drove into the town first, to leave the heavy luggage at Ghasitoo Ram, the Commission Agent's shop, from where it would be picked up later and taken by bullock cart to the village. No one explained this plan, but I was getting adept at piecing bits of recognizable Punjabi together to arrive at some sort of meaning . . . not always accurate.

I told Carol how we all went to the house of a family friend after that. We were given lunch and invited to take a nap. When I woke up, it was all confusion: Where was I? On the *Corfu*? In Bombay? On the train? Someone was sitting over me, waving a fan of woven reeds back and forth. It was the young wife of the family friend. She had sat all afternoon seeing to my comfort in a house that had no electricity.

Orange light through the drawn curtains of the room suggested that the sun was going down. It was time to go. Punjabi thank-yous and goodbyes were being said and responded to. There were smiles and gestures for me. Soon there would be no more trains to board, no more ports to disembark from, no more crowded city streets to be guided through, no more open drains to jump across.

At sunset the tonga-driver dropped off the six of us, and we started down the dirt road that Tej said led to Ambala, but had been unused by through traffic since Kipling's time. We had to turn left off it for the last mile into Majra. In the presence of Hari and the cousins from Amritsar, Tej's manner had taken on a new, hard-to-define tone. Brusque was

45

not the word: offhand and managing were. Or it may have been that the unfamiliar sound of Punjabi on Tej's lips became aggressive and abrupt-seeming.

The sun had turned into an orange ball, bloated and obscene as it lowered itself onto the prostrate horizon. Parrots screeched and crows cawed as they headed for their nests in the *sheesham* trees by the side of the road. Deep yellow laburnum blossoms hung in languid, back-lit festoons, and the leaves of the occasional teak trees fluttered and crackled like flat fans in the dying wind. The fields stretched beyond in an unbroken plain of cracked clay where the stubble from the harvested wheat still thrust its sharp, dried shoots.

"Watch out for these, Bhabi," Hari said, turning to me. "They can go right through heavy shoes, even."

These were the first words that he had spoken directly to me since we stepped down from the train. His voice had the same timbre as Tej's, livened by a Punjabi rhythm superimposed on English.

When we reached the turn-off to Majra and rounded the bend, Tej and Hari, the cousins, and I found ourselves directly facing the setting sun. It threw into silhouette everything ahead of us—the tall *sheesham* tree windbreaks bordering the fields, the stray birds that hadn't reached their nests yet, the mud houses of the village as we got nearer. Presently we reached Majra pond. It was just as Tej had described it once in a letter, and I knew without being told that the building standing at its edge and mirrored darkly in it, was an abandoned mosque, crumbling at the walls, weak in the minarets. There had been no one to see to its upkeep for three years now.

There still remained a little way to go. Smoke from the fires of dried cow dung rose in the dusk, filtering the orange and diffusing whatever light was left into a soft, even glow. Its subtle fragrance, like old wood burning, or some exotic incense, filled the air.

"It's just beyond that tamarind tree," Tej said and pointed to a spot a few yards off where great shadows had formed in the gathering darkness. In the afterglow, we proceeded past the tree, past a compound wall, and finally reached a wooden gate seven feet high.

46

It opened at our coming, and inside the yard was a bouquet of disembodied faces. Expressions of unself-conscious curiosity, suspicion, and shyness were held for an instant in bold relief by the light of kerosene lanterns. Family and servants had gathered for this, as had onlookers from the rooftops of nearby houses. Then out of the dusk a short, brisk, motherly figure emerged and took me in her warm, plump arms before I had a chance to go through the ritual of touching the hem of her garment. Tej had coached me to do this with older people as a mark of respect and good upbringing. The others materialized out of the deep dusk—Pitaji, a tall, heavy, military presence against the lantern light; then Goodi and Rano. Beside them was a third person.

We two must have looked at one another for a moment too long. I could feel the breaths of the others stop. They stood watching us. Tej created some business with the luggage. Hari turned to help him. Mataji, Pitaji, the girls, and the cousins from Amritsar formed a tableau in the half-dark. I took a step forward. An unanticipated question crossed my mind: was I supposed to touch the hem of *her* garment? She was, after all, older than I. Something powerful held me back. Where was Tej to advise me what to do? To get me through this moment? There was no one to give a hint. And she kept standing there, a tall, full figure in the light of the kerosene lantern that made a shadow of her features at the same time it shone through the dupatta—sheer as a dragonfly's wing— that was drawn over her head and that partially covered her face.

From behind her darted another form out of the dark. It was a child wearing a turban sizes too big for him. The occasion for breaking the impasse had presented itself. I bent down to chuck him under the chin. He slipped away, to hide behind his mother. By the time I straightened up, Dilraj Kaur had turned to order one of the servants to bring us tea, and everybody had started talking at once.

5

By the time Uncle Gurnam Singh arrived from Bikaner in the first week of July—in a jeep, with all his retinue, out of a whirl of dust and confusion, filling the village with excitement and wonder—the heat of the premonsoon summer had taken possession of our very flesh and bones. The dry winds that whipped through the dun-colored landscape in May and June had given way to a relentless, moisture-laden, yellow dust-haze that not even the smallest breeze disturbed. There was a breathless suspension of sound, except for the drugged hum of crickets in the hibiscus hedgerows. And all conversations centered on when the rains would come. The monsoon had been drenching and flooding the streets of Bombay for over a month and was moving north in its own time. Pitaji, like farmers everywhere and always, scanned the skies morning and evening, looking for clues.

Everything was ready to pop, and the uneasy relationship that had grown between Dilraj Kaur and me since my arrival six weeks earlier, was, like the heat, locked in with the lid on. In the beginning we sometimes caught ourselves studying one another, she perhaps wondering if my pubic hair was the same color as the pale blond of my head; I trying to figure out if she shaved hers, as I had heard Indian women do. Surely she plucked her eyebrows, though; those straight lines seemed too neat to be true, too classic to be achieved without some help. Classic. Statuelike. Greek goddess-like. She was, in fact, a reminder that Alexander's soldiers had done more than fight in Punjab. They had left a veritable Juno behind in the form of this twentieth century descendant. The broad brow, the straight nose, the full jaw, the grey eyes testified to that.

48

She lived her life within the family occupying a couple of rooms set aside for her and Nikku. I lived mine with Tej, whose attention I shared with the sitar, farm work, the overseeing of the new house for the family going up on the village outskirts, and with all the people, friends and family, who naturally gravitated into his magnetic field.

Tej's space and mine was the mud-walled room at one end of the compound. Mataji had installed us there together from the start, in what we took to be a triumph of logic over social taboo. Tej was, after all, my only link to the new world around me. It made sense for us to be together. Our room had two small windows with heavy wooden shutters that kept out both heat and light. On the packed earthen floor was spread a Persian carpet, a possession from pre-Partition days and one of the few belongings the family had salvaged when they made the move to east Punjab in 1947. Pitaji, back from tank warfare in the North African desert, had just retired as a Major in the Indian Army, and instead of being able to settle in his home village southwest of Lahore on the Pakistan side of the border, had to start all over again in Majra, where the government had allotted him some land in compensation for the farm he'd lost in the upheaval.

The carpet, then, was a constant reminder of the past; the mud floor, present reality. And my present reality was life amongst the resettled family that was soon to become mine. Even after two months, there were the extravagant presences outside the door of our room, the watchful eyes from behind the bamboo screens in the veranda, the cautious scrutiny at close range. I was still a novelty, an exotic, potentially dangerous—and therefore beguiling—creature from another world. In the presence of others, Tej needed to make it seem that I was not (as they may have feared) yet another disruptive force dropped down in their midst, that I was not going to make everything fall apart. He was still his own man, his own boss, their son, and not my plaything. Alone with me, he insisted on taking responsibility for the whole of India, minus its splendor, and for all its mass of people. For every fly on every item of food in the bazaars, for every peanut shell littering a train compartment, there was the look in his eyes that took personal blame for it all. It belied the take-it-or-leave-it attitude he wore like a suit of armor. I wanted to tell him that all this was not his fault. That it didn't matter anyway. But I didn't know how.

On the day of Uncle Gurnam's arrival, then, lunch had been finished, and everyone was ready to draw curtains, bolt the doors and the wooden shutters, and settle down for another afternoon, amongst a whole summer of afternoons, without electricity.

But then there came the seldom sound of a car engine, of tires spinning in the dust of the unpaved road into Majra, and as the vehicle approached, the groan of the overloaded chassis. Rano and I climbed up the bamboo ladder to the roof to find out what was going on. Ram Piari was not far behind. Moti and Jim and Lal barked, and Gian, acting on the reasonable assumption that ours was the only house in the village likely to have a visitor who owned a car, flung the gate to our compound open in anticipation. A jeepload of men and boys, laughing and talking loudly, was rounding the bend beyond the Majra pond, passing the abandoned mosque and heading our way.

A moment later, Nikku and Goodi were beside us on the roof, while the yard was filling up fast with the rest of the family.

"It's Uncle Gurnam Singh!" Goodi cried.

"Who's with him?" Rano asked.

"I can't tell from here," Goodi said.

"I want to see too," Nikku said, getting in between the girls to have a look.

"I don't see Aunt Gursharan," Goodi said. Her voice breathed disappointment.

The Punjabi came too fast for me to follow after that. It had to do with the other occupants of the jeep, names that were unfamiliar to me and relationships too complicated to sort out.

Before we knew it, the jeep had drawn up inside the compound, in front of the main room of the house. Welcoming shouts of "*Sat Sri Akal*" greeted the newcomers. Mataji and Pitaji came forward as Uncle alighted from behind the steering wheel and lifted a little boy (his youngest son Surinder?) down from the front seat. Rano and Nikku, Goodi and Ram Piari were already down the ladder again, while I struggled to descend the swaying bamboo contraption with some shred of dignity, aware that a misstep would find me sprawling at its base. I would end up being the center of concern, if not laughter. Already, neighbors had crowded the roofs of adjacent houses to find out what was going on. Amongst them was Veera Bai, the girl from the village who swept our yard everyday. A smile hovered on her lips ready to break into a laugh if I were to oblige them all with a spectacle.

Tej and Hari went to receive their bear hugs from Uncle and the others, and Dilraj Kaur, her face modestly veiled by her dupatta, touched Uncle's feet. By this time Nikku was by his mother's side and Uncle was patting the top of his head.

It was time for me to step down from the bamboo ladder, and face the questioning glances of the newcomers that asked what Tej's memsahib was like, what he saw in her; what their daughters would do for husbands if Jat boys should go on marrying foreign girls like this.

I came forward with my palms together in greeting and the demure expression I had perfected when meeting elders for the first time. Tej managed it so that he was at my side as Uncle gave me his blessing. He inquired about the health of my parents, asked how many sisters and brothers I had and registered sincere concern when I told him I had no brother. He wished me prosperity and happiness anyway.

It soon became clear that one of Uncle's passions, even as a guest, was taking charge and ordering others to get things done. Mataji's younger brother by two years was at his best at this, making it somehow an honor—a privilege even—to be allowed to do something for him. He issued instructions to the retinue of friends, poor relations, people who wanted favors from him, and servants, who like vassals of a maharaja, accompanied him wherever he went and who were now climbing out of the jeep. I had become familiar with the Indian habit of dispensing with introductions and knew that before long all these individuals who had come along with Uncle would get sorted out, and I would come to know in good time who each one was.

Pitaji, Tej, and Hari, and the cousins from Amritsar, gathered around the recent arrivals while Mataji, the girls, Dilraj Kaur, and I returned to the kitchen to relight stoves, warm

up the curries, and make fresh rotis for their lunch. Udmi
Ram was already mixing a new batch of flour-and-water
dough for them. A dessert was hastily concocted of fried
bread slices soaked in cardamom syrup and fresh cream.
Furious flies, disturbed from their siesta, buzzed angrily as
they searched out new places to settle down in.
Through the kitchen door I watched as the baggage was
being taken down from the jeep and carried away to the main
room of the house. Uncle Gurnam Singh came into view
from time to time. Something Tej had said made him laugh.
Casual, curiosity-driven neighbors had meanwhile joined the
crowd around Uncle, who stood leaning on a walking stick,
one foot thrust out in front of the other. His full, dark brown
beard was glossy from recent brushing.
In the kitchen it was all orderly confusion. Doing the cooking at floor level while sitting on low stools beside the stoves
was a procedure worked out over centuries. It suited the
climate, and the tools and equipment at hand; it also operated on the premise that there would be servants to fetch
and carry and to hand you things. But to my Western eyes
this arrangement created a certain mess and inefficiency. In
the midst of it, there was a conversation I felt I was not
supposed to understand. Uncle was as usual the subject of
it, and his sudden and unannounced presence in our midst
added spice.
"It's a disgrace," Mataji was saying to whoever had the time
to listen.
Dilraj Kaur stopped what she was doing. "What, Mataji?"
she said.
Mataji glanced around as if wondering whether to pro-
ceed. "It's Gurnam Singh," she said with a meaningful glance
at Dilraj Kaur, "and that woman in his village."
Goodi and Rano looked at one another. Dilraj Kaur sat
down on a low stool beside Mataji. Udmi Ram almost forgot
the dough he was kneading for the tandoori roti, and Chotu
dropped a plate he was wiping. The sudden crash of shattered porcelain broke the sudden silence that had overtaken
the room and made everybody jump. It was the occasion for
Udmi Ram to box the boy's ears.
"What are you slapping him for?" Mataji shouted to the

cook. "He's a child. He makes mistakes. He just has to be more careful. Don't let that happen again, *beta*," she said to Chotu.

Dilraj Kaur waited for Mataji to go on.

"I have to have it out with Gurnam Singh this time. I hear he sees that woman every day. He keeps her like a concubine," Mataji continued in a voice meant for only Dilraj Kaur to hear.

Dilraj Kaur made a suitably discreet remark in reply, and glanced briefly in my direction in the abstract way she had come to adopt in recent weeks.

"And that is not all," Mataji went on. "The woman is a widow with a small child. Can you imagine?"

"Some people are without shame . . . the woman, I mean," Dilraj Kaur said, warming up to the conversation and at the same time eager to show where she apportioned blame. "Who can imagine such a creature?"

"It's all Gurnam Singh's fault," Mataji said. "He needs to have some sense put into his head. When I think of what it must be like for Bhabi Gursharan Kaur . . ." she broke off to wipe her face with her dupatta . . . "I wonder how she stands it. She has given birth to five children for him, and this is all she gets in return in her old age: a husband old enough to know better, acting like a sixteen-year-old. Who does he think he is!"

Uncle's age was clearly a factor that made the entire business all the more crass. But other ideas were crowding in. I wasn't able to string them together; it was more in the way of a feeling that wasn't quite right. It had to do with the expression on Dilraj Kaur's classic face when she glanced at me. She who usually had no time for small talk, whose conversation typically consisted of practical matters like, "pass the salt", or "hand me the ladle", had found a subject to her liking.

"And that woman," she said, "how old is she?"

"She must be too young for him, whatever her age is," Mataji replied with a dismissive gesture that was as much of the Punjabi language as the words she was speaking.

Dilraj Kaur steered around to another point. "She must

53

have cast a spell on him," she said. "Such women go to any lengths."

By now their dialogue was being listened to by everybody in the kitchen. Mataji was silent for a moment while she transferred the dessert into a serving bowl.

"But he hasn't actually taken her into his house, under his roof, has he?" Dilraj Kaur went on.

"I should hope not," Mataji said.

"That would, of course, be worse," Dilraj Kaur observed, almost to herself. She allowed a small silence to settle over the room.

When the conversation started up again, it took a philosophical turn and became too abstract for my meager Punjabi vocabulary, tightly confined as it was to a few basic words and close attention to body language. Like a deaf person, wearied of lip reading, I tuned out their talk and took off on my own thoughts of what Uncle's concubine must be like.

As lunch was being gotten on I thought about how the presence of a young woman in his life added to his image, at least as I'd received it during the past hour and through family gossip all along. He belonged, surely, to an earlier age when landlords lived their lives in a kind of security that would never be enjoyed again. His youth had been a time of unlimited money, influence, and family lands. He behaved as if all these feudal delights were still at hand and his to savor. Moreover, he was in a perpetual state of activity, finding himself either in the midst of a lawsuit or a village feud, or both. He was a champion of lost causes, and lately he had graduated from local to state politics.

How can anyone so devoid of social consciousness be so charming, I wondered. It didn't fit. He should be making everyone angry or resentful or envious. My liberal outlook should be offended. My liberal friends in Berkeley would be appalled. Ripped out of context, Uncle wouldn't do. He'd be an embarrassment, a denial of some of our most precious beliefs about human dignity, a throwback to a feudal age mercifully dead, in most places anyway.

But there was a spot for him here. I thought about it as I watched him hold the company in thrall at lunch (even Tej was upstaged for the time being), and I became convinced it was altogether appropriate that Uncle Gurnam Singh should have a concubine; why not? This would complete the picture. I wondered why Mataji was so exercised over the whole affair. Even Mama would have liked to have her say, had some magic carpet brought her onto the scene here. "How can you approve of that man?" I could hear her ask. "It's bad enough for him to slight his wife and keep another woman. But don't you see anything wrong? I know you better than you know yourself, and I can't believe you could have grown up in our house, a Graziani, and still think that man's okay." For a moment I wondered if all the values I had grown up by had deserted me. Have I changed? I wondered. Was I right then, or am I right now?

At the same time, the vague apprehensions that had been lurking around in my head earlier, trying to take on some coherence, were settling down into an idea I did not want to explore further, since I had a suspicion that where it led, I didn't want to go. I would get back to it later, and meanwhile get Rano to fill me in on the parts of the conversation I had missed.

As it turned out, Rano's job as translator picked up as Uncle's visit progressed. Something was always going on: an outing for everybody at the nearby canal headworks, a shooting party for the men at dawn, a side trip to a city in the next district that the cousins from Amritsar had declared famous for a particular kind of sweet Uncle fancied. There were anecdotes to share; verbal fireworks to listen in on; arguments about almost everything that quickly settled down, as Tej would say, "as fast as the bubbles on a pool of pee." Even when we didn't go along, there was always someone of Uncle's original party who stayed behind.

Shiv Kanwar Singh, for instance. He had fought in the Second World War and at the merest prompting would take from the pocket of his saffron-colored kurta a much-worn snapshot of a blonde Italian girl he had once known, the two of them . . . he in the uniform of the British Indian Army, and she in a tight skirt and peasant blouse, smiling broadly into the camera. She had an uncle in Rappallo who had shot off his trigger finger to avoid conscription into Mussolini's army. A young fellow, called Brother John because of some private joke, stood or even sat at attention wherever he was, and except when eating, went around with a shotgun resting in the crook of one arm. His grandfather had fought in the Afghan wars, had brought back a tribal woman from the Frontier, and had installed her as his favorite wife. She lived to be ninety.

Their companion was Santji, an allegedly pious old man. His claim to the title of "Sant" was never quite made clear, but his dark blue tunic and carved wooden prayer beads gave him the external bona fides. He had lots of stories to tell, but none about himself or his family, if he had ever had one.

On the fringes of their circle hovered Ramu, a vague, sleepy boy who was Uncle's servant. We rarely saw Uncle's driver, Banwari Lal. His services were in perpetual demand as the jeep made repeated trips into town for one thing or another. He was short and wiry and resourceful, and his hair was cut long at the sides and short at the back.

Imagine us, then, sitting around, drinking tea and arguing about what to wash our hair with. It was one of those evenings when Uncle, Tej, and Pitaji had gone off on a visit to a neighboring landlord, leaving those who stayed back the job of entertaining themselves.

"No soaps at all should be used to wash hair," Santji began. He waved his hand in a gesture that discouraged all opposition when the others seemed about to take issue. "Even water is bad enough."

The cousins from Amritsar shook their heads doubtfully and gazed into their mugs of tea. For Sikhs, with uncut ropes of thick hair, the subject was one to raise debate, since everyone had his own theory about the best way to manage a shampoo. Ramu looked from Santji to the others. Uncle's little son, Surinder, and Nikku ran through the company bent on some chase game of their own. Mataji poured another round of tea and I passed the pakoras. The hot vegetable fritters turned out to be only a momentary distraction.

"Look at my hair," Santji went on. He lifted his turban off like a hat, and showed everybody the twisted and coiled mass of healthy mane, then put the turban back on again, giving it a smart tug as he did so. "I have never poured water on my hair in all my sixty-three years," he said. "Oil and lots of massage. That's all that's needed."

One of the cousins—Jeet?—asked how that helped. He said the best thing was to rub chick-pea flour into dry hair before washing it in water, and to follow this up with a lemon or curd rinse.

"Curd stinks," Brother John said. And that was that.

Shiv Kanwar Singh, ever ready to talk about his war experiences, regaled us with stories of washing his hair in diesel oil from the tank he drove in the North African desert. "There wasn't even water to drink," he said. "So where was the question of getting water to wash our hair? We would just take some diesel from the tank, and it worked fine."

And so the days passed. The real reason for Uncle Gurnam Singh's apparently impromptu visit did not come to light until his week-long stay was almost over. We were sitting on our charpoys after dinner one evening. A light breeze that had come as gently as the kiss of a mosquito scattered the dust-haze and revealed the rare sight of bright stars, soft glowing planets, the moon!

"Bhaji," Uncle said to Pitaji and the whole company at large, "I'm trying for a ticket from the party headquarters to run for the State Assembly when the general elections come up." He paused for the announcement to sink in.

Mataji was appropriately thrilled; her younger brother would be a Member of the Legislative Assembly of Rajasthan, an M.L.A.!

Pitaji looked uneasy. It was no secret that when funds were low, Uncle Gurnam Singh would take a loan from a relative (usually Pitaji) to tide himself over, and everyone knew that election campaigns cost money—the more so as this one would be the first in independent India. All that driving around from village to village through the Bikaner sand dunes in the diesel-hungry, trouble-prone jeep, all that entertaining and feasting to create a *political base,* as Uncle termed it! Party funds would cover only a fraction of what he would have to spend; the rest would have to come from his own (or some other individual's) pocket.

"I'm going to need your help, Bhaji," Uncle Gurnam Singh went on. "I need smart workers, people around who can lend

57

a hand with things. Do you think you could spare Hari for a few weeks?"

Pitaji leaned back on his charpoy against the still rolled up bedding he used as a bolster and gave a soft groan of relief. "Why not?" he said. "We can manage by ourselves for a few days, can't we, *beta*?" he asked Tej.

Tej said yes. What else was there for him to say? But I knew he was rapidly calculating how much more of his precious time looking up some newly-found musician friends in Ladopur or practicing the sitar was going to be usurped by the work he hated, when Hari would not be there to do his share. Hari of course brightened at the prospect of a few days away from the farm and the excitement of going along with Uncle. For my part, I wondered if Hari would indeed be back in a "few weeks," in time for Tej and me to get on with our much-delayed wedding. It was to be a civil ceremony, and for that we needed to go forty miles away to the District Headquarters in Ambala. The date was not ours to choose, but waited on the convenience of the District Commissioner who was to officiate. In all these weeks he had not answered our letter asking for an appointment.

"I'll go to Bikaner too," Mataji declared. "Bhabhi Gursharan Kaur will have lots to do," she added pointedly. It was the opportunity for Mataji to see for herself what was going on inside Uncle Gurnam Singh's household, and she was not going to let it go. She would size up the situation, see what Gursharan Kaur was going through, would get her brother to see reason and realize what a shameful position he had got himself into with the concubine. I played out the scene in my imagination as Rano, her large eyes earnest and intent, whispered translations of snatches of the conversation there in the dark, illumined now by a single kerosene lantern on the unpainted wooden table by Pitaji's charpoy. For one fleeting instant, something in her expression, something about her eyes—not on the surface, but deep inside the pupils from where the person who was Rano looked out on the world—reminded me of Tej. I felt drawn to her on his account; I felt an immediate kinship.

Monsoon

6

The family pattern broke up the next day like shifting pieces of a kaleidoscope. Mataji and Hari went off to Bikaner with Uncle (who had yet another loan from Pitaji in his pocket, got at the last minute). Because Nikku made a great fuss, he too was squeezed into the overloaded jeep, on the lap of Brother John, which he shared with the shotgun. Dilraj Kaur had to attend a wedding in her brother Arjun Singh's village in Faridkot, and one of the Amritsar cousins—Sukhdev?— was deputed to escort her there, gentlewomen never being left to travel alone. Tej and Pitaji, Rano and Goodi, and I stayed back to see to the Majra house and to await the monsoon.

All but the minimum of farm work came to a standstill amidst the hushed waiting. The dust-haze and the humidity returned, clamped down even tighter over the part of the earth we occupied. In a wash of homesickness, I tried to remember what July in Berkeley had been like, and failed. I supposed there would have been wild oats covering the dry, yellow hills of California, and on their gentle slopes, the neat, patterned shade of the occasional clump of oak trees. As soon as the image surfaced, it floated away like the scene in a mirage.

At the same time, uneasiness over my status within the family grew as the days without rain followed one upon the other, and the silence from the District Commissioner in Ambala remained unbroken. Tej and I bickered through the long afternoons in our little Persian-carpeted room, once the joys of the flesh had been savored and the sweat wiped away. Three days after Uncle Gurnam Singh drove off with half the family, the lid flew off.

61

"I need to know where I stand," I said. "I've been keeping quiet, trying to get the hang of things here. Just seeing what's going on. Where I fit in. I can't go on wondering what other people think of me. Mataji has put us in the same room together, as if we were man and wife."

"That's because we are, or will be soon enough."

"Not soon enough for me,"I said.

"Do you think I'm enjoying this wait?" he asked. "It's bad enough without you making it worse with all your imaginings."

"They're not imaginings. You don't know what it's like, dealing with the women in this house," I said.

"Don't try to draw me into your squabbles," Tej said. "I refuse to take their side and I refuse to take yours. It'd be a mess if I got into your kitchen quarrels."

"They're not even quarrels," I went on. "Nobody says anything outright. There are lots of innuendos and sneaky asides and meaningful pauses. I'm tired of it. I don't know how to handle it."

"I say it's all in your head."

"I say it isn't! Rano told me what they said the day Uncle arrived, about his having a concubine and all . . ."

"What's that got to do with you?" Tej said.

"That's what I need to know," I said. "The way *she* was going on and on about that kept woman, keeping the whole kitchen eagerly tuned in to her talk. It wasn't lost on *me* that she was forcing a comparison."

"*She.* Who?" Tej wanted to know.

"Who else but Dilraj Kaur?" I said. "Mataji just goes along with whatever she says, without pausing to think. I don't believe Mataji would hurt my feelings on purpose. And the girls are friendly to me. But for how long? Under this kind of constant bombardment? Rano told me . . ."

"Rano should keep her mouth shut," Tej interrupted.

"Just listen to me," I said. "Rano told me the gist of what they were saying about Uncle Gurnam Singh the day he arrived. How the woman is too young for him. How shameless she is . . . things like that. I just want to know if that's what they think of me."

"That you're too young for *me*?" he asked facetiously.

62

"Of course not," I said, furious with him for not taking me seriously. "You know what I mean. Dilraj Kaur is continually suggesting I'm not quite pukka, not quite legitimately here. She's forever bringing up this woman of Uncle's in ways that bring out her similarities to me."

"Look here, what do you want me to do?"

"I don't know," I said and began to cry. "It just seems like things will never get resolved, never get spelled out, we'll never get to Ambala, get married, get settled . . ." I chanted.

"Why do you keep insisting on everything getting defined? Where's the need? Sooner or later the District Commissioner will give us an appointment, we'll be married, and everything will be okay. In the meantime . . ."

"In the meantime, I have to put up with all of Dilraj Kaur's nastiness, I suppose."

"Why don't you lay off her?" he said, getting really impatient now. "She's an unfortunate woman. Her husband is dead . . ."

"Her *first* husband," I corrected him.

"Her *only* husband," he said pointedly. "What I am trying to ask you is, who would want to trade places with her? With only that little son to love her? When Hardev Bhaji died, her whole life was over. She broke her bangles, tore her hair, threw away all her fine clothes." Whenever Tej, or anyone else in the family got on this subject, their language took on the flavor of myth in the retelling. "She even wanted to die on his funeral pyre," he went on. "We men had to hold her back from making the supreme sacrifice . . ."

"That doesn't give her a license to make my life miserable," I broke in. I had heard the story too many times now. It had become family folklore, this grief of Dilraj Kaur's and her desperate acting out of it.

"Let's drop it," Tej said. It was more of a warning than a suggestion.

I knew he hated to come to grips with things. He hated defining relationships, pinning things down, drawing lines, receiving ultimatums, looking at circumstances from an either-or perspective. He hated me for insisting on it now. His way out was to turn to the sitar, or to go see the musicians in the gurdwara. I wasn't going to let this conversation go the way of all the others if I could help it. "Well, she appears to have *your* sympathy, anyway," I said. "You're always leaping to her defense like some . . ."

He was on his feet, standing over me. "What is that supposed to mean?" he demanded.

"No more than what I said."

"That's already too much," he shouted.

"After all, she did have you to herself when you got back, those seven months before I arrived," I couldn't help saying.

"What?" he exclaimed, seizing me by the shoulders and looking at me hard. "Say that again, and I'll . . ."

I will never know what threat he was about to make because just then a deep rumbling from far away came bursting in upon us, and his words were lost in it. We both stopped and listened. It was followed by yet another deep rumble and a rushing sound unlike anything I had ever heard before. In an instant, the sky closed down and turned the sun off. The rushing sound soon became a roar, the wooden shutters began to rattle, and the door to shake on its iron hinges. We ran to the window to look out, and as we unbolted the shutter, it was ripped out of our hands before we could stop it and went banging rhythmically on its hinges against the outside wall. The sky was a roiling mass of low, black clouds amidst a garish yellow glare now, and lightning stabbed the ground in repeated thrusts. The smell of sulphur and the continuous blasts of thunder fueled our excitement and exhilaration as we fought our way to the roof, our clothes whipping about us and dust forcing its way under our eyelids and between our teeth. Palm trees in the distance were bent double, snapped back, and hurled forward again. Branches were torn off the *sheesham* trees in our yard. Pitaji was in Abdullapur for the day, and the girls, who had gone to visit a friend in the village, returned laughing and running against the wind in a wild, spontaneous celebration. On the distant horizon to the east we could see it advancing—a moving sheet of water. The earth sent up its pungent female fragrance as it received the first hesitant drops of rain. And then the sky opened up to pour out the monsoon.

Bucketsful! The whole village heaved to life as if it had been a corpse miraculously revived. From the courtyard below, Rano shouted something to us about tea and some sweet, fried pancakes made of semolina and syrup that she and Goodi were preparing.

"We'll be down in a minute," Tej shouted back.

Hilarious bursts of laughter and splashings around could be heard from our rooftop vantage point as we watched neighbors fling open the doors of their houses and pour out into the rain. We ourselves pirouetted in a crazy, impromptu dance, laughing at our sodden, clinging clothes and at our hair plastered to our heads and necks. When our laughter died down, we looked at one another and knew the dance had taken us as far as it could on the rooftop. Back in our room, wet clothes flung off, wet hair thrown back, we went into the final *pas de deux*.

That night we were serenaded by thousands of frogs in the village pond celebrating their liberation from summer hiding places. It was a surprise the next morning to find the sun out, a bright and glittering ball, and every bit of dust blown away. Steam rose from the fields as heat hit the drenched earth and drew forth grass and weeds that grew inches in a day. Inside our compound the hard-packed clay of yesterday had become a no-man's-land of mud over which busy brown centipedes hurried, frantic to get to the outside walls of the house and climb up them toward some goal known only to themselves. They shared space with spiders of vermillion velvet, no bigger than holly berries, that polka-dotted the landscape. Butterflies flew out of hedges; whole new generations of houseflies swarmed. By night mosquitoes, all but wiped out by the heat of summer, made their come-back, while fireflies—twinkling green lights—made love in the mango trees.

The monsoon turned out to be a humid, hot celebration of all life, except human. Ants competed for the sugar in the sugar bowl, flies for the cookie crumbs, mosquitoes for breathing space. Rats gnawed holes in the doors. Lizards had the impudence to die in inaccessible corners where their corpses rotted. Winged termites flung themselves against the light of the lanterns until they died.

By day, our enthusiasm burned away in the sun's rays that came directly now with the disappearance of the dust layer in yesterday's sky. All energy drained away in the sweat that followed the least exertion. Freshly washed clothes that were hung out to dry in the morning and were exposed the whole windless day to the dazzling sun were still damp at nightfall. Mangoes began ripening faster than we could eat them. We filled whole buckets of water with them, lifting the fruits out one by one, sucking them, and comparing flavors until we were up to our elbows in juice.

Before long the much-awaited typed notice from the District Commissioner in Ambala arrived. Our marriage ceremony was to take place shortly.

"It's fixed for next Monday morning in his office," Tej said, "in the District Headquarters." He handed me the letter.

"It looks official, anyway," I said. I resented the fact that someone we didn't even know or care about, and who didn't care about us either, should be deciding on such an important date.

Tej drew out a second mimeographed sheet from the envelope. "I, AB, take thee, CD, to be my lawful husband, or wife, as the case may be," he intoned.

"What?"

"It's the marriage vows, I guess," he said laughing as he handed me the sheet. "What we're supposed to say under oath."

I read it over a couple of times. It had a certain poetic quality, short as it was. It was above all a stark statement that took care of every eventuality of gender. Was it enclosed with the District Commissioner's letter so that we could rehearse it? Or were we to study it? Was it supposed to give us a clue about what we were getting into?

We boarded a train from Abdullapur station early the next Monday morning after a wild ride on a tonga through a rainstorm. I wore rubber boots and a nylon sari to my wedding. My mind presented me with a brief flutter-cut to a recurring girlhood vision I had had of myself in yards of white tulle and a bridal veil decorated with orange blossoms, carrying a bouquet of pale pink roses and lilies of the valley, my father offering his arm before escorting me down the aisle of the church. Organ music. Flowers. Happy faces greeting us in our progress. Mama crying into a newly-bought

66

embroidered, lace-edged hanky; Nicoletta, a flower girl in organdy; Gloria and Julia, bridesmaids in pastel pink. The light through the stained glass windows filters in. Everything is in soft focus and slow motion.

And then, quite surprisingly, we were in the waiting room of the District Commissioner's office and being called into his august presence. I looked around and saw there was nobody to give me away. Mama and Papa and my sisters didn't even know at that moment that I was standing amongst shelves of untidy, dog-eared files, mended chairs, and scarred desks, getting married—with Tej beside me (he, AB and I, CD), and the only witnesses drawn from interested onlookers from the next room.

I held out my hand, and Tej took out the gold wedding band. The jeweller in Abdullapur had made it to order weeks ago. As Tej put it on my finger, I made a vow to myself never to forget the expression in his eyes: it said, "Whatever happens, we are like no two other people. There are no two other people quite like us. Not now, or ever."

7

Two days later we rolled and pitched along on a Himalaya Roadways bus that had a floppy gear shift and a driver with remarkable nerves. Local mountain villagers and city people from the plains, who had come on a pilgrimage, shared the space in an uneasy coexistence. The bus crawled like a confused centipede over the last mile of the hazardous road from Ghuntor, an outpost twenty miles behind us, and we came to an abrupt halt amidst billows of powdery red dust and the bleatings of a pair of baby goats belonging to one of the passengers up front.

Tej and I were on our honeymoon. AB and CD, legally joined and on our own at last. This was supposed to be Ranikaran, a retreat in the Himalayas famous for its hot springs and the Babaji, a holy man, who lived there. But there was no habitation in sight. The trip from Ambala had taken two days, first by train to Pathankot, and then by bus, in a circuitous route through the mountains. On the way, Tej wanted to show me Bhakra, where one of Asia's biggest dams was going up.

"How would you like to live here?" he asked as we stood watching midget bulldozers, earthmovers, and tractors scurrying around hundreds of feet below.

He looked at me, perhaps expectantly, perhaps anxiously, a smile waiting to take hold, but not quite making it. I knew the question had not occurred to him, just at that moment, although he wanted to make it seem that way.

"Why not?" I said, taking a lungful of air. The landscape was hilly and rocky, with low, thorny shrubs shrouded in dust in spite of the rainy season. Here and there a pine tree struggled for life, its lower limbs having been amputated by villagers looking for firewood or building material. We stood holding hands and looking over the busy abyss. I tried out an image of Tej. He's leading a team of electrical engineers by day; coming home to me at night to offer sitar serenades, hugs, and kisses. We're pioneers. In the Wild *East*. Best of all, we're by ourselves. What shall I have done all day? Stitched curtains? Swept and dusted? Played house?

"Why not?" I said again, honest and cautious at the same time. "Why do you ask?"

"Maybe I'll try for a job here," he said, still with the waiting look in his eyes. "They're inviting applications. It's what you'd like isn't it? For me to get a job? I know how you feel."

People were always knowing how I felt—Mama, Carol. Now Tej. "How *do* I feel?" I asked.

"You'd like it if I got a job so we could move away from Majra, from the family," he said, letting go of my hand.

"I never said that."

"You didn't need to. It's plain enough. But let me tell you one thing," he said, keeping his tone light. "We couldn't afford a servant, and you wouldn't last a day keeping house on your own. You don't even know how to light a stove."

"If I had to, I could learn. Nobody ever lets me do anything in the kitchen. They treat me like a cretin."

"They're trying to spare you some drudgery, and you take it as an insult. *Wah*, Memsahibji!"

He knew and I knew that "they" meant Dilraj Kaur. Hers was the magic name to light a verbal fire between us, so we both backed off.

"You've got it partly right, and partly wrong, *meri jaan*," I said. "I'd like you to get a job so you could make use of your degree. You didn't need to spend two years in graduate school to run the farm for Pitaji." This was a sentence I'd rehearsed enough times. It gave me a little thrill to have spoken it at last. But it came out sounding different from what I had imagined. I looked up at him to see how it had settled.

He didn't say anything.

"And if you're going to throw up those two years and all that slogging, why not sacrifice them to something you love?" I went on. "You hate farming and I know it."

69

"How would you like being the wife of a musician, then?" he asked, seeing the direction I was going in.

Up to then, this had been the great unspoken topic between us. It had often enough flitted from him to me and back again, unverbalized and fluttery as the wings of a hummingbird. It had never allowed itself to be grabbed. Now here we were with nets, trying to get hold of the iridescent wings.

"I *am* a musician's wife," I said in answer to his question.

"You know what I mean."

"I guess so," I said.

"I don't need to tell you there's no money in it, to speak of," he said. "And the traveling and all . . ."

"I know."

"Musicians lead terrible lives," he went on. "At the mercy of patrons, if they're good; trying to find one, if they're not."

"I know that too." I waited for him to continue.

"And then, you've got to perform whether you feel like it or not, when and where they decide. Shorten the performance to fit in a program while people in the audience sit and pick their teeth and scratch their arses."

"I'm listening," I said.

"Besides, you're dealing with other musicians all the time. They don't want to hear you, you know. If you're good, they're jealous. If you're mediocre, they're bored. They're the worst bunch of backbiters in the world."

"What are you telling me?" I asked.

"I'm saying . . . I can't imagine doing anything else!" he exclaimed. "But I have to start—imagining something more practical." His voice rose and fell like a musical phrase reaching some final resolution. "You know how the family feels about music," he added flatly.

No one had ever said it, not in my hearing at any rate, but I could guess the views that that family of non-music lovers would have. Once in Berkeley, Tej had told me how his parents had encouraged him when he was a child with an overload of talent and how they had been proud to see him perform for friends at every opportunity. But when he reached college age, the sitar was something he was supposed to pack away, along with the model airplanes, electric trains, and air guns. It was as if real life had no place for operators of mechanical toys, players of sitars.

Although the idea of moving out of the tight world of Majra was not new to me, I'd been waiting for Tej to bring it up. That would give it a better chance. Now the prospect of him and me living our own lives, on whatever terms, and whatever that meant, presented itself as a delightful possibility that I was free to explore the rest of the journey to Ranikaran.

It had been Tej's idea in the first place, this trip to Ranikaran. It had something to do with the death of his guru, Pandit Shankar Dayal. A promise he had made the dying musician; a vow taken. In any case, it was odd to have chosen an ashram to spend a honeymoon in, a place where flesh has to give way to the spirit, and abstinence from all kinds of earthly delights is the rule. But we were here to get the Babaji's blessing before returning to Majra to begin our married life. And in truth, Ranikaran turned out to be no Shangri-La. There was no Ronald Colman in a mandarin suit meditating amidst trees that sprouted paper cherry blossoms prolific as popcorn in a theatre lobby. No Great High Lama.

In the first place, we arrived just before nightfall, dripping wet. We'd walked the last two miles from the bus stop in a rainstorm. The three Indian families on pilgrimage had all got down and vanished, invisible as forest deities, into the mountain scenery as soon as the bus came to a full stop. Unburdened by sitars, excess baggage and a certain naïveté, they had made it to the ashram ahead of the storm and were already settled in, while we floundered around, looking for the path, finally finding the way, and getting drenched in the process. An old Sikh priest in a pink turban met us at the ashram entrance, which was festive with fluttery, wet, multicolored flags festooned above the gateway. He led us downstairs to the river level onto a crowded veranda where everybody was drinking tea. It was being served by a burly fellow. Marvelous smile. Build of a truck driver. Massive shoulders. Sinewy arms. He was tending a big brass kettle of boiling water set in a shallow pool of the hot springs lined with flat stones that had been artfully constructed to provide a perpetual stove.

We must have looked like watery ghosts when we arrived on the scene. The elderly couple from Madras, the Delhi businessman, his plump wife, and their two young boys, and the husband and wife from Bombay with their teenage daughter, all stopped what they were doing to take us in with a single shared look of surprise, amusement, and unconcealed curiosity.

At the same time, there were so many details to deal with, my eyes ached. Then, a word from Tej that made everybody laugh was enough to turn everything on again, to wind everybody up. The men came forward with introductions all round and all sorts of questions. How had we managed to make it through that storm? How had we got delayed in the first place? The women and children, lost in the unfamiliar sounds of my American English, crowded around looking puzzled and entranced. The hefty Sikh serving tea offered us big brass tumblers of the sweet, spicy decoction, fragrant with almond, poppyseed, and cardamom.

Tej held the ready-made audience transfixed with his embellished version of our trek through the rain. How it had taken us more than an hour and a half to cover the two miles. How we kept slipping on the wet stones on the narrow trail, nonexistent in places, and the Kumbh River swollen and angry below us. In the rain and the gathering darkness it had been one-step-at-a-time all the way. I found myself hanging onto his every word as though I were, like the rest, waiting to find out what was going to happen next.

"And of course the worst of it was, we didn't know where we were going," he said. He lapsed into Hindi with these last words and stopped long enough to take a swallow of tea. The old man in the pink turban made another appearance, this time to show us to the last remaining room. I wondered where the Babaji was.

The ashram itself was a rabbit warren of a place, hugging the steep banks of the river at a point where some hot springs boiled over. Except for the cement stairways, the building was a split-level improvisation made of packing box material not very expertly fastened together with nails and screws, strips of metal, and even twine. Cubicles were placed in no kind of order or symmetry. They'd just been added at various times with pragmatic abandon. Windows were larger-than-usual open spaces between the boards, and interior "doors" were ragged curtains under which people's comings and goings could be observed.

The others who had come up on the bus with us, and whose names were now familiar to us—the Subramaniams, the Aggarwals, and the Malgaonkars—had added their own dash of chaos in the process of settling in. The place was all suitcases and boxes, brass water jugs, dripping saris, soggy socks, women with loosened hair flicked out to dry, puddles on the cement steps, towels, and bare feet. And everyone was talking at the same time. Tej said it was Tamil, some Delhi Hindi, some Marathi. The sounds ricocheted off the walls in a mad cacophony of liquid vowels and gutturals that refused to blend.

All the while, the hot springs steam-heated the building as they burbled beneath the rocks that the ashram was constructed upon. It was said that the Babaji's own room was originally a cave, and that he spent the whole winter in that warm womb of a place, cosy and comfortable even after the snows began to fall in late October. Was he there now, I wondered.

Three hours later, after a change of clothes and settling in, Tej and I were beginning to come to ourselves once again. He sat tuning his sitar, and I decided to paint my toenails by the light of the kerosene lantern in our room in celebration of the occasion, the act a physical one, yet chaste enough. Warm waves of air blew in from the water at regular intervals through gaps in the wall, and from time to time a curious face—of a village child who had helped serve us dinner, or the two Aggarwal boys, or the teenage girl with the Malgaonkars—would dart from behind the curtain that served as a door. Pairs of bare feet could be seen beneath it, hurrying back and forth.

"I never saw so many things, so many people," I declared, examining the first coat of nail polish for smudges.

"Umm," Tej mumbled, looking up abstractedly from the instrument.

"So many things, so many people, in such a small space. Little rooms every which way, passageways, stairways, railings,

73

bridges, cubicles, belongings—everywhere! It's like an over-crowded, miniature golf course."

"That's no way to look at it," he said. "What are you so worked up about? I hope you weren't expecting a fancy hotel up here, or something."

"I'm not worked up. It's just that all these impressions are making themselves felt. Those women and children down there couldn't take their eyes off me all day on the bus, nor could the men, for that matter. I feel like a complete sideshow all by myself, when all I'd like to do is sit down and be one with them. Don't you see?"

"Look, you imagine a lot of stuff and want to take me along with it. If you're crazy, I don't have to be too," Tej said. "It's not part of the deal."

Having made that pronouncement, he went back to the tuning of the sitar, fiddling with the frets, bending his ear to the strings, tightening one, loosening another, frowning, tense, in pain. All the while he kept his eyes on me and nodded from time to time, but with his ear to the strings, as preoccupied as it was possible to be.

"Instead, I feel hemmed in," I went on, "as if everybody's pushing and shoving, only we're not going anywhere. There's probably nowhere to go from here, except into the river."

"Why don't you have a look around before you rush to all these judgments," he said in a loud voice, resting the sitar across his lap. He was sitting cross-legged on his spread-out bedroll on the slanting, wooden floor. "You'll be able to see things more clearly tomorrow morning."

Even as he spoke, one of the Delhi businessman's little boys brushed aside the curtain long enough in passing to cast a bright, awestruck glance into the room.

"See what I mean?" I said, getting up. I felt like striking out for somewhere, but I didn't know where. My voice must have come out louder than I knew, because an anxious voice from behind the curtain said, "Is everything all right?" It was Mr. Malgaonkar. His eyes, big with curiosity and alarm, were visible for a flash through a tear in the curtain.

"Fine, thank you," Tej replied in a voice as normal as he could make it.

"Just wondered," Mr. Malgaonkar said, and made his way

74

back to his room. We could see him urging his reluctant wife and daughter from the scene.

"Well that's settled, anyway," I said.

"What's settled? Nothing is ever settled," Tej declared gloomily. "Nor is there any reason it should be."

He picked up the sitar again and made a final effort to hone its tune to a fine point. Then he began the alap, the slow first movement of his favorite raga, "Megh Malhar," one to be played in the monsoon season. It was a wistful utterance, tinged with regret, and it was as if in the plucking of the strings of the instrument Tej were communicating with a spirit that could understand him as no human being could. I felt left out. I sat down again to listen in spite of myself.

Several improvisations on the raga in the alap followed one another in great, soft sighs. This is our wedding night, I said to myself. It was something I had lost sight of, what with the long bus ride and all the traveling before that. It seemed as if I'd been on the road for months, with only a brief, intense stopover in Majra. Perhaps it was the struggle through the rain, the anticlimax of actually being here. Of all the times I had imagined my wedding night—great filmy abstractions—nothing like this had ever surfaced. Meanwhile, Tej's fingers hovered over the same four notes of the raga, worrying them into a shimmer of sound.

Outside our room was the small bustle of people gathering around—footsteps on the cement stairs, creaking on the wooden floors. I got up and looked out. The Aggarwals and the Malgaonkars and their children were sitting crowded together in the narrow hall. The elderly Subramaniams were standing at the door of their cubicle at the upper landing of the stairs. Enchanted. Tej moved into the second phase of the raga, increasing the tempo, composing now, melody after melody. And finally came the climax, a cascade of sound and rhythm at unbelievable speeds. An occasional "*Wah-wah*" was heard outside, registering approval, delight, surprise, as Tej, like a magician pulling several rabbits out of a hat, drew out unexpected variations from the instrument.

All rancor between us subsided with the final notes of the raga. Deep night had fallen. No stars, no moon. An overcast sky. There was a shuffle of feet outside in the passageway as

75

the audience got up to leave. In the next cubicle the Delhi businessman and his family were settling down for the night.

"This isn't what I expected, Meena," we heard Mr. Aggarwal say.

"It's not a proper ashram," his wife declared. "Not like any we've visited before, I don't think."

"I wonder where the Babaji lives?" one of their boys said.

"He doesn't seem to be anywhere around," Mrs. Aggarwal said.

"It's a funny place," the other boy remarked sleepily.

Tej and I sat cross-legged on his bedroll facing each other, sharing a grin.

"It's like no ashram *I've* ever seen," the wife went on. "No priests, no Babaji, no reading from the scriptures. No discourses. This is supposed to be the abode of the gods, Shiva and Parvati. Dancing."

"The cosmic dance," her husband chanted in agreement.

"But it's only the other visitors wandering about. As if on a holiday. Those Bombaywallas, and the South Indians."

"The Sardarji with his memsahib. And then a sitar recital. Pukka rag—classical music—in the middle of the night," Mr. Aggarwal said.

"I didn't see anybody praying," Mrs. Aggarwal said.

Tej looked at me. "Let's have a look around this place, memsahib," he whispered. "I'm not sleepy yet, are you?"

We tiptoed out through the maze of packing-box rooms like cat burglars, not wanting anybody to hear us. We went down the winding stairs to the covered veranda that ran the length of the building and separated it from the sacred tank of spring water. Steam billowed out as the chill breeze off the river hit the boiling water that gushed out of the rocks below the gurdwara, housed in the ashram at ground level. A soft, steady rain was falling now, and instead of mingling with the water of the cold river, it darted here and there on the surface, just as the clouds of steam that rose from the hot springs failed to merge with the flood, but instead rebounded from it in great bursts of vapor. The pool was divided in two by a bridge that could be crossed in five strides. A low railing divided the body of water from the veranda. The bench along the wall of the building, and that which earlier in the evening was the center around which the life of the ashram spun, was empty now.

Tej and I walked along the veranda, looking at the pictures of Hindu gods and goddesses which papered the outer wall of the building. They had been clipped from religious magazines and old calendars. Some had been hand painted by devotees. Gory scenes depicting battles and tortured heroes from Sikh history shared the space with pictures of Krishna sporting amorously with the milkmaids and Parvati worshiping the Shiva lingam. An ornate wall clock hung over the door of the cave-room which the Babaji was supposed to occupy. Its shiny brass pendulum and carved wooden case gave it authority and rendered Time important. Tej lifted the cover of a transistor radio that sat on a shelf beside the clock. It had been hand stitched by some devotee out of silk brocade and bristled with stiff frills and flounces. At the far end of the veranda was a separate enclosed tank for women to bathe in, and some more stairways, this time leading up to a multitiered terrace.

"That's it," Tej said, taking my arm and putting it around his waist. We stood like that, absorbed in the scene, our eyes accustomed to the night now. All of these details clamored for attention. None of them blended. Everything was cut up, partitioned, refusing to mingle. Every item declared its independence from everything else, and at the same time demanded to be taken into account. It was more than I could take in. I closed my eyes. The damp air had penetrated my lungs, made my hair fuzzy and Tej's beard curl. Our clothes were damp, our skin felt like wet rubber. It kept feeling hot, then cold.

"Come," Tej said, reaching down and putting one hand in the pool. "Let's try it out. It feels warm."

The pool itself was in contrast to all the separateness and divisiveness of the surroundings. A constant stream of boiling spring water flowed into it and warmed the water from the icy river to a temperature just right for bathing. Tej drew me down beside him on one of the rock ledges in the shallow, warm, sulphurous water. It had a texture of its own. I had the conviction it was flowing through me, that I was dissolving into it, losing myself and at the same time gathering it all to me. The cells of the body renew themselves—almost a completely fresh set—every year. In that pool, it happened all in a few minutes to me. A great shedding of old cells. Fresh ones taking their place. New nuclei!

The drizzle of rain continued, but it became one with the pool. All the complexities of the scene outside were dissipated. At the same time, the lines that divided Tej and me were impossible to maintain, even if we'd wanted to; they were erased, washed away by the flowing water. His loose shirt and cotton pajamas billowed out around him; my dupatta lost its veil-like quality and became a floating wreath around my shoulders. Without even touching him, I was certain that his flesh beneath the wet clothes was warm and solid, and familiar, as familiar as my own, and that I'd make my home on one of Jupiter's moons, if need be, to live out a lifetime with him.

Minutes later we emerged from the pool and headed towards our room, simply cold and wet now and eager to dry off. A figure came toward us out of the shadows at an unhurried pace from across the little bridge. It was the server of tea, the maker of dinner, the truck driver with the marvelous smile.

"Good night, children," he said in Punjabi-accented English. "Sleep well."

8

Back in our room, Tej carefully replaced the sitar in its case, and I stretched out on my bedding against the wall opposite him. I speculated about what it must be like to be him—a man. What does it feel like to have a man's body, I wondered. Those muscular shoulders, long legs? What does it feel like to rise almost six feet above the ground, to be able to see over the heads of crowds? To look down on everybody? How would it feel to have large hands like that? To manipulate the things of this world with fingers almost twice the length of mine? What to do with that long back? The tight, muscular hams? How would it feel to touch your face and encounter a soft, silky beard? To touch a chest that is flat and downy? To clasp forearms that bristle with hair? How to move the big bones and muscles, to establish a rhythm of walking stride by stride instead of step by step? What must it be to hold possession of such a body? And how could it not affect the mind inhabiting it? Did Tej even half realize the power it gave him over me? One drop of his semen could throw my whole system into top gear, could start a baby.

What was it like, I wondered, to be Tej: the human being that he was. The behavior learned from family and kin lay fused like a firmly bonded veneer on his outward self, I thought. But in what conflict to his inner self, the one that fell in love with me, someone of his own choice, and experienced feelings contrary to the values he received while growing up. "He's walking a tightrope too!" I exclaimed to myself in surprise. "Between two ways of life. And he can't get off."

By now, all the other pilgrims had gone to sleep. I could hear Mr. Aggarwal lightly snoring, or was it his wife? From a room above us, a girl cried out in her sleep. Somewhere

79

amongst the web of human life in that architectural nightmare of an ashram was the Babaji. Was he awake or asleep? Praying or meditating?

A light breeze kept blowing the curtain back and forth as though with the comings and goings of busy phantoms, which, now that the lantern was out, possessed the room. It had become damper, the room more permeated with the smell of sulphur. Gigantic sighs and superhuman whispers raced through the window.

"What's that sound?" I said.

"Which one?"

"I can't hear it just this minute, but it comes at regular intervals," I said. It sounded like the hoarse whisper of a giant.

Tej raised himself on one elbow. His silhouette was solid against the luminous night sky as it streamed through the hole in the packing box wall. "Where do you think it's coming from?" he asked.

"For all I know, from inside my head," I said. "I just begin to fall asleep and then I hear it again."

"It might be Shiva and Parvati," he whispered in a straight voice. "You heard what the lady said."

"You don't really . . ."

"Believe that?" he asked.

"Yes," I said. "You don't really think they're here." I strained to see him in the dark, but his features were in shadow.

"He's the god of destruction and she's his consort and between them they're supposed to be able to dance up a storm. This is, after all, their legendary home."

"Are you serious?" I asked.

"The next valley is named after her. Not for nothing."

"Come on. What does that prove?" I said. "It's just folklore."

"No," Tej insisted. "It's what the sound tells me. I hear it now. What you heard."

"I don't believe it," I said. "You're making it all up."

He laughed and lay down again.

"If you want it to be Shiva and Parvati, why not?" I said, wanting to have the last word. "We haven't even seen the

80

Babaji yet, but you insist he exists. Do you think we'll see him?"

"I suppose so," he mumbled, turning over.

"Maybe we'll see him in the morning?" I suggested.

"We're leaving in the morning," he said, barely audible now.

"There'll be time to meet him before we leave, won't there? After all, he's the reason we've come up here."

It was getting harder to make sense of all this, with my eyelids refusing to stay open and my breathing slowing down. "Tej," I said, "isn't it odd? I can see myself lying down here; I can see the two of us, your sitar and our gear and everything. And at the same time I can see us trudging through the rain up that slippery path, and earlier, all of us bumping up and down over that dirt road, squeezed into the bus all morning. Did we really do all that? Or am I dreaming?"

"We did," Tej reassured me.

"You know," I said, staring into the darkness of the room, "sometimes I wonder if life is going to be just a series of disconnected comings and goings. At the end, will I look back and see a meaningless hodgepodge of pictures that are unrelated? That have no development?"

"Do you suppose," I went on, not caring now whether he was listening or not, "that we experience life in the same way as we look at a motion picture? With that defect in the human eye they call persistence of vision? I once read that because of some peculiarity, our eyes hold onto the image of a subject for a bare instant after the thing we're looking at has moved. Moving pictures are just a series of still pictures, but our eyes don't perceive the gaps in between; we are fooled into thinking that everything is moving. Isn't that odd?" He didn't answer.

"In our lives, are we really moving along? Or does it just seem that way? Do we suffer a kind of psychological persistence of vision too, that makes us think we're going somewhere when we're not? It could be that our lives, like the motion picture, are just some stills that we connect together so that they will make sense."

There was a moment like a blacked-out motion picture screen before the M.G.M. lion roars or the 20th Century Fox klieg lights scan the sky. Then the stills flashed by in my mind

81

like rushes from a hastily filmed sequence. They needed editing, but there they were: scenes of Tej and me in Berkeley.

Actually, Carol and me at International House, to begin with. By the time we were graduate students we moved in, I the better to find out about India and, more to the point, to meet Indians living there.
One Saturday night Carol and I took the F Train to San Francisco, along with a couple of Hungarians from the International House. They had recently arrived from Shanghai where they had got bogged down while awaiting their U.S. visas. For eight years. I had a photographic assignment to cover for the college newspaper, and the others came along because there was nothing else to do in particular. Carol and I were made to feel somehow inadequate, since we did not share the Hungarians' passion for bridge, which they played two-handed on a little board as we sped along in the train. Besides, years of travel with uncertain documents across hostile borders had made both understandably gloomy and prone to lapse into Magyar in the midst of conversations. Mama would have declared them too old for Carol and me. But I wasn't dreaming of marrying either one, nor was Carol. They had simply turned up looking adrift in the International House dining hall a couple of days earlier, and Carol and I had introduced ourselves. When we suggested the jaunt to San Francisco to hear a Berkeley student, a musician recently arrived from India, play an instrument called the sitar, they seemed to think it was a good, if puzzling, idea.
Our destination was a small hall that had once been a neighborhood theatre in North Beach. Once inside, we discovered a Sikh in a pastel blue turban and pinstripe Nehru coat about to occupy a raised dais in the middle of the stage where a snug group of expectant listeners was waiting to be enthralled. There were plenty of empty seats in the rest of the auditorium.
The Sikh musician had just made his entrance and was acknowledging the applause. He sat down and settled his right ankle over his left knee, and with the face of the sitar toward the audience, he began to tune it, plucking the strings, and making adjustments. No unnecessary gestures;

everything deliberate and sure. He sat with the instrument resting against the outer part of his right thigh. The long shaft of the instrument's neck, held at an angle, crossed his left shoulder and extended above it. He played a few notes. The fingers of his left hand moved along the strings while he strummed with the right. Details I devoured!

The Hungarians soon became bored and shifted around in their seats. Carol was working hard at enjoying herself for my sake. Of our group only I sat captive in the web of music that came spinning out of the exotic instrument. It was full of beginnings with no endings I could discern. There were exciting shiftings of tempo and rhythm, especially when the accompanist on the drums joined in. But I felt somehow suspended somewhere between pleasure and puzzlement. I was so lured away by those sounds insinuating themselves into my ears, that I nearly forgot what I had come for.

As soon as the concert was over, I left the others to wait for me in the lobby while I got to work. I went up and introduced myself to the musician, busy all the while figuring out what shots I'd attempt. He was on his feet, getting ready to pack his instrument away. All movement of his hands were controlled, with an economy of motion, an absence of fussiness. There was a precision about everything he did that proclaimed he knew exactly what results he intended. Close up, it was the eyes I settled on, not the hands, nor even the sitar, for that matter. They were direct and half-smiling and enigmatic all at the same time. How did one fly into the life of one such as he, I wondered, getting ahead of myself somewhat. How did one find out what made such a one tick? What fueled the powerhouse, charged the batteries? Was he wondering the same about me? Something in his look made me check myself out to see if everything was all right. I had my arms and legs on straight, but what was I doing with my hands? Having them full of camera helped. Gave me something to hang onto. And something to talk about, as it turned out.

"So you're a photographer, a lady photographer," he said, with a nod at the Rollei and a reference to my gender which I didn't know whether I liked or not.

"Yes. For *The Daily Californian*," I said. "Mind if I take some pictures?"

"Go ahead," he said, sitting down again. The accompanist sat wrapping his drums in cloth, ready to pack them away, and a faithful handful of admirers still hung about the stage. "Do you want a picture of the instrument? The sitar's made of a gourd; a neck of wood; some strings. Simple." He got aside so that I could focus on the instrument and turned it so that the intricate design in ivory inlay was shown to advantage.

"No. I want you in it too," I said, waving him back into the viewfinder frame.

And so this is Tej. Tejbir Singh. I've got him so that his face, black-bearded and moustached, fills up the frame with a wonderful smile, the sitar nowhere in sight. He's amused at something I've said about how difficult such an instrument must be to learn. I don't know whether he's amused at my naïveté or at the way I worded my remark. But it's a good laugh, a surprised laugh, about something unexpected that he's enjoying. When I lowered the camera again, I found him, the smile gone, staring at me with the exactness of a photographer lining up a shot.

"Well, thanks," I said.

"My pleasure," he answered in what sounded like a clipped British accent. Except there was nothing brisk about it.

I wanted to go on hearing that voice, but there wasn't anything else to say that didn't seem inane, so I said good-bye and hurried out to find the Hungarians and Carol.

After that first meeting I used every means I could devise to scrape up an acquaintance with Tejbir Singh, to know him, gain the intimacy of his thoughts. But I had to wrest him away from his friends first. He would be in the midst of them, laughing, gesticulating, speaking Punjabi, if it were a Punjabi group, telling jokes that sent the others into seizures of laughter while I smiled uncomprehendingly on. Or he would be playing the sitar in the midst of students he had acquired by the dozen. His presence was enough to occasion a gathering. Girls in shoulder-length bobs, white buck saddle oxfords, and pleated skirts, their faces made bright with red lipstick, sought him out, wanted his company, dragged him away, smiling and protesting.

Here's a sequence from last spring. I've managed to maneuvre Tej away from all these people. We're on the Berkeley campus, sitting in the sunshine amidst a Milky Way of pink-and-white daisies on the dark green grass of Faculty Glade. Beside us Strawberry Creek gurgles past.

All this is to put us against a backdrop: we were acting out our lives in a particular time and place, and this was it. There were innumerable cups of coffee in the International House coffee shop and lots of time spent sitting around in the Great Hall. For two people with no home to go to, no car, and no money, a lot of time is spent in restaurants, parks, theater lounges.

When June arrived, casual dates turned into weekend trips. By the time we went to Yosemite, we were moving into each others' lives with the speed of light, and our time was running out. Tej had to go back to India before month's end. The engineering scholarship that supported him was almost over.

We watched El Capitan levitating in the moonlight, its rock face stark white and shadow-racked. It was freezing up where we were, sitting on a bench in front of the hotel, on top of everything. We bent to the breeze, cheeks stinging with the cold, breaths barely inches away as we talked. Feeling like conspirators and using fictitious names, we had taken separate rooms at the hotel. Between kisses we stared down at the shadowed valley hundreds of feet below and talked about the future.

During the silences, I tried out some possibilities, ran them through, saw how they worked. But they didn't. I couldn't see myself continuing with my studies at the university. I couldn't see myself at home again. Lots of friends from International House were heading for Europe, and visions of the cold German towns, battered by the North Sea and six years of bombing, sent shivers through my blood.

"Will you get married," I said into the darkness. "When you get home?"

"I don't think so," he said.

"I thought all Indians got married."

"I don't think I will."

"Why not?"

"Because . . ." He hesitated while the wind through the pine trees filled the empty spaces where his words should have been.

"Go on," I said, not wanting to listen, but having to.

When he spoke again, his voice came from the other side of Saturn. "I don't know what to say," he said, looking straight at me.

"Just say why not," I said. "Tell me why you don't think you'll get married."

"Because I already am," he said. "I already have a wife."

I awoke from sleep with a start if indeed I had been asleep. Had I been talking to myself? The rain had stopped. A puff of steamy, sulphur-laden air came blowing through the Ranikaran ashram window as the boiling springs rebounded from the cold river water into which they plunged. I turned over, pulled the blanket close around myself, and closed my eyes.

"Ho! Over there! Look!" Tej cried out in his sleep.

9

All night I dreamt I was awake. Maybe I was. I never lost conscious contact with the slant of the floor and kept flinging my arms outside the blanket when I felt hot, tucking the blanket around myself when I felt cold. It was always damp; I was always listening for the restless presences that whirled and stomped through our space. The sulphurous sighs and breathings. Were they from underground? From the boiling powerhouse below us? What grand events were going on beneath Earth's mild crust to send these forces to the surface? What busyness? Down there, whole continental plates were shifting and sliding like moveable burners slammed around by a cosmic hand. Down there, it was molten rock, furnace-fiery. Volcanic torrents struggling to break through: A soup cauldron set over a fire. What a miracle we tread on it, this earth, I thought; dare lie down to rest on it, without fear of going up in flames, without terror at losing our balance on the shifting crust!

Or were these beings made of the air above us? Did they sweep down from the wild range of icicle peaks that loomed on the northern horizon? We had held them before us in our vision as we trudged up to Ranikaran through the rain. They had been just visible between the clouds and the steep rock walls of the lower range of mountains that closed off the northern end of the valley. Miles away. They had stood, substantial and three-dimensional, behind the veil of gathering mist and spray from the river like jagged sentinels guarding the edge of the world.

It was later than we thought next morning when we got ourselves together to leave. All around us were the sounds of the others rushing to pack, and running down to the pool for a perfunctory bath before going back down the hill to the bus stop. The frail old man was busy again, this time collecting the bedding that had been borrowed from the ashram by the other pilgrims. The Aggarwal youngsters, their bare feet thudding on the hollow-sounding floor boards, raced up and down, taking a last look at the place.

The adults were down by the pool, all lined up, drinking tea on the veranda. The Malgaonkar girl, neither adult nor child, sat reading a Nick Carter thriller. A little shadow of downy hair darkened her upper lip as she pronounced each word silently to herself. From time to time she looked up from her reading with quick black eyes and took a sip of tea.

The sky had cleared, and the morning was cloud-free bright. The three women sat appraising each others' saris and jewelry and exchanging addresses. The men were taking on the problems of the planet and were already up to their waving arms in a political argument in English. Fresh American troops had landed in Korea! The news was just now coming over the Babaji's radio. It diverted everyone's attention momentarily away from Tej and me as we all strained to hear the details of this two-month-old war over All-India Radio, Jullundur. The news came in crackles and spurts like one of Admiral Byrd's nightly broadcasts from Antarctica of more than a decade earlier. There was a sense of something historic and momentous taking place, but we couldn't pinpoint what. I leaned toward the set for more facts, but by then the news bulletin was over, and Tej and I were being offered tea by a little girl from Ranikaran village who had come to help the hefty Sikh with the job.

By morning light, he looked even more carelessly thrown together than he had the night before. His wiry grey hair sprang out from under his hastily wrapped turban, and his beard bristled every which way as he went about the business of preparing for lunch, now that morning tea was taken care of.

While Tej and I and the others sat there drinking tea, I tried to imagine what was happening in Los Angeles or San Francisco or wherever my friends might be—the ones who still remained to live their lives out on familiar ground—as news of the Korean war flashed. What supermarket turnstiles would they be passing through at that moment? Zooming out which freeway offramp? Going through which revolving door? Mama and Papa, Nicoletta and Gloria and Julia would be going across the street to Aunt Teresa's to watch the news because she was the only one with a television set. Lots of people in motion, going somewhere, on the move, not sitting still long enough for me to catch them in my mind's grip. Was there really going to be a Third World War after just five years of peace?

For the others in Ranikaran, the news had come as a brief, bright interlude between tea and leaving to catch the bus. For the makers and servers of tea it hadn't even been that. There was a war underway. Fresh troops had arrived this morning. It was all taking place in our part of the world. Yet Korea seemed more remote than the moon and the events there no more relevant to the people around me than a lunar event.

Someone had turned off the Babaji's radio. Perhaps it was the server of tea, because he was sitting outside the cave entrance now with a small crowd of pilgrims and Ranikaran villagers around him while he pounded mint and dried pomegranate seed into the chutney that was to be eaten with the rice and curry at lunch. His pestle was a rough, well-worn *deodar* branch, and the mortar a hollowed-out stump. A helper from the village had already tied raw rice in a bundle of muslin cloth and had placed the raw lentils, water, and spices in a tight-lidded brass utensil and set both preparations in a shallow bed of the boiling springs to cook.

"It takes exactly half an hour," the cook said in broken English for the benefit of the Subramaniams, who would not have been able to understand Hindi or Punjabi, and perhaps for my benefit as well. "It's always the same. Never varies," he went on. "Chapattis and rice and potatoes are all cooked in exactly half an hour. Rice pudding takes one hour, and sweet rice two."

"Tell us about this place," Mr. Malgaonkar said.

The cook stopped grinding the chutney to give the man his full attention. He sat resting one arm on a wooden stand where he kept drinking water, and supported his left ankle on his right knee. He gripped his left foot with his left hand

89

as he talked. "The tank—this pool here—is completely emptied every five days," he said solemnly.

He went on to recite (with his eyes half shut) how long it took for a complete turnover of water to renew the pool as it flowed in constantly. Amidst the flood of facts, he told of how the Kumbh River originated in the fabled Mansarover Lake that India shared with China, flowed underground for many miles and emerged at a point upstream which Shiva and Parvati were known to inhabit. It was Guru Nanakji, the first Sikh guru, who discovered the hot springs under a rock during a visit he made to Ranikaran. "This has always been a sacred place, you see," he wound up.

"Are there any interesting plants or animals here about?" Mr. Malgaonkar wanted to know, his curiosity apparently still unslaked.

"There are walnuts and wild almonds," the grinder of chutney replied. "Mushrooms, too. And besides, many medicinal plants grow here. We even find wild rice growing near the village and a tree whose bark is used for making paper."

"How long have you been here?" Mr. Aggarwal asked.

"A long time," the cook said. "I wandered around the plains of the Punjab for thirty years before coming here. I've been here ever since. Right here," he said.

"In Ranikaran?" Mrs. Aggarwal asked.

"No, I mean right *here*."

"Not even upstairs?" Mr. Aggarwal asked in disbelief. "But here? Just this veranda and all?"

"Within sight of the pool," the man replied with a broad smile.

"And the famous Babaji?" somebody asked. "Where is he?"

"The Babaji?" he repeated, his smile breaking into laughter. "I don't know. It's what the village people call me. Every old man is Babaji to them, isn't it? I suppose I'm a Babaji." The idea appeared to delight him.

Just then the wall clock struck eight solemn notes, and everybody looked at their watches to check the time. All at once hurried good-byes were being said, donations were being pressed into the hands of the Babaji, and there was a rush to gather up baggage and head for the bus stop. Each tried to get ahead of the others to secure a window seat on the bus.

On the way down the hill, Tej and I overheard Mr. Aggarwal and his family.

"Imagine, wasting our time with that talk about boiling rice and all," his wife exclaimed. "How long it takes to cook dal in the hot springs, and all about the fruit trees. Medicinal plants! I don't know what all. No discourse, hardly a mention of Shiva and Parvati, no speech about the gods or the sacredness of the surroundings."

"It's a funny place," her husband said.

"He's an odd Babaji," she said.

"We don't have to come here again, do we?" one of the boys asked.

10

The whole of Majra was hot and flooded with muddy water when we got back from Ranikaran. After continual rains, the pond had spilled over its banks, and happy black water buffaloes sloshed and bobbed in its depths. Flies and mosquitoes were busy recreating themselves in geometric progression. The landscape kept tossing up grass and slime, gushing a tide of mould, shrubs, and hedges, while mangoes continued to drop from the trees. The sudden greening was awe-inspiring and complete. A tubewell was being sunk, a tractor bought. Paddy nurseries, great patches of chartreuse on the landscape, were being readied for transplanting.

"It's been raining here almost every day," Mataji declared with smiles and hugs for both of us. She had come back from Bikaner sooner than expected in order to be there to welcome us home, and had brought Nikku with her. "But we were expecting you three days ago," she said to Tej. "What happened? Never mind. You're here, and that's all that matters." She popped ceremonial sweets into our mouths and exclaimed, "So you are married now."

The rest of the family gathered round, and we distributed the souvenirs we'd brought everybody from Kulu town on the way down from Ranikaran. Nikku came up to receive a hug and a present from Tej, and smiled shyly at me, wondering whether he should come closer or not; then, deciding against it, he ran off to play with the toy truck we had given him.

"I wish you'd have a religious ceremony as well," Mataji said as she had Udmi Ram bring us some tea. "What is a civil ceremony after all? It's hardly a wedding. Nobody there to witness it, no friends to entertain, no blessing from God. No . . ."

"Whatever suits the young couple suits us," Pitaji said, cutting her off. Then he turned to us to give his blessing. "May you have a long, happy married life. Always be good to each other," he said, giving each word its weight as he clasped our hands together.

"But Bhaji, we feel cheated out of some new clothes," Goodi said, lightly enough, yet I had the feeling she wasn't joking. "In a proper wedding we're supposed to get some presents from Bhabi's parents—like salwar-kameezes and chiffon dupattas for our brother's wedding." Rano gave her an ungentle nudge and Pitaji frowned.

Hari was still in Bikaner, helping Uncle Gurnam Singh establish his *political base,* and Dilraj Kaur was not due back from Faridkot for another two weeks.

I felt I had come home, finally. I allowed myself to take heart. Things would be different now that Tej and I were married. Majra was my place. I belonged. Tej and I spent hours at the building site, where work had come to a standstill with the onset of the monsoon. The plastered brick walls, the cement floors, and the roof were in place and stood awaiting completion, like a half-finished movie set. Work had begun on the cabinets too, but nothing had been finished.

One afternoon Tej and I sat together on a woven mat spread down in the room that was to be ours, planning furniture arrangements. The room faced the east from where the cool monsoon winds came. Tej had brought his sitar and began a raga especially for barsat: the time of year for lovers and poets. The sitar itself responded to the humid, fecund season with a new, full-throated richness, free of needle sharpness and "stringness." He began with an alap whose low, slow notes were more tentative than assertive and voluptuous without being syrupy. Something was going on inside me that was in harmony with the raga, and I came to understand what it was only five days later: I was pregnant.

The kitchen once again became the hub of the women's lives. Mataji was brimming with gossip from Bikaner. "He's so stubborn," she began on Uncle Gurnam Singh. "I tried all the time I was there to make him promise to stop seeing that woman. For Bhabiji Gursharan Kaur's sake."

"What did he say, Mataji?" Goodi wanted to know.

"Never mind," she answered. For a moment she busied

93

herself with giving instructions to Udmi Ram about lunch. Then she said, taking up her theme once more, "He didn't say anything! Just laughed, the way he does, as if it were a big joke!" She spread her open palms in front of her and shrugged her shoulders in a gesture of helpless incomprehension.

"What about Aunt Gursharan Kaur?" Rano asked.

"I can't understand her," Mataji exclaimed. "She's too good. A saint. She doesn't say anything, and tries to stop me from saying anything to that man. I'm ashamed to say he's my brother."

I too wondered about Aunt. Self-effacing? Self-sacrificing? Loath to assert herself? A clinging vine? A doormat? What made her that way? And if she was all that everyone said she was and Uncle all that he was purported to be, what was Aunt Gursharan Kaur getting out of life?

"He's under that woman's spell," Mataji continued. "The money he squanders on her! Dilraj Kaur has always said it. She's evil, greedy, a drain on everyone." There followed a Punjabi saying I had come to recognize because Mataji used it so often—whenever she was on the subject of a destructive woman: "A little cloud looking like the feathers of a partridge; a woman eating cream on the sly: one brings down rain, the other the ruination of her family. The wisdom of this saying can be depended upon."

"I can't understand this about Mamaji Gurnam Singh," I remembered Dilraj Kaur saying on an earlier occasion, in this same kitchen, this beehive buzzing with female malice as long as she was present. "How he fails to recognize the true worth of Mamiji, his real wife, his first wife?" She paused then to allow the words to take hold. "Her goodness is there for all the world to see. Only he's blind."

It became clear that Mataji had not been able to open his eyes to his folly. Her mission had failed. There had been nothing for her to do but return home.

The rains continued through days of mango eating, paddy transplanting, and playing on the swing that had been hung from the neem tree in the yard. Goodi, her pigtails flying in the wind, would squeal like a child the higher Rano and I pushed her. Because I was a bride and this was my first rainy

94

season with the family, I was given extra turns, higher pushes, more dizzying heights to swoop down from. And all this accompanied by songs about brides, about me! The artificial breeze stirred up by the movement of the swing disturbed the leaves and shook from them their pungent, penetrating odor. On nights we could spend outside, spotted owls on the prowl cooed us to sleep amidst a chorus of frogs and the lullabies of crickets. Barnyard smells mingled with the fragrance of jasmine. Now that we were married, at least in the eyes of the law if not in Mataji's, and with parenthood only months away, the future all at once became something to seriously plan for.

"I have to look for a job," Tej announced one evening to the company at large.

"Where's the need, *beta?*" Mataji was quick to ask.

"I've got to do something with myself," he said. "Make use of the degree I have."

The others looked at him as if he'd momentarily lost his reason. But I knew he hadn't. He had said nothing further to me since that day in Bhakra, but his desperation about the future was never far from the surface and erupted in momentary bursts of temper with the way things were going on the farm, his preoccupation with trivia, his sudden retreats into silence or long hours spent in Ladopur with musician friends he'd made, *ragis* from the gurdwara, or occasional performers passing through.

Later that night, as we lay on our charpoys under the mosquito nets, Tej said to me, "They didn't even *hear* me."

"I guess they never thought about your going away and getting a job," I said.

"Well, I have. Especially now, with the baby coming." He drew the mosquito nets aside and rested his hand firmly but gently on my stomach. My eyes were inside his head, and I could see the warring images that thronged there: the months and years devoted to music, placed like offerings before a shrine and all these at odds with the demands of farm and family and his need to make a living, especially now, as he said.

"Yes," I said again, and felt for his hand. It was warm and I could feel the pulse in his fingertips.

"You know as well as I do that I never could have made it as a musician," he said, almost to himself.

"You wanted to have a shot at it, though."

"That's another thing." He hesitated. I could hear him draw in his breath.

"What?"

"To have spent so much time on it. So many years. So much effort. I'm not a child any more. It's taken me this long to know I'm good. But not good enough."

"You *are* good enough; better than good," I said. "But sometimes other things crowd in. It's too hard to manage."

"Especially with no other musicians worth the name around," he said. "No tabla player to practice with; no one to back me up with the tanpura."

"Things you want sometimes get set aside," I said, and remembered the unexposed film in my old Rollei. I was going to say something more but Tej went on, as if he hadn't heard me.

"I got spoiled in America," he said. "Every note I struck was great by their standards. People didn't know what to listen for. I got worse instead of better, with no critics to keep me from getting sloppy. Then I lost heart when I got back here. I saw Panditji only once before he died, and he spent the entire meeting telling me how awful my playing had become. How I'd have to start all over again. When he died I knew I could never find another guru like him."

He went on to tell me about the first time he heard Pandit Shankar Dayal perform. He was just a schoolboy. His uncle Manjeet Singh from Amritsar had got some tickets to the Harvallabh Music Festival in Jullundur, a week of all-night affairs for true music lovers. Out of doors. In October.

"He insisted I go with him," Tej continued. "Said it would be part of my education. Four maestros were performing that night. One on the sarod, the others all on the sitar, with top names as their tabla accompanists, Uncle said. The most famous of the soloists, Panditji from Bombay, wasn't to play till the end, so we settled down on the lawn to wait. Uncle had brought along a dhurrie to sit on and some bolsters to lean against, but the ground felt damp and cold and hard all the same.

Tej paused a moment to raise himself on an elbow and rest his chin in his hand. "Can you picture it?" he asked. Then he completely lifted out of our way the mosquito nets hanging between us on our charpoys. I turned toward him to listen. "There was hot, spiced tea, courtesy the organizers, served in earthen cups. Some hot, salty snacks, too. People came and went; listened to the music or carried on conversations, as they felt like. A bunch of fanatical music lovers sat at the feet of the performers, keeping time, coming out with sounds of approval. Encouraging the performers. You've seen how they do, haven't you? Some listeners got bored, got up and walked around; came back again. I did too. I spent lots of time that night looking into the faces of the crowd."

"What did you see in their faces?" I asked.

"A kind of craziness, like some religious experiences bring on," Tej said. "I wondered what it must feel like to be able to have that effect on people."

"Then?"

"By midnight the crowd had thinned out. The real devotees stayed on. Those at the back moved forward, settled themselves into more comfortable positions. Some had waited all night long just to listen to the ustad and his famous tabla accompanist from Bombay. The percussionist was such a skilled artist, that he once forced a famous Kathak dancer off the stage in tears because she couldn't keep up with his intricate rhythms on the drums."

Tej went on remembering aloud the events of that night while I tried to create from his words a feel of what it must have been like for that weeping dancer, for that boy with his uncle from Amritsar: a tired and sleepy schoolboy, wandering amongst the crowd of grown-up music lovers near midnight. Staring into their rapt faces.

"Rumors started going the rounds," Tej went on. "The ustad's train from Bombay had been delayed; he was in a bad mood; he had drunk too much, was refusing to perform; he had quarreled with his mistress and was in no humor to play."

He said they kept waiting, but no one got up for tea or chatted with friends. He whispered to Uncle; asked him why everyone was so quiet. And his Uncle looked at him with this fierce expression and told him to be still.

97

Tej then described a frail little man with dyed hair and a forlorn expression who appeared out of the night, carrying a sitar and wearing a gold-colored silk kurta-pajama suit.

"But what was he *like*," I asked.

"I'd never seen anyone like him before," Tej said. "He came in, and when he acknowledged the applause from the audience, a gold chain around his neck shone, and diamond rings on his fingers sparkled. Admirers and students hovered around him. One handed him a big, white handkerchief. Another took a red sacred string bracelet from him that he'd carefully undone from his wrist. Another handed him a freshly made betal nut "paan" which he tucked into his mouth. As he sat down, he threw a Kashmiri shawl over his shoulders; it fell in ripples around his feet. The whole thing was like some kind of spectacle," Tej said. "It really woke me up. Uncle settled back on his bolster; he was prepared to be carried away."

The ustad interrupted the tuning of his instrument to talk to the Punjabi audience in Hindi sprinkled with Urdu, and to acknowledge the presence of old friends in the front row. When the maestro saw Tej's uncle, he smiled and salaamed. His voice was barely audible; he shrank into his shawl so that he was all but invisible in its folds.

"And then he started to play," Tej said. "He began with the alap in raga Bihaga."

"One for the midnight hour," I said, remembering a time Tej himself had played it for me.

"Well, the crowd settled down. There was a sigh of approval you could hear from all over the audience. You know, when the music is good it joins both the performer and the listener. It's a bond closer than that between lovers."

"You've told me that before. Tell me more about Panditji," I said.

Tej paused a moment before going on. "When this little man began to play, he became a giant; a god," he said. "He filled up all the space around us. It was his presence. His music. And like a lover, he led us along. He wanted us to understand what he understood and to feel what he felt."

Tej described how sometimes the ustad would mime the meaning of the music with movements of his right hand as

98

it hovered over the sitar, or with nods of his head, or with facial expressions. Sometimes there would be a broad, ecstatic smile on his face, as if he had seen God. At other times he would be in pain. He cradled the neck of the instrument to him as if holding a reluctant lover. The notes became plaintive, shy, expressive of longing, hope; some were mildly complaining; some joyful. All this during a conversation between the louder notes and those played as softly as possible. There followed a dialogue, one to be conducted on either side of an arabesque screen. Speaking of secret love? Of mourning that dare not be expressed? The ustad looked into the eyes of the audience, inviting them to eavesdrop on this tête-à-tête, this small drama. He wanted them to understand the agony of a hidden love.

"I listened to every note," Tej said. "Every phrase. I was a restless boy with the concentration of a grasshopper, but I had a pretty good idea of what the music meant and the grown-up feelings it dealt with. I don't think I moved a muscle all that time."

Finally he described how the ustad and the tabla player began the final passage. The *gat* was a celebration! It was joyful. It was raucous. There was laughter in the music. Notes were shooting into the night like fireworks. And then came the final contest between the tabla and the sitar.

"It drove headlong to the finish in a kind of frantic dance," Tej said, "a rhythmic extravaganza." He stopped for a moment. "I was ten years old and I knew what I wanted to be when I grew up," he said. "Well, that was a long time ago, wasn't it? Before I became an electrical engineer."

We both fell silent while the sounds of the night hummed around us.

"Whatever it's to be, I'm with you," I said at last, but by then he had turned over, covered himself with a sheet against the dampness of the night, and fallen asleep.

Tej followed up his declared intent of getting a job with a batch of applications for engineering jobs advertised in the newspaper. At least one would have seen us in Bhakra. All kinds of government "schemes," as they were called, were being "formulated," but these did not materialize in the form of job offers.

"It could take months," he said one day, and resumed farm work.

Dilraj Kaur arrived, as she said she would, in the first week of September. She was escorted by her brother Arjun Singh, a big landlord from a rich family, with maroon socks that matched his stiffly starched turban. He was not singular in his cleverness, but this escaped almost everyone's notice, as Tej pointed out once, because whoever has a full granary, even his mad family members are thought to be clever. I recognized this as one of Mataji's favorite proverbs.

Arjun Singh and Dilraj Kaur had arrived by the morning train from Faridkot, and Pitaji had sent the cousins from Amritsar and Gian on the bullock cart to bring their baggage. Would the roles Dilraj Kaur and I acted out be different now, I wondered, as I watched their arrival from inside our room in the old house. They walked through the gate surrounded by flurries of butterflies, against a sky as blue as an Iranian tile. She was all white chiffon dupatta and cream satin salwar-kameez; new earrings hung in cascades of gold filigree on either side of her face. She was tall, withdrawn, important, waiting for others to come to her. No one would have believed she had just walked two miles through mud to get here.

Goodi was the first to run to meet them. She had put on a freshly starched salwar-kameez, and her fine new muslin dupatta was a streak of red flying behind her. She gave Dilraj Kaur a deferential hug and a smile. Nikku was next; he threw his arms around his mother and clung to her knees. Everyone was there, crowding around; servants on the fringes. Except Tej, who only now was coming back from overseeing the transplanting of rice shoots. As he came up, the crowd around Dilraj Kaur and her brother parted, leaving a space between them and Tej. It held me riveted.

Fall

11

Four seasons had passed since Tej planted that woman in my head with his disclosure that night in Yosemite. She had grown there like some monsoon vine ever since. I had come to wonder if there would be any place left for other thoughts.

How the revelation that Tej was already married triggered what happened next that night, it is hard to say. The logic of it is missing, as is the ethical component. Instead of doing the sensible, the right thing and saying good night and good-bye, there we were, within minutes, both of us in my room in the hotel on top of the mountain, making a universe of our own out of ourselves, embarking on explorations too long postponed, making up for time lost holding hands, walking in parks, trekking the hills of San Francisco, kissing under eucalyptus trees.

Now the moment had come that I had always agonized over. And I was unprepared. As it turned out, I needn't have worried. There was no occasion for doubts, for games and maneuvers. All misgivings fell away as we ourselves, a constellation of arms, legs, and bellies, joined the slowly turning, shifting stars, the great spinning galaxies, and the slow moving planets in that starry Yosemite night. The sky against which they all whirled, and each at their own pace, was black with excitement. Great shiftings and changes of place were going on. In the midst of it, a rope of silky black hair came rippling down, once the turban was discarded. It lay coiled between us as we made our re-entry the next morning.

It was the room again. Helen and Tej, and . . . a third person. "How much of a wife is she?" I asked.

I was on my side, leaning on one elbow, facing Tej as he lay on his back. The long rope of hair was coiled again into a tight knot on top of his head. He looked at me for one sharp moment, then abruptly got up, throwing the sheet around himself. He sat looking out through the gauzy curtain in front of the window by the bed without giving any evidence that he saw what was outside.

"Tell me," I said. "I need to know."

"What do you need to know?" he said, still staring out the window. "I'm married. That's all. What else is there to say?"

"There's a lot you can say," I persisted, placing myself between him and the window so that he had to look at me. "For a start, you can tell me who she is. What's her name? Where is she? Do you love her? Do you have children? How long have you been married? Do you reduce her to jelly like you do me . . .?" I started sounding hysterical, even to myself. I had to stop.

"She has nothing to do with us, now," was all he said.

"She has *everything* to do with us. She's so real I feel her in the room this very minute. She's all over the place, she's . . ."

"Be still," he said, without raising his voice. "I tell you, she has nothing to do with us. And never will have."

"How can you say that?"

"We have found each other, haven't we? Can you say *no* to that? Can you go back on that? I hadn't intended we should come together like this. But we have in spite of everything. Ten thousand miles couldn't keep us apart. Nor can she."

"Are you saying we have some kind of special bond or something? Is that it? While you go back, as you have to, to your wife? That this was all too beautiful a mistake not to have been made, and so on?"

"I'm not saying anything like that."

"But isn't it? A colossal mistake? Too beautiful not to have been made? Charles Boyer fed that line to Olivia de Havilland in *Hold Back the Dawn*. It fits in here okay. It's about time for the orchestra to come in with the love theme before the fade-out, The End, and the lights come on."

"You're not making sense," he said, "I'm trying to tell you I can't spend the rest of my life without you."

"Are you saying you're in love with me? At least this morning? Right now?"

"I don't know anything about love," he said. "You talk about love, whatever that means, and quote dialogue from some half-assed movie I've never seen. People fall in and out of love so easily here. Come down to earth now. Look at life as it is. Look at me as I am," he insisted. "That's all I'm asking for. I'm without too many prospects. I told you I was already married, and that's true. But at the same time it's not what you must be imagining."

"Then . . .?" My voice was once more doing what I wanted it to do, which was to sound casual without being flippant and interested without being desperate. He hadn't thought about the next bit, I guessed, because he was clearly thinking aloud, improvising skillfully enough, but it was unrehearsed all the same.

"I'm asking you to come with me, just as I am, to a dusty Punjab village, where life is meager, boring, and hard." He looked at me and then away. He had gone too far too fast.

"You told me last night you didn't think you'd ever get married. So what kind of proposal are you making?" I tried not to sound sarcastic, because I really didn't feel anything but a certain puzzlement about where I fit in. Was I to be his soulmate? Baby-sitter for his children, if he had any? Friend? Buddy? Lover? The possibilities went on presenting themselves. "I don't know how I'm supposed to see myself in your dusty Punjab village. I don't see that we have anything to say to one another, but good-bye."

"What I said last night about not getting married has nothing to do with anything this morning," Tej said. "Everything's changed now. Last night I was trying to keep my life uncomplicated and spare you too. But now everything's changed."

"You keep insisting on that!" I was ready to burst. My head ached. "What has changed in the meantime?"

"Do I have to spell it out? Don't you feel differently now? Do I have to tell you everything? Can we ever go back to being the same two people?" The rhetorical questions kept pouring out.

I drew aside the window curtain that made a fog of everything outside, hoping to break the impasse by a moment's business with our surroundings. El Capitan was revealed, basking in the early morning sunlight now, golden-faced and craggy and somehow reassuring.

"What I'm saying is, I don't know how I'm supposed to go with you," I said finally. "Am I supposed to consider myself engaged? And if so," I went on hurriedly, "how can I be to a man who's already married? It's insane."

"Listen to me," Tej said. "I want to put you in a bottle, push in the stopper, twist the cap, keep you in my pocket. I want to have you with me always. I don't know at this moment how we can work it out, but . . . I want to marry you. Divorce in India is impossible, but a man can marry a second time, under the law. It's legal. You must know . . . a man can have more than one wife."

I was still trying to absorb the part about being kept in his pocket. I wasn't sure whether that was what I wanted out of life. However, if I was to be in anybody's pocket—and that's the way life up to now had looked to me; one was in someone or the other's pocket all the time: parents', friends', whatever—I could think of no one's I'd rather be in than Tej's. Besides, he went on opening up a new kind of logic, like some sleight-of-hand. It made sense until I thought about it carefully, soberly, in the way everyone else in the world would. Absurdities fell into place like fake flowers in a magician's posy, as if they cohered into some rational whole; improbabilities became possibilities, at least for as long as he talked.

Tej told me she had been his elder brother Hardev's bride, his own Bhabi. He had been just a teenager when his brother married her, and he could scarcely remember a time when she was not part of the family. When Hardev died in a shooting accident, she became a widow with a son, Nikku, who was three years old at the time. Tej went on to describe how intolerable life is for widows in India.

"But Punjabi farmers—landlords—have a remedy for it," he said. "Sometimes the older brother's widow is married to the younger brother. They are not married in the traditional way, but are placed under the *chadhar*, 'under the sheet'." He described a ceremony where a sheet, like a canopy, is held over the couple while they sit in front of the holy book, the *Granth Sahib* and the priest pronounces some words over them, making legitimate their sharing of more-than-symbolic bedclothes afterward.

"This ceremony allows them to live like husband and wife. The real idea behind this is that whatever property there is due to the widow and her children, will remain in the family: she's supported by the family. Her children have a share in the lands and can claim it when the time comes," Tej said.

It took me a while to take this in: first, the two of them, Tej and his widowed Bhabi, sitting "under the *chadhar*" so that later they can go to bed together if they like, all quite properly. Was she beautiful? Was she demure, this mother of a little boy? Had there been many witnesses? Wedding guests? And then it occurred to me that Tej wasn't talking about the other, excellent reason for this kind of arrangement. A sexually hungry young widow on the loose could only come to grief (in Indian terms, where her remarriage was unacceptable) and the family shamed and disgraced.

"I was twenty-five at the time," Tej went on. "She's five years older than me. She didn't want it any more than I did. She was, after all, still in mourning for Bhaji Hardev. But I was just about to leave for California. The family kept insisting that we go through the ceremony before I left. As a formality. Her brother was also pushing for it, for all the obvious reasons. I didn't have much say in the matter, and neither did she. They kept telling me this would not matter if I ever wanted to get married the traditional way."

"What did *she* say about this?" I asked.

"What?" It was as if I had interrupted him while he was talking to himself.

"Your wife, your sister-in-law, your Bha . . ."

"Bhabi? Nothing. How do I know?" He broke off as if everything had been said on the matter.

I couldn't let him leave it at that. Yet I felt so bruised and bounced from taking on so many ideas, one after the other, that I didn't know the right questions to ask. Yet I asked some. The notion of sharing a husband with another wife was terrifying. The whole idea, now that it was laid out before me, was terrifying. I had already set my foot on a path of life that I hoped would lead somehow to India. But with all these land mines? Going under the circumstances that only now were becoming clear amounted almost to a dare. It would be only slightly easier than climbing Mount Everest. Yet, I had to see if I could do it.

As I replay it, I see us in that room that morning as on a racing carousel amidst clothes, cast off and left where they fell; sheets and blankets and pillows creating a muddle on the unmade bed. Things were happening faster than either of us had reckoned, and in ways we could not have foreseen.

As for Tej, he had not even figured things out. He just wanted to marry me and take me home. Or take me home and marry me. Nothing was clear at that moment. There was merely this overwhelming fact that we both knew: We had created a world between ourselves that made the only sense we could verify, and that not rationally, not intellectually, but along nerve endings and pulses, inside guts and spleen, through the liver and lymph.

A year had gone by since that morning. And here *she* was again. Real. In the flesh. Not just a hazy idea, a faceless presence in the background of my mind, something I'd have to confront later. But back in our midst in Majra, as if she'd never gone away. I tried to drive the memories away, of earlier conversations I'd overhead: of Dilraj Kaur making much of Aunt Gursharan Kaur as Uncle's first wife, his only wife; of Mataji saying, "What is a civil ceremony after all?" Was the *chadhar* more binding than a District Commissioner's seal on a piece of paper?

I could feel the muscles of Tej's back stiffen as he hesitated momentarily before exchanging handshakes with Arjun Singh and the obligatory hug between equals. His back was to me, but I could see the expression on his face. He would be smiling his fake smile, the one he reserved for rare occasions when nothing else would do. The two men were saying something to one another. Some gestures. Tej trying to postpone the meeting with Dilraj Kaur.

There was this pounding, leaping heart that seemed to belong to somebody else. But it was mine. And there was that feeling again, that certainty that the scene before me was one I had no place in. It didn't need me in it. Everything, everyone was complete. Nikku was holding onto Tej's hand now.

He and Tej and Dilraj Kaur made a threesome who spoke the same language, were born to the same customs, and who shared a culture thousands of years old. It wiped out the previous two weeks in an instant. Getting married hadn't helped. I was still an outsider, an alien. A sense of unbelonging raged inside me for a dazzling moment. And then it occurred to me that if anyone was about to go crazy, it would be me, all by myself. And that would not be fun.

I moved closer to the window then, and parted the curtain further to get a clearer look at what was going on outside in the yard. A spectator, I had the time and the occasion to seize upon every gesture, on every regrouping of the actors on that outdoor stage onto which Dilraj Kaur had so recently made her re-entrance.

There was no one left between her and Tej now. They stood facing each other with several feet between them. And then, with just the right timing and the intuitive genius of knowing exactly what to do next, Dilraj Kaur took several steps forward. Her dupatta fluttered prettily about her head. A barely perceptible smile hovered over her lips. Her grey eyes looked briefly into Tej's before she lowered her gaze and sank down to touch his feet before he had the presence of mind to stop her.

Without thinking, I ran my hand across my stomach. Whatever else was happening, the life inside belonged to me—for the next few months, anyway. A day may come, I told myself, when this home, so recently settled into, may cease to be that place I'd been looking for. Staying on like this would not be worth my loss of sanity. I'd have to get moving. I remembered the Ranikaran Babaji and was certain that at that moment—while all this was going on here, all the comings and goings, the formal greetings and farewells at the gate—he would be sitting at his cave-room entrance, going nowhere, dispensing tea and his little speech about the hot springs to today's batch of pilgrims. They would go away as disappointed as the Aggarwals, while he sat happily by his pool, as he had since the day he discovered it for himself.

The time had come when I couldn't postpone my entry much longer. I had got my cue. It should not be said that I was being aloof. A memsahib. It should also not be felt that

109

some lack of confidence was making me jealous and mean and unsure of myself. I let the curtain fall in front of the window, smoothed my hair, squared my shoulders, put on my best, cheeriest smile, and moved into this high-density scene, visible, but undefined, like an out-of-focus figure in a grainy photograph.

12

When the rains finally wore themselves out toward the end of August, work on the five hundred acres of farmland belonging to the family claimed everyone's attention and energy. The swing in the neem tree was taken down for another year and another bride. It was just about the time my pregnancy was making it a queasy way to spend time anyway. Meanwhile the family had received the news of the expected child with the kind of joy and enthusiasm known only in lands where babies are always welcome gifts of the gods.

With Hari still away in Bikaner, the workload for Tej was doubled. Everyone had a job to do, except me. Or if I had one, I didn't know what it was. Whenever I offered to pitch in, I was told I should not exert myself. Was it because I was pregnant? Because I was not capable of doing the task? Because I couldn't even learn? The message wasn't clear. I couldn't settle down. A character in search of a part, I wondered what would become of our baby if one day I found I could no longer settle for this wandering about on a busy stage without being part of the action. If I simply bolted. Even my walk-on part in the kitchen appeared to be dwindling as Dilraj Kaur resumed stewardship of that vital department. Whenever I asked Udmi Ram or Chotu or Ram Piari to do something for me, they always looked to her first to see if my request should be carried out. She was "Bhabiji" to everyone, while I was simply "Bhabi," minus the respectful suffix. To my alarm, I found myself wallowing in such concerns.

"Bhabiji says that the woman Uncle sees all the time is using black magic on him," Rano said to me late one morning. "As if there was such a thing."

111

We were taking out some lassi to Tej who was sitting in for the tractor driver that day. The man had suddenly quit over an issue that was never made clear to me: he had been caught fornicating in the sugarcane fields with the wife of another worker, or had been cheating on the diesel bill. Whatever the case, Tej was stuck with the plowing and was already waiting for the buttermilk, just out of the churn, that we were bringing him.

"Don't you believe in black magic?" I asked Rano as we turned into the broad, tractor-furrowed path leading out to the fields.

"Of course not," she said.

Rano is a no-nonsense type. She has gone to good schools all during Pitaji's military career, and has had the sense to make use of a convent education as far as she's gone.

"But the others do?" I asked.

"I suppose so. Mataji says she doesn't give any importance to such things, but then sometimes she gets influenced. And Goodi thinks anything Bhabiji says is right."

"How would a person use black magic, Rano?" I asked. "What would that woman in Uncle's village be doing?"

"There's usually some old woman in a village to go to who would tell you what to do, give you some advice," Rano said. "For a fee, naturally. Or some favor or something. Here in Majra, it's Veera Bai, the sweeperess."

"You mean Veera Bai is a sweeperess by day and a sorceress after sundown?"

"Not all the time; not every night," Rano said. "Just when the mood comes on. Whenever the spirit gets inside her. Then everybody comes to know; they say 'she's playing.' Whoever wants her help goes to her hut that evening."

"But Veera Bai's very young," I said illogically. "Does she really have magic powers?"

"Not Veera Bai, but the spirit that comes into her, they say. She casts out demons and . . ."

"And?"

"She might give a person in trouble a message from the spirit, some act to carry out, some penance to perform, some charity to offer," Rano said. "Usually it's something silly. Maybe she would have them sticking pins in a photograph

112

of an enemy, reciting a mantra or something like that. Sometimes they tie up a lock of a baby boy's hair in a red cloth to bring him bad luck, to cause his death, even."

We reached the spot where the new tubewell had just been installed and turned toward the open fields. Our path took us down a lane of newly-planted eucalyptus trees that were intended as windbreaks to protect the leechee and mango groves. Underneath the trees, Egyptian clover—green fodder for the livestock—spread damp, fragrant leaves. We made our way over the ruts in the half-dried mud made by the tractors, bullock carts, and cattle. The sun shone down like a spotlight.

"But what do you think this woman in Uncle's village is up to?" I asked Rano.

"I don't know, Bhabi. Maybe she would be wanting Uncle to like her or be under her influence. Then, you see, she would put something in his drink when he came to see her. Something given to her by the *kala jadoowalli*, the sorceress." Judging from the tone of her voice, the whole idea was insane or outrageous or both, as far as Rano was concerned. At the same time she found it amusing.

A few fields ahead we could see Tej on the tractor going back and forth across a plot being readied for wheat sowing. An acre beyond that Dilraj Kaur was supervising the transplanting of the paddy plants from the nursery to the fields. She was a black-umbrella dot on the landscape. Scores of *chumaries*, ill-clad, barefoot Harijan women from our village, bent to their task in the calf-deep, muddy water, while she cajoled, bullied, and rallied them on. She stood locked together with them in this cliché of rural backwardness and oppression. The *chumaries'* aching backs went into the food we ate, the clothes we wore. Their sweat earned us our livelihood. This apparent exploitation was one of the issues Tej and I could never resolve between us. It was the subject, on one occasion, of one of our most furious fights. He ended up saying I didn't understand the system because I hadn't been brought up in it.

Pitaji, seeing me rush out of our room crying that day, called me to him with a wild gesture of alarm. "What is it, *beti?*" He cried. It was the first time he had seen me like this,

113

and his voice was full of concern. "Don't feel troubled, *beti*," he said. "Tej sometimes takes things too far. He's rash. Stubborn. Difficult. But a wonderful boy, really." His voice trailed off. Pitaji was a big man, strongly built, with a military bearing. At the same time, there was an expression of such gentleness in his eyes at that moment that I felt reassured and comforted. "Remember, Mataji and I are here to look after you," he said. "Think of us as parents, not as in-laws."

I had no words to reply before he went on. "We Punjabis are like that. Ready to fight, always taking offence. It's our nature. It's because we're fighters, have seen so much bloodshed. Our villages have been turned into battlefields time and again. It has made us tough. And we quarrel a lot too, don't we? Well, we've seen too much: babies torn from their mothers' arms. Women and young girls carried off. All the young men and boys killed; as recently as three years ago, in some villages."

"I know. I understand," I said. And I suppose I did, to a certain extent. But understanding is not the same thing as condoning, and I explained to Pitaji what Tej and I had been arguing about.

"In a world free of imperfections," he said, returning now to his usual pontifical tone of voice, "those who have would sit down with those who do not. But . . . ."

I had to admit, if only to myself, that so far the attempt had never worked out on a sustained, large scale anywhere in the world, in spite of goodwill, bright intentions, and honest efforts.

"In the meantime," Pitaji continued, "we provide jobs, they earn their living, partake of feasts on our family birthdays, and enjoy the celebrations with the rest of us when the harvest is over."

"What are you thinking about, Bhabi?" Rano's voice interrupted my rerun of the event that had taken place more than a week ago.

"Nothing," I lied. "Or rather, I was still thinking about that woman in Bikaner. What is she like?"

"I don't know much. Mataji says she lives separately from Uncle's family. In another part of his village. And everyone agrees that's a good thing. She has a little land, you know, but no munshi, no one to oversee it. Uncle goes to see her every day, almost. Spends lots of time with her. Lots of money on her and the little girl, too. Maybe she's poor," Rano added, trying for some rationale.

"Maybe she's beautiful," I said.

"Who knows?" Rano said. "Mataji hasn't even seen her. Everybody says she's young, though. Too young for Uncle."

"That appears to be the big objection," I said.

"Bhabiji says that nothing too horrible can be said about such a woman," Rano went on.

"What do *you* say?" I asked her.

She looked at me, trying to discover my views from the expression on my face. She had the same straight-at-you look Tej had and a forthrightness about her that the adults in the family continually sought to tone down. A door was opening in her mind, into a corridor she hadn't been down. "I don't know what to think," she said finally. "And you?"

"I don't know, either," I said. And I didn't. A pouting creature in harem-pants, seated on a pile of silk cushions, kept coming to mind. A Persian carpet, jugs of wine, and plates of sweetmeats. Gauzy curtains, hovering servants. She would be spoiled, demanding, and unreasonable. But she kept Uncle spellbound. I had lived in Majra long enough to know all this was not a likely portrait of Uncle's concubine, but what was? Was she beautiful? Attentive? Understanding? Aunt Gursharan Kaur was—or had been—all of these things, by all accounts. Perhaps it *was* black magic, *kala jadoo,* that was behind that girl's power over Uncle. Who could tell, I asked myself, as I watched the black umbrella in the distance move across the field of paddy being sown. Suppose there were such a thing? The black umbrella was joined by a streak of red against the mud color of the watery paddy field.

"Is that Goodi?" I asked Rano.

"Yes. Bringing Bhabiji her lassi," she said. "Bhabiji likes hers sweet."

Winter

13

Four months later I sat down to write to Carol Thorpe again. "Dear Carol," I began. "It's the Christmas season already, and I hardly realized it until the other day when I felt inspired to mass produce these homemade Christmas cards for friends and family—so far away! The urge came in answer to some primeval cry for a celebration of the winter equinox, I guess. I felt Christmasy in my bones, looked at the calendar, and saw the big day was a mere week away.

"I have been wanting to reply to your letter, the one telling about your breakup with the Dante professor. By now you have no doubt decided that everything was for the best. I've often wondered, though, why single men never attract you! Well, no matter. The Right Man will come along one day, and you will know it when he does.

"We're in the midst of winter. It's cold, dusty and dry, with piercing winds that rage all day. The sky is often overcast with blue-grey partridge-feather clouds, and the misty ball of a sun hangs like a frosted Christmas tree ornament in it. The sugarcane is high, the wheat fluorescent green and growing, and the brilliant yellow mustard fields stretch into the distance. During the daytime, the girls and I go gathering wildflowers and brown berries in the fields. At night, we sit around the fire in the new kitchen.

"Yes, we've finally moved into the new house. It was finished just a month ago, and I must describe it to you so that you can picture everything. It's an 'L'-shaped, two-storyed brick building with broad verandas at ground level. Tej and I have our bedroom and bath on the ground floor, and so has his brother Hari. The living room and a kind of reception center for casual guests, who are not friends of the family, are also

119

on the ground floor. Above us, Tej's two sisters share a room, and Mataji has her room next to theirs. Pitaji's is next. Then there are a couple more rooms upstairs for guests."

I stopped at this point to look up and across to one of those rooms, the one at the opposite end of the "L" from ours, where Dilraj Kaur and Nikku stayed.

"The kitchen and store are quite separate from the main building," I continued. "Outside the courtyard beyond a wall are sheds for machines and cattle. I guess it would have been simpler if I'd just drawn a picture. But you remember I'm no good with pencil and paper.

"Anyway, we all have our dinner in the kitchen where it's warm. Chotu helps the cook, Udmi Ram, roll out fresh rotis of cornmeal, and Ram Piari ladles out fresh ginger-flavored, pureed spinach, buttery and hot from the earthen cooking pot.

"It's crowded in the kitchen and smoky from the wood fires, and Ram Piari has to pick her way over our feet and reach across our laps to hand us our trays of food because we're all sitting on low stools as close to the fire as possible. Nobody wants to leave after dinner to go to bed in a cold room, so we stay on, telling stories. The elders remember relatives long gone about whom innumerable legends abound: the grandmother on Pitaji's side who in the seventh month of one of her eleven pregnancies, fell from a horse, got her foot caught in the stirrup, was dragged several feet before being rescued, and delivered the baby at full term, with no complications at all; then there were the family eccentrics, military heroes, a great-grandfather with seven wives, one of the girls a Paharan, a hill girl from the lower Himalayas, who must have been as exotic a creature as I am in this scene."

I stopped to wonder if I too would be the subject one day of a winter's tale told beside a kitchen fire. Nikku as an old man, Goodi as a grandmother—would they remember the girl from California with the round face, the straw-colored hair, the green eyes like a cat's? What, will they say, became of her?

And then I wanted to pour it all out to Carol. Unload

120

everything. What I had written up to now was true as far as it went, but there was so much more I needed to get rid of.

"Well, I've made everything appear picturesque and full of cheer," I continued. "But life is not all wildflower gathering and stories by the fireside. If you want to know the absolute truth, I'm as homesick as it is possible to be. I have not received even one letter from Mama since I got married last August. I guess she can't forgive me for not taking her advice, throwing up everything and going back to California. Papa has written a couple of times, but mostly to say how badly off Mama is without me, and how much Nicoletta and Gloria and Julia miss me.

"I'm homesick for the Christmas tree lights, the party times, the shopping, the going home for the holidays, all the relatives. I never thought I'd miss them so much: the sound of Italian being spoken, the taking of communion, the going to mass, the candles!

"We've moved into the new house all right, but we've brought along all our problems from the old one. It was not, after all, a case of cramped quarters, mud walls and floors, and a makeshift, outdoor shower room for bathing that brought everything to the point of desperation, but ourselves."

I wanted to tell Carol about Dilraj Kaur. How street-smart, or village wise, she was. Like the day we were all getting ready to attend a wedding in Ladopur. A big occasion! Excitement!

"I'll help *choti bahu* get dressed," Dilraj Kaur announces to the household at large. She always refers to me in the third person, and always communicates with me through other persons in Punjabi. I suspect she knows English well enough to do without an interpreter. But it suits her not to speak it.

Well, here is a friendly gesture at last. Surprised and happy, I put myself into her hands. I'm already getting installed in red finery with gold embroidery. The ornate but elegant salwar has extra-wide, fashionable cuffs, and the kameez has a tight-fitting bodice that flares away to a full hem. It's a wedding present given to me by Mataji, and the only outfit I have that would befit the grandeur of the Ladopur wedding we are going to.

"Let me do that," Dilraj Kaur says, easing the kameez over

121

my thickening waist and midriff. She helps me on with it and is giving the shoulders a little pat to settle the seams straight when she offers to do my hair as well. I hear her whisper something to Goodi about how thick and dry and uncontrollable it is. She stands off and gives me a narrowed-eyed look. "A little hair oil is needed," she says. "Get me some, Goodi, from the cupboard over there."

I watch in the mirror in disbelief. The usually meticulous, sure-handed Dilraj Kaur, who never lets slip a cup or saucer or plate, who never breaks a vase, who never spills even a drop of curry while cooking, fumbles now with the bottle of hair oil as Goodi hands it to her and allows half of it to spill over my lap.

"Oh!" she exclaims, allowing the bottle to slip from her hands. "I'm so sorry! What can be done now?"

Mataji and Rano come running in from the next room, and in the confusion, everyone is talking and exclaiming about what a pity it is. The upshot is that nothing is done, nor can anything help. There are offerings of clothes to borrow. But the close-fitting style is such that one person's salwarkameez cannot fit anyone else. There is nothing for it except for me to stay home from the wedding and watch from my window as the whole family sets out together. All except Rano, who pleads a headache and says she'd rather stay back. Rano's a good teller of white lies and this one makes me grateful to her. Dilraj Kaur rides with the women in the bullock cart, managing to be in command, even in such a vehicle. The men go on foot.

"She did it on purpose," I told Tej that night after everyone had returned well fed, and satiated from an afternoon and evening of eating and drinking and socializing.

"How can you say that?" he asked.

"I know it," I said.

He muttered something about women's intuition and tried to laugh it off.

"That's not funny," I countered.

"Why would she deliberately spill hair oil on your clothes?" he asked in a tone of voice adults reserve for unreasonable children. "It doesn't make sense."

And I suppose it didn't to him. But it did to me. And I

said so. "It was an ingenious way for her to see that I was cut out of things."

"You're being childish if you think Dilraj Kaur is interested in 'cutting you out'."

"That's no way to look at it," I said. "You don't solve anything by saying I'm childish, do you? You just don't want to face up to the fact that your Bhabi is devious and mean."

"Not so mean as you are with your baseless accusations every third day."

"It's natural for her to resent my being here," I said, ignoring his last remark and trying to keep my voice at a sensible pitch.

"She may think anything," Tej said.

"There you are again," I said. "Not taking account of her. Bringing me onto this scene was wrong—at least in her eyes. You've hurt us both by it. I didn't anticipate this. It's you she should be taking it out on, not me."

"You seize upon an idea and just won't let it go, will you," Tej said. "You refuse to understand that Bhabiji Dilraj Kaur has nothing to complain about. Nothing, no one has been taken away from her by you. Besides, I wouldn't expect her to behave as you make it appear. She's an unfortunate person. I'm disappointed in you for not having more feeling, more compassion. You should be above such petty thoughts. They only spoil your looks." He paused a moment. "And I like your looks, *missi-bawa*." He took my face in his hands and kissed me on either cheek, then held me at arm's length for a moment.

I couldn't return his gaze. Instead, I buried my head against his shoulder. My heartbeat rattled in my ears. Rage and frustration were making my head pound.

"You are naturally disappointed because you couldn't go to the wedding. It was a silly affair. All show and bad taste, and I wished I could have got out of it," he said, stroking my hair, holding me close to him.

A millon little suns exploded into being along my bloodstream, whirled their lifetimes out, and collapsed one by one upon themselves, as I reminded myself that when affection is truly offered—love, even—you don't turn away. I hugged him back.

Remembering that occasion was enough. I didn't need to write it down in my letter to Carol. Nor all that about how homesick I was. Instead, my thoughts went back to an earlier time when all these maneuvers and manipulations of someone like Dilraj Kaur would have seemed petty and inconsequential and not worth thinking about: back to Berkeley after that weekend in Yosemite.

It was Monday morning, and the idea of running off to India with Tej bounced off reality and got knocked about in the process. Everything in my life said *no!* Family considerations. Friends. The degree I'd worked so hard for. The photography, the technical skills mastered to the point where they were beginning to respond to the ideas I had in mind. Above everything else, the widow-mother-sister-in-law-wife occupied my head where she banged on my conscience and demanded to be taken into account. How could I do that to another woman?

I persuaded Tej that I needed to be by myself for a few days. Questions bloomed like carnivorous lilies, and I had no answers. He stayed away. Questions remained. It gradually occurred to me that what I was doing was preparing myself for saying a belated good-bye. It was just at a time when rumors of my impending flight to India with Tej started making the rounds of International House. The irony of it struck me. Everything was out of sync, like the shutter and flash of a camera working at odds. I had no energy or will to set right my friends, least of all Carol.

When the week was up, there was Tej. He'd come during the coffee break after dinner to sweep me away through the swinging doors of the Great Hall, out into the night. An effervescence in the cells, a tingling in the nuclei set in.

But I stuck to my resolve and told him we'd have to say good-bye for good when he left for India. I must have said a lot of things, all sensible and right, arrived at with effort. And he must have countered them all with his own reasonable-sounding assurances about how nobody would really be hurt by us: an idea I wasn't ever able to accept. Not even as I recalled the scene.

We stayed up talking all night under the eucalyptus trees

124

by the Forestry Building, ignoring the cold and the campus police. By one o'clock in the morning I would have been locked out of International House anyway. Tej and I watched the dawn come up behind the football stadium and then went our separate ways, wrung out and vacant. I had stayed firm. For the first time in months, we parted without saying when we'd see each other again.

I resumed my letter to Carol. "Remember that morning I missed breakfast? I ran into you in the International House coffee shop. We had a long talk. You didn't know, but my life was falling apart, leaking away, oozing through the cracks. I didn't like the feeling. I needed a cup of coffee and a cigarette.

"I squeezed through the crowded coffee shop and found a table by the big plate glass window facing onto Bancroft, sat down opposite it, and waved you over. You were picking up an order from the counter and had turned around to find a place. There you were, a smiling reminder of the familiar amidst the phantasmagoria of the past week. But you soon started in on whether I was going to India with Tej. You didn't call him Tej; you called him my "Sikh friend," as if by avoiding naming him, you would somehow not have to acknowledge him as a person, someone real. It appeared you wanted to say a lot, or at any rate, ask a lot of questions, all of which were designed to exclude him from my much-discussed future. I could understand why you were behaving like this, Carol. Other friends, too, had given us no support, Tej and me. Not his friends; not mine. As a pair, we were threatening. Subversive. Dangerous. We upset everyone's idea of how things were supposed to be; we were under-miners of one another's cultures; wreckers of tradition and custom.

"You kept digging around the same idea. Trying to find out what in the world I was after. Adventure? Excitement? Satisfaction of curiosity? A good screw?

"I was exhausted from sleeplessness and the previous night's tug-of-war between everything I wanted and every-thing I thought other people wanted *for* me. I longed to be left alone before I dissolved away in a fit of hysteria. Smiling vacantly and looking out the window were my strategies for

125

turning off your questions and avoiding a scene in which I imagined myself standing up and screaming, or alternatively, sinking into a flood of tears. Perhaps you would give up at last, but you didn't. Instead, your words were getting lost in the din of my own thoughts when, without having time to prepare myself or an opportunity to pull myself together, I happened to look out the window, past you, past the steps up to the coffee shop.

"And there was Tej, walking up Bancroft toward International House, wearing a fawn-colored Nehru jacket and light tan pants. He was still half a block away and would have been lost in the crowd to eyes other than mine. I watched him as he came up the hill. He was lovely about the neck, silky about the beard, a mover without excess motion.

"A single conviction took hold for a period of time that was briefer than a second and brighter than the sun: I had to marry that man or no one else. I had denied some loyalty deeper than family and country and culture when I had believed otherwise. Going away with Tej would be going home. I stood up. He was nearing the steps, now, in just his particular way of walking, like nobody else, not another person in the world. All I knew was that wherever I went, whatever I did henceforth, I wanted him to be in on it. I rushed out to tell him so."

14

I took up a fresh sheet of writing paper to continue. Then stopped. The letter was getting out of hand. I was telling Carol more than she would be able to understand and much more than I wanted her to know. I went back to the part where I described the sitting around in the kitchen at night. Then I tore up the rest.

In its stead I'd have to put in something concerning our daily lives that she'd like to hear about. Things like the week-long visits from family friends, old army comrades of Pitaji's and their wives and grown-up children. The men off shooting partridge and wild buck; the women and children on long walks through the fields at sunset or into some cooking project for tea time. Very romantic. A scene from a nineteenth century Russian novel!

Not so romantic were the frequent callers from Ladopur, petty but powerful officials and their wives who were motivated more by what they needed from our farm (sugarcane, garden vegetables, flowers for garlands meant for special occasions, chickens by the dozen for wedding feasts, honey, milk, eggs—whatever was in season or available or both) than by friendship. Pitaji liked to oblige them because he was a genial, generous man, and it also made certain official transactions go more smoothly.

Hari finally got back from Bikaner in November and out of the orbit of Uncle Gurnam Singh that would have threatened to keep him going around and around for months more, if Pitaji had not written several letters saying he needed Hari at Majra. Hari came back grown up, pounds heavier, sporting a thicker beard, and full of news.

It surprised no one that Uncle was unsuccessful, for the

127

time being at any rate, in getting a "ticket" from the party. But he had had a great deal of fun during the attempt. Hari was ready with stories of whirlwind tours of villages, Uncle's speechmaking before wildly appreciative supporters, Brother John's arguments with Santji and Shiv Kanwar Singh, and the repeated breakdowns of the jeep that driver Banwari Lal had to cope with in the middle of sand dunes and date palms, miles from the nearest village. Midnight suppers on the road became a nightly feature. Wayside meals at *dhabas* were always the same: stringy goat meat in watery, chili-peppered curry, with burnt tandoori rotis.

"It was Mamiji Gursharan Kaur who did most of the work, though," Hari said. "She did more than any of us. There was always a bunch of people back in the village to feed and bring tea for at all hours. And she always had a smile for everybody."

While he was saying this, an image of yet another smiling server of tea crossed my mind and for a moment I couldn't place it.

"What about that other woman?" Mataji was quick to ask.

"Oh," Hari said. "She's moved into Uncle's house. She and her little girl."

Mataji had her mouth open to say something further, and Dilraj Kaur shook her head in disbelief. But Hari hurried on to other stories of his stay with Uncle before he could be further grilled on that lively man's indiscretions. Hari clearly enjoyed his role as newsbringer, but found no relish in the more prurient bits so eagerly awaited by Mataji and Dilraj Kaur and Goodi.

Would I need to tell Carol all this?

In any case, I'd tell her about how, all fall, Tej had been spending less time looking up musicians and trying to find a tabla accompanist, and more time trying hard for a job. But not succeeding. Then there was this bizarre process taking place in the family all the while as I watched helplessly on. A neat magnetization: Dilraj Kaur at one end; I at the other. The rest of the family were being drawn like bits of iron filings to our opposite poles. Pitaji and Rano and Hari remained open and unself-conscious with me; but I got the impression that "people" were saying I kept to my room too much. Wasn't I feigning morning sickness, just to get out of work? Didn't I find too many excuses to visit the Mission Hospital in Ladopur for prenatal check-ups? Weren't the two Scottish nursing sisters there, Jean Campbell and Ina Mae Scott, trying to get me back into the Christian fold while pretending to deliver only professional care with their tea and scones?

These messages came more through body language and facial expressions, tones of voice, and studied silences, than from anything concrete. They also came through Goodi, who had become Dilraj Kaur's mouthpiece. Opinions, feelings, judgments were conveyed to me via Rano, who in passing them on tried to soften them for my benefit and in the interests of maintaining harmony in the household. Rano was a peacemaker. I would describe for Carol how she operated. I'd tell her about the morning Rano and I were taking Jim for a walk.

"Goodi and I were talking last night," Rano began.

"And?"

"Before we went to sleep. You know how she is, pretty childish, really. Anyway, she was telling me what Bhabiji has been saying. And, I don't know if Goodi got it right or not, but she said Bhabiji in a kind of joking way remarked that you seem to have cast a spell over Pitaji, he spends so much time talking to you. More than anyone else in the family."

"What?" Jim was tugging at his leash, and my exclamation as I kept him in control came out in a burst of breath that gave it more force than intended.

Rano looked at me. Is this the wrong topic to have started, she perhaps wondered. Whatever, she plunged ahead. "That's what she said," Rano replied. "Goodi said that Mataji looked up from her knitting—she was working on that grey pullover for Hari—and gave a little laugh. Not amused, but uneasy. Maybe she didn't know what to say. Anyway, Bhabiji said, 'Haven't you ever noticed? Every evening before dinner they sit there together listening to All-India Radio Jullundur and talking for I don't know how long'."

"'So,' Mataji said, 'then what?'

"'Nothing,' Bhabiji said.

"'You must have something more to say,' Mataji went on.

"'Isn't that enough?' Bhabiji asked. Then everything was quiet. Goodi said Mataji seemed to be thinking about what Bhabiji had said. Udmi Ram had been hovering around like he does, with the tea things and all, and Ram Piari and even Gian had been listening to every word. They're all terrible gossips. They must have repeated that conversation to every servant in the village by this time. Anyway, Goodi says Mataji seemed really upset then, all of them there and all. Her face got red and she put away her knitting and didn't say another word until dinner time."

I stopped a moment to take this in and to sort out some impressions. What I came up with was as much ado about nothing as anyone could possibly imagine. Tripe and trivia and nonsense. Yet I had to give Dilraj Kaur credit for seizing upon such meager material and wrestling something sensational from it, or at least disturbing to Mataji. Plus food for the gossip-hungry. Laughable. Pathetic. Dangerous.

"So what do *you* say?" I asked Rano. "Is it another case of black magic?"

She laughed. "I should not have told you all this probably. It's so silly and stupid. Still you need to know. Bhabiji can make trouble for you."

"Why would she want to do that?" I asked, not that I didn't know a reason or two, but I wanted Rano's ideas on the subject.

"She must be jealous, Bhabi," Rano said.

"Of me?"

"Of course. Her position in the family was different before you came," Rano said.

"How?"

"She got more importance then. The only daughter-in-law and all. She probably envies you also." Rano said.

"For what?"

"You're younger. You have a husband . . ."

"She's your brother's—my husband's—wife, too." I stopped to let Jim have a sniff around and mark out his territory on a tree stump.

"Only in name," Rano said.

"What about before I came?" I had to ask.

Rano looked embarrassed. Pretended she hadn't heard me.

130

We started walking again, neither of us saying anything, but I with a mind full of questions I couldn't ask.

Meanwhile, I rang mental changes on the envy idea. Did Dilraj Kaur feel jealous of my education? I asked myself. Not likely! She would think it was useless and something that made me masculine.

"I suppose I disgust her a little bit, too, don't I?" I said to Rano after a few moments.

She looked confused. Alarmed. "What do you mean?"

"My ritual cleanliness is about nonexistent," I said.

"Oh," she said. "You mean not touching certain utensils at certain times and all. Well. Yes . . . Maybe. Sometimes you handle food with your left hand; sometimes you taste something while you're cooking it."

"Is that bad?" I asked.

"It's just not the custom," Rano said. "But Bhabi, please don't take it ill that I've told you."

"Why didn't anybody tell me before?" I wanted to know.

Rano rummaged around for a reason. "I suppose we just took it for granted you knew and didn't care about doing things our way."

I wondered what other innocent practices of mine offended. Using toilet paper or some available substitute instead of water, perhaps? Offering to shake hands with a man? How many times had I unwittingly been the source of embarrassment to the family, I wondered.

At the same time, my value in my own culture had not been a piece of baggage I could bring with me and unpack at this destination for everyone's delight. Like ice, it was substantial and weighty enough when I started out. But when I carried it off, it melted and dribbled away, just leaked out, and I had nothing to show for it at the other end. And nothing to save me from committing blunders.

It was not news to me that Dilraj Kaur believed in black magic, or that she could do me harm. But the matter of Pitaji and me was. Who could have imagined evil intent in our listening to the six o'clock news from Jullundur every evening, bending our ears to the sputtering, static-filled portable radio speaker as we strained to hear the English-speaking newsreader? It's true, life in Majra was conservative. All that

131

covering of heads and turning away the minute a man walked
into the room. But from the start I had enjoyed a kind of
immunity from observing purdah and had supposed everyone took it for granted. Tej himself had declared it unfeasible: "You'd be forgetting to cover your head all the time. It's
better if you just don't start doing it at all. It's an old-
fashioned custom, anyway."

These things hadn't seemed to matter up to now. Pitaji
liked to keep up with what was happening in Korea, and to
have someone hear his views on it. I'm a good listener, and
no one else in the family had the time or the inclination to
hear Pitaji's pronouncements on the state of the world.

"What do you think, *beti?*" Pitaji would say, addressing me
by the same term he used for his own daughters, "Will Mac-
Arthur dare to cross the 39th Parallel?" His voice had a timbre all its own. It was resonant, slightly nasal, and not
particularly deep. But it carried. And while I'd think about
how to answer, he would go on, keeping time to the rhythm
of his words with jabs at the air, his right hand, palm held
toward me like a policeman's, discouraging all dissent. "I can
tell you he won't. He won't dare cross the 39th Parallel. But
he should. The Americans always play fair and most of the
time play safe. It doesn't get them anywhere, but they do."
He would pause for this to take effect. "Look at this country:
Nehru reaches for the Chinese with one hand and has the
other out for American aid. And the Americans oblige him,
don't they? Extraordinary! India is a nation of calamities,"
he would go on. "No matter how much help we get, it would
never be enough. Some new problem would come up. Look
what happens to farming, to agriculture, if the monsoon fails
just one year: famine, misery. More calamities."

These views would be delivered in impeccably grammatical
English with only rare lapses, and an overlay on the native
Punjabi of a Scottish accent, a speech mannerism that Pitaji
had picked up as a boy in a Presbyterian mission school.

I took up my pen again and tried to picture Carol still in
Michigan, receiving this letter from me after so many
months. What would these random details mean to her?
These anecdotes? If they were a puzzlement to me, what
sense could she make of them? We belonged to different

worlds now. The one I was in was as untranslatable as a Martian's would be. I tore up everything I had written and picked up one of the Christmas cards I had made. Old magazine cut-outs pasted on heavy white paper procured with difficulty from Ladopur. Lettered with poster paints. Under the cartoon of a snowman, I wrote: "Dear Carol, Will write a proper answer to your long letter soon! Belated holiday greetings and all good wishes for the New Year! Meanwhile, keep in touch. Love, Helen. P.S. I'm pregnant. Baby is expected end of May! I'm doing fine."

There was just time to put it in an envelope and hand it over to the boy with the B.A. and the black umbrella who would be coming by on his bicycle any moment to pick up the Majra mail.

15

I would not have known it was Christmas Day if I hadn't
ticked off the dates on the wall calendar in our room every
morning, and if Pitaji had not wished me a *Bada Din-ka mu-
barak*, which is as close as you can get to saying Merry Christmas in Punjabi.

I had sent off cards to family and friends, with long letters
to Mama and Papa and Aunt Teresa. Now there was the tree
to trim. Actually a palm branch I had spirited into our room
the day before without anyone taking notice. I had to feel
my way along in this. I didn't want to seem to impose some
esoteric religious ritual on an unsuspecting family. The truth
is, I anticipated a reaction like *my* family's would have been,
had some Hindu or Buddhist in their midst come up with a
celebration. Alarm bells would have gone off, and excitement
would have erupted in Italian exclamations of dismay and
disapproval. I didn't want my tree-trimming rite to cause a
disturbance like that in this household where I had, after all,
been received as a family member with kindness and a good
measure of love as well.

So I went ahead with as little fuss as possible, searched
everywhere for a suitable evergreen, and finally settled on a
palm branch. It was installed in our room on my red steamer
trunk that occupied one corner and doubled as a table. The
trouble was that by Christmas morning the branches were
already drooping and threatening to turn brown and crisp
in the dusty cold. The branch was firmly set in a sturdy vase
weighed down with moist earth, but that hadn't helped to
preserve its original freshness. I propped the container
tightly against the wall so that the "tree" wouldn't topple over.

Tej was interested and amused for a while, and contributed

134

some of his own ideas for decorating it before heading out to the sugarcane fields where laborers were already cutting and stripping the stalks before loading them onto the tractor trailer. I had to rely principally on using foil from candy wrappers and cutouts from magazines pasted on thin cardboard for the ornaments. Tinsel was easy to come by; I had stashed some away in anticipation.

I had to admit it was not the traditional Christmas tree, but it was a gesture to the past, to what I had grown up with and so recently parted from. The lights were a problem, though, with no electricity; still, I reminded myself, there were Christmas tree lights before Edison. However, with the unsteadiness of the palm branch, I had to give up the notion of balancing candles on it and had to settle for placing some around its base. I stood back and looked at the display, trying not to be aware of the makeshift origins of the ornaments and ignoring the drooping leaves.

Life was good, after all. The warm spirit of Christmas, of the winter equinox, of whatever it was that kept inhabitants of the northern hemisphere alive and hopeful, century after century, through the dark days—lighting lights against winter's sunless sky, keeping in mind that spring was never far behind—entered my bones, cheered my heart.

A persistent memory kept surfacing, searching for a place to settle down in the scene: a Santa with the beatific smile and the carelessly wrapped turban of the Ranikaran Babaji. I stopped a moment to consider him, the real Babaji. He would be in his cave-room now. Snow all around. Warm inside. It was somehow reassuring to contemplate this certainty. It brought to mind past Christmases and made me wonder about future ones. Playing Scrooge. The holiday time invites comparisons.

Christmas Past. I couldn't fail to remember it, the previous Christmas. I had to recall it now, for remembrance' sake, and for my own sake, to come to terms with it. I turned my mind to it, as I had to, and dragged up images of traveling on the train from Berkeley that last time, of being met at the Los Angeles Union Station by Mama and Papa and the girls, sharing hugs and kisses (the feel of little girl flesh and muscles and bones; the smell of freshly washed hair and clean clothes). Middle-age rotundities, muscularities: Mama was plump and short; Papa lean and tall and bouncy. There was occasion for the usual argument about which sister would sit beside me in the front seat. Six-year-old Nicoletta won by reason of her being the youngest. Gloria and Julia flanked Mama in the back seat. I kept turning around, looking over my shoulder, hearing all the news at once, all the anecdotes they had saved up just for me, while headlights of cars from the opposite direction illumined their features in intermittent flashes: smiling, eager, excited.

Homecomings were always like this, thanks to Mama's genius for event-staging, custom-establishing, family-reinforcing. Faced with the impossibility of transplanting Old Country traditions in the unreliable soil of California, the household she grew up in did the next best thing: they invented their own. Meeting me like this had become one of her rites and rituals subscribed to by everybody.

Driving at night through the great grid of Los Angeles, along its streets threaded with lights all the way down to the ocean, I never failed to be gripped by its magnitude: Where did it end? The ride was all questions without time for answers, tuggings at my sleeve, old family jokes brought out once again, the latest concerns that had everybody wound up. And Aunt Teresa? She would be waiting at our house for us, and there would be homemade ravioli stuffed with lamb and spinach, and polenta on the stove, and some Barbera to wash it down.

Once home, it was all of us bursting through the door, Aunt Teresa hurrying out of the kitchen to welcome me in her embrace, and the air redolent of garlic and butter and *salsa ala Piemontese*. Out came the glasses and the bottles of wine. My sisters displayed the house I grew up in for my inspection, now that I no longer lived there. Nicoletta demonstrated how bouncy the new sofa was: Julia, blonde and blue-eyed and self-consciously fourteen, and Gloria, more confidently sixteen, posed on the new bar stools beside a counter that had replaced the partition between the kitchen and the living room.

Would I ever be welcomed anywhere like this again, I wondered, as the keen sense of this as the last Christmas with

136

the family for a long, long time froze my bones. When I boarded the train again, I would be bound for a point far beyond Berkeley.

I sat there at the counter in the midst of the family, receiving more hugs and kisses (cousins arriving now from Rosemead and Glendale), pregnant with this heavy load of subterfuge which lay cradled in my insides like some secret child, loveable only to a mother. Now that I had finished all the work for my M.A. I was going to join Tej in India in the spring. We were going to get married. There was something of a fantasy in the notion considered in the present context. The plan belonged to another set of characters, in another place, at another time, far removed from the present. Even to rehearse the plan in my own mind seemed novel, exotic, unlikely. Yet I knew that I was going away to spend a lifetime with him. My mind reeled with astonishment and fear at the certainty of it. I had just a few more weeks to spend here, and no one amongst this bright, happy, noisy company had even heard of Tejbir Singh's existence. I'd sent out some feelers that I hoped would prepare them for my going off in March. To Europe. Perhaps to India. I hadn't been specific. But there was not a hint so far that I wasn't coming back.

"Why India?" Mama asked when I tried the idea out on her for the first time. "Everybody else you know is going to Germany, or somewhere in Europe, anyway. It's what you told me yourself, Helena." She was ironing clothes and set the iron down on its stand while she turned toward me, a hand on her hip. "I don't know why you wanna go anywhere outside these United States. We have everything here, Helena. Everything."

It wasn't the first time she had said this. I had never had a reply. We did indeed have everything. Yet everything wasn't enough for me, nor for any of my friends. We were all on our way. To Munich, to Berlin, to Paris, Vienna, places we'd waited out a war to see. In my case, I was going farther, staying longer, perhaps never coming back.

I moved through the holiday in a state of well-concealed panic that saw me through shopping for presents, hiding them away in cupboards to be wrapped later, decorating the house, the tree, going to mass, helping Mama prepare the

Christmas breads from old recipes brought over from Piedmont, playing at being big sister, obedient daughter, the family's hope and pride onto whom were hung bright dreams, like tinsel along the branches of a fir tree. It anaesthetized me against the unendurable and kept my concentration fixed on getting across the tightrope and onto the other side.

I struggled to keep my wandering attention on what the others were saying, keeping a smile ready in case it was needed, or an answer to a half-heard question. There were times I would discover my mother staring at me when she thought I wasn't looking, as one does at a loved one of whom some dreadful fate is suspected: a terminal illness, a financial disaster, an irreparable loss. Her eyes pried and penetrated as she tried to figure me out. She knew something was up. And so did Papa. But I'd have to keep my plans secret for a while more. Christmas was not the time to drop the bomb. It would have to be later. After New Year's.

This memory needed closing down now, required a dissolve to another scene. Why not the present? Majra. The room Tej and I share in the new house, looking out on the garden in front, and beyond it, on acres of sugarcane. The crop is sweetest this time of year. There's a flat horizon's worth of cloudy sky and the leafless branches of the *sheesham* trees are being whipped by the wind that races through every noon, raising dust-devil dances across the yard. Against the fluorescent green of the Egyptian clover fodder crop, the trunks of the *sheesham* trees are stark black. Mauve ageratum, looking like pale but vibrant purple dandelions, hug the irrigation channels. Alongside them wild orange-and-yellow lantana flowers glow amidst the shrub's dark green foliage. It's cold and damp after a recent rain and gloomy inside the house with no electricity into which to plug a heater. At the same time, it's too cold to sit outside. The clouds are high and thick and dark on the horizon, light only where the sun shines through in a shapeless luminescence. Each spot of color arouses a physical response—a glow along the ganglia—made more intense for sharing space with darkness: like happiness whose face is glimpsed in the mirror of its opposite.

I return to the business of trimming the palm-branch

Christmas tree and wonder what to do for a star. I'm working on this, cranking up whatever creative forces lie inside, discarding idea after idea as unfeasible, ridiculous, or both. I'm concentrating so hard that I don't hear—am unaware—that someone else is in the room, has come in through the open door, parted the curtains that hang across the opening and stands watching me. I have the feeling that Nikku has been waiting there for some time before I turn around and discover him.

"Chachiji, what are you making?" he asks, addressing me as "aunt," the wife of his father's younger brother. His voice is a husky Punjabi voice, and he speaks English in words, not phrases, grabbing them out of a bag and hoping they will say what he wants them to mean.

I go over and draw him inside the room. I'm thrilled! This is the first time he has ever come to me, the first time he has ever spoken without being spoken to first. His eyes never leave me for a second. He's still, after all these months, trying to figure me out, with no idea where I've come from.

I try to make it easy for him. Put a hand on his shoulder, a little, bony-boy shoulder, lean and sinewy and tough for a six-year-old. He doesn't wince. I show him what I'm doing, and try to explain why I'm doing it. "People where I come from put up Christmas trees this time of year," I say. "It's fun."

"Oh," he says. I can see he's puzzled. Wondering how sticking a palm branch into a vase and hanging candy papers from it can be fun. His eyes search the tree for details. He's wondering what's important and what isn't in the setting up of such a display.

"I have seen some photos," he says, "but . . ."

I guess he wants to say this looks like no Christmas tree he has ever seen. "I know," I say, "this doesn't look like those in pictures." It's just symbolic, I want to add, but I know that would be no explanation. "It's as near as I can get to what it should be," I say, wondering why I feel I need to apologize for it. "There aren't any real fir trees around."

He sits down on a low stool in front of the red steamer trunk, leans his elbows on his knees, and rests his chin in his

139

hands, contemplating the results of my work. "You need a star on top, don't you, Chachiji?" he says.

"Yes. I was just trying to figure out how to make one," I say. "What can I use?"

He looks at me. Confused. Have I said something wrong? He's not used to having his opinion sought. Nobody ever asks him what he thinks about anything. Probably scared to say. Feels put on the spot. Can't imagine what I want from him. Shrugs his shoulders.

"Well, I'll figure something out," I say in answer to my own question. He looks relieved. His round-faced, round-eyed look makes him appear plumper than he is. His hair has been pulled into a knot on top of his head, and the turban has been tied tight as a tourniquet on top. It gives him a quizzical, mature expression. Sometimes he looks like a little wise man. He's lost a tooth, and the gap adds to the impression he gives of a clever gnome. His smile is broad and friendly when he allows it to brighten his cautious features, but he has learned early not to give too much away.

"Chachiji," he says, getting up all of a sudden, "could I put some of these on?" He picks up one of the ornaments still lying beside the tree.

"Sure," I say, "Go ahead."

"Where shall I put this?" he asks, still holding the ornament.

"Anywhere you like," I say. "Put it where you think there's a good space for it."

"And can I make some more?" he asks, already looping the thread of the ornament over a palm leaf. Before I can say anything, he steps back and says, "Is this all right here?"

We're busy now, the two of us, filling in gaps, trying to reach a balance, so that no part of the tree appears more sparsely decorated than another. I get out some more candy wrappers, another string of tinsel, some silver foil that just might make a star. We're sitting there, on the Persian carpet, on the floor with scissors and twine and glue, and candy wrappers in a heap in the center. The tree is loaded, but Nikku is just getting into the whole process. He's forgotten me as he twists the wrappers into shapes more imaginative than I've been able to devise.

"This one is a bell," he says. "They go on Christmas trees, don't they?" He holds up his latest invention. Hardly a bell, but that doesn't matter. For a moment I am ready to believe him, accept the crumpled bit of shiny paper as a bell. "And this is a peacock," he says of another creation. "A blue peacock. This is his tail. Okay?"

When he's exhausted his fund of ideas, after a tiger and two camels and a monkey have been added to the tree, he sits back and says, "But we have to have a star."

His words are coming together faster now. Sometimes there's a Punjabi word or phrase thrown in when the English term hops out of reach.

"What about this?" I ask, handing him a larger-than-usual piece of foil that has escaped getting twisted and cut up and strung.

"Yes!" he cries. "I know: we can put some glue on the back and put it on this." He proceeds to attach the flimsy piece of foil to a bit of cardboard. "Do you have a *kanchee*, Chachiji?"

"*Kanchee?* You mean scissors?" I hand him a pair.

When the glue has dried, he hastily cuts out a more or less five-pointed shape, not exactly a star. He holds it up with a look of accomplishment and pride. "*Changa hai?* Okay?" he asks. The star spins around on the freshly attached string, catches the light from the window and sends it off to the four corners of the dark room and back again.

"It's great," I say. "*Bhout changa hai.*" And it is.

"I want to put it on the top of the tree, Chachiji," he says. "Okay?"

He looks at me a moment. Coming back to where we are. Realizing who he is; who I am. We've never really had anything to do with each other before! I see a wave of alarm wash over him. He's all of a sudden awkward, all hands, feet getting in his own way, fingers not doing what he wants them to do. Eye-hand coordination all fouled up.

"Go on," I say. "It's okay. Put it right there on top. Tie it with the string. I think it will stay up all right."

He picks up his handiwork. Love in his fingers, in his eyes for this thing he has made, the five-pointed-not-quite-a-star of foil. A little glue has got smeared on the right side, but he doesn't see it. The star of Bethlehem about to rise yet one more time, shakily, unsteadily, lopsided, flashing light. Nikku leans across the red trunk to reach the top of the tree with one hand, and he's gripping the star in the other, holding it so tightly it's as if he expects it to escape him. He tries several angles, makes his own six-year-old calculations. He wants to get it right. His hand is shaking with the effort at precision, and he looks back over his shoulder for my help. But he's not looking at me. He's looking beyond me, and I understand in less time that it takes to draw in a breath that what he sees has brought him back to where we started from half an hour ago. Even before I turn around to look behind me, he has dropped the star onto the red trunk and has started to wipe his hands on his pants. Even before I turn around, I know what it is that has seized him. His mother strides into the room, and without looking at me, without taking notice of the tree, or uttering a word, gathers the boy up into her arms as if to protect him from some evil force and hurries out without looking back. Nikku doesn't dare speak, but gives me one blank glance, full of alarm, in which there is one confused element of apology—for what? To whom?

16

The New Year began with a hailstorm and a rainbow. It was tea time, and the family sat around the fire in the kitchen, eating a homemade sweet. It was a crumbly mixture of sugar, almonds, raisins, and quantities of clarified butter all held together by parched wheat flour. Mataji had spent the entire morning preparing it. Nobody had stayed up the night before to celebrate the coming of the New Year; nevertheless, the weather was remarkable enough to make us all take note of the day. Pitaji recalled that when he was a boy a similar combination of atmospheric events had preceded a bumper crop of wheat in May. "It was the year my cousin brother Sumeet got married," he said, "to Hukum Singh's eldest daughter."

"He married *Harbans* Singh's daughter," Mataji corrected him. "My older brother went to that same wedding."

"Hukum Singh's daughter," Pitaji repeated as if he hadn't heard her. "We all went to the wedding in Cheecha, near Lahore. He was a big landlord, and the celebrations lasted for five days. There were two hundred people in the marriage party from the groom's side."

"Five hundred," Mataji said.

Everyone looked suitably impressed, even though the story must not have been new.

"Anyway, the entire barat was fed, the whole groom's side. Housed, too, in the village all that time," Pitaji went on.

"That girl brought twenty-five sets of bedding in her dowry," Mataji said. "But she turned out to be a trouble-maker. Right from the start she got everybody fighting with everybody else."

"That was a long time ago. She's a grandmother now," Pitaji said, settling the issue.

I sat staring into the wood fire as one conversation flowed into another. Talk involved people and places too far away; too long ago. I, on the other hand, had my own recollections to sort out, and the fire's unpredictable flames helped give a moveable, changeable focus to the events in my mind: transitory and ever changing close-ups, mid-range shots, longshots in quick succession.

It was New Year's day. Just exactly a year ago.

"Mama says you're talking about going to India instead of looking for a job," Papa began. "If I thought for one minute you were going over there to get married, I'd do everything in my power to stop you. It would just kill Mama."

I was too surprised even to try to deny what he was saying. His words came without warning. Where had I betrayed even a hint of my plans, I wondered. How had he been able to guess? To hit the spot so accurately, all in one shot? I turned from what I was doing and looked at him, a wet dish in one hand, the dish towel in the other. I was finishing up after breakfast. The others had gone to Aunt Teresa's across the street where the Rosemead cousins and their families were to have lunch. Papa must have stayed back to have it out with me, to get a clear answer, without Mama's hysterics and my sisters' alarm and confusion. It was just he and I. I didn't know what to do with the dish cloth. I guess I kept twisting it in my hands. This was it. The occasion I had rehearsed for. But the initiative had been taken away from me, and I didn't know whether to feel relief or panic. The things I had planned to say, the arguments I had aimed to present, were useless. The whole story of Tej and me and our decision to marry, once I joined him, got told out of sequence, in bits of stammered phrases. It sounded unreal even to me.

"That's a fine idea," Papa said. "You are going to meet this guy in Bombay . . . after being apart seven months, did you say? He's already back in the Punjab." (He pronounced it *Poonjob*) "And you're here? Helena, you're crazy. Your Mama and I can't understand you. What makes you think he'll be at the docks to meet you? What makes you think he'll be there, huh?" He threw up his hands in disbelief.

All the time he was talking, he paced up and down in the

kitchen, stopping to bang his fist on the bar counter whenever he wanted to emphasize a point. I tried to say something, give him a word of reassurance, talk about my sense of destiny, remind him the world was getting smaller, that I wasn't really going so far away, and that my thoughts would always be with the family, but he kept interrupting me. In English and Italian, by turn. I even tried an appeal to universal brotherhood, but it only made things worse.

"Let everybody live like they like," Papa said. "We don't have no trouble. They don't have no trouble. You don't owe him—what's his name? You don't owe him *nothing*. You owe *us*. Your *family*. Forget about what's going on in India. The Hindus can take care of themselves." There was a pause. "They eat rice, don't they? A no-good diet. Can't keep a man going. You'd get sick on it." He stopped for a moment and then said in a quieter voice, "Why don't you stay and get your Ph.D., like you wanted to? You'd be the first in the family, honey. We'd be so proud . . ."

"I don't want to get a Ph.D.," I said, my patience and eagerness to be understood all at once abandoning me. "To hell with a Ph.D. What would I do with it? Teach other people to get Ph.D.'s in the same subject? Grow old and crazy in the process?"

"Shut up," he said. "Stop shouting. Listen to some sense. I'm trying to make you see what you're doing. You're the stubbornest person I ever saw. Headstrong. Your head is of stone." He tapped his own forehead to make the point. "It's no good. But if you insist on going ahead with this crazy plan—like I said—I'll do everything in my power to stop you, Helena!"

And he did. He used words, arguments, threats. He used love, memories . . .

A long time ago. Smiling faces; happy shouts. Fleeting. Disconnected. Across an expanse of sand, competing with the sound of waves sloshing against the wet beach, the tide coming in . . . It's Santa Monica, the day Mama and Aunt Teresa got the bad sunburns and quarreled about which of them always got fussed over more, who got more sympathy, aroused more interest, got more attention. The sun is in my eyes, but I'm smiling as if it is expected of me, since I'm standing in the parking lot at the beach in front of the new Studebaker. The spare tire fastened at the back is a rubber halo behind my head.

The conversations of the grown-ups, half in Italian, half in broken English, wash over me in a comforting tide at first. Aunt Teresa's laughter, my father's asides, Uncle Oreste's jokes, Grandmother Graziani's sibilant scoldings through false teeth as she sits shielding herself from the sun under the multicolored umbrella. The jokes end in jibes. Mama is feeling aggrieved about something someone has said.

"Whatsa matter, Fran, honey?" my Papa asks. "She didn't mean a thing."

I feel I should understand all of it. I'm left out; bypassed. Nobody actually brings me into the conversation. At the same time, I'm the center of attention on an outing like this. I think it is because I am somebody special. It must be true: I am the only seven-year-old amongst all these adults.

"Hey, tyke, whose pal are you?" my Papa says in English, lifting me up in his arms, putting me on his shoulder, making me feel important. Blue eyes; coarse, curly brown hair; white, freckled skin; muscular body wet from the surf.

"Papa's!" I giggle, self-conscious with love and wonder.

Three sisters arrive in turn to claim everyone's attention. Papa, Mama, aunts, uncles, cousins, all get caught up in these fresh births. Death takes Grandmother Graziani, Uncle Oreste. Aunt Teresa moves across the street. High school has to be gotten through; a war has to start; boys I have known since kindergarten are in boot camp instead of in classrooms.

About that time, Carol Thorpe moved in two doors away. Her father kept bees and worked on the swing shift at Lockheed; her mother made Scottish tarts with coconut and jam and what she called shortcrust. Her brother played the tuba in the high school band. Within a week, Carol fell in love with Andy down the street and talked me into walking with her past his house every evening after school, as though we were going somewhere. He would be practicing boogie-woogie piano—just the bass part. We could see his silhouette through the screen door. Andy, battling acne and a bad case of adolescent voice change, was enough to satisfy Carol's appetite for romance. To me it seemed she was settling for a starvation diet.

Summer nights followed tedious summer vacation days when there was nowhere to go, nothing to do. By contrast, the throbbing Southern California evenings, once the sun went down, offered numberless, undefinable escapades, leaps into fantasy and glamor. Barely eight miles away klieg lights scanned the Hollywood skies, heralding the coming of the stars. Plantinumed, sequined, minked, escorted goddesses rose like Venuses from waves of shiny black limousines while cameras clicked and flashbulbs popped. The lights searched the skies in restless, bold diagonals, crisscrossed each other, and searched again. Carol and Andy would have gone to the beach. Even now they would be watching the grunion swim in by the tens of thousands, turning the waves into liquid silver with their flashing bodies in the moonlight. There was nothing for me to do but lie awake wondering when I would start living. While I waited, I found some temporary time-fillers: school work, movies, and India, each in its way a road out.

"Why are you so interested in India?" Mama often asked. "It's too far away. They worship cows there."

I didn't tell her my reason because I didn't know myself. Part of it may have been the very remoteness Mama looked upon with such suspicion. Part of it was surely something else. When others in my high school geography class went after the pyramids, the Coliseum, or the Empire State building during a project on famous buildings of the world, I settled on the Taj Mahal at Agra. Did I choose it? Did it choose me? I decided to do a poster of this tomb built by Emperor Shahjehan for his favorite wife: a tribute to love! In undying marble! The drawing arranged itself in my mind first, from details I had been able to make out from a small black-and-white illustration in an encyclopedia: the fine bits of floral inlay in the marble, the paths that lead to the mausoleum, and the evergreen trees that line them. When I started to draw, I walked those paths, climbed those stairs, disappeared through that grand entrance.

The poster needed something more: gilded highlights would do it, I thought, and gold paint was the answer. I had to show what would happen with sunlight on those trees, on that central dome, on those minarets. Even then I knew that what I had perceived as other-worldly grandeur, I had rendered merely garish with my gold paint. I never stopped looking for yet one more detail to add to the picture to make it right, and at the same time for a way that would one day lead me up those actual paths whose reality I had to see for myself. An obsession! Nothing and no one was going to stop me. . . .

"Do you understand? Nobody, nothing is going to stop me!" I heard myself shout.

Papa stood openmouthed, drop-jawed speechless. He was looking over my shoulder toward the front door that I heard swing open at that instant. I turned around. Mama had come back.

"What's wrong?" she wanted to know. She had the intense look that crises always brought on. Her antennae were up; she could sense trouble, ordinary trouble, across a room. This was something else. Her entry itself was like an accusation. She looked from one to the other of us. "What's wrong?" she repeated.

"Ask *her*, Fran," Papa said, jerking his head in my direction, but not looking at me.

I could feel the blood hotting up my face; my heart pounding.

"Well, what is it, Helena?" Mama said, trying to keep her voice from flying away.

"I'm going to India to get married, and . . ."

"You see, I was right!" she said, cutting in. She looked at Papa. "I told you, and you wouldn't believe me, Mario. Months ago! Months ago! We could have done something. But no, you wouldn't listen. Now it's too late."

"It's not as if I were going to war, or something like that," I said. "I'm going to get married to the man I love, and who loves me."

"Be quiet, Helena. You don't now what you're saying. I know you better than you know yourself. I know you could not be happy—nobody in our family could be happy—living so far away. Living with strangers. Eating strange food. No-

148

body speaks English. Not even Italian. How would you spend your time? Who would look after you? How would you get along with all those foreigners?"

"Mama, *I'd* be the foreigner there," I said.

"Don't try to be smart," she said. "You know what I mean. I'm your mother; I gave birth to you," she accompanied her words with hands on her heart, tears in her eyes. "After nine long months. I loved you so!" She looked out of the corner of her eye at Papa.

"It's true, Helena," he put in. "We know what's best for you."

"Then why did you go to all the trouble and expense to educate me?" I asked. "What is an education for if not to help a person manage their own life, be responsible, be an adult?"

"That's a fine question to ask," Papa declared. "After all the sacrifices your Mama has made—the cheap meals she's had to serve the family, the cheap cuts of meat, the cheap wines, the day-old bread. The clothes she denied herself! My God, honey, she had nothing decent to wear to your cousin Mary's wedding. I couldn't even afford to buy her a new dress. Your room and board had to be paid, every month. Your tuition, every semester. All those books . . ."

"And your Papa driving that Safeway's truck day in, day out," Mama said. "Sometimes sixteen hours at a stretch. And now you ask why we did it!"

"Yes. That's what I want to know. Why did you educate me? Why didn't you keep me in the kitchen, rolling out ravioli dough? I wouldn't have known the difference. You could have married me off to a railroader or short-order cook, straight off the boat from the Old Country."

"Shut up about railroaders and cooks. They're honest, hard-working men; union men, like your Papa. Not a bunch of Reds, anyway," Mama shouted.

I hadn't wanted to say that about the railroaders. I wanted to die for having said it.

"We wanted the best for you, kid," Papa said simply, almost apologetically. "We still do."

His words got to me. I hugged him and stifled a sob. "Forgive me, Papa," I said into his lapel. He put his arm around me as he used to when I was a child.

149

"We didn't expect you to turn on us," Mama said.

"I'm not turning on you," I said, facing her again. "It's that my experience of life up to now has been different from yours. It's made it hard for us to understand each other. I keep saying things that hurt you when I don't want to. I've had doors in my mind opened up; I've got to go through them. It's my own life." I was picking words out of a bag of ideas gleaned from books and movie dialogues. And not the less sincere for that.

"I knew we shouldn't have let you go away up North to college," Mama said, taking up a favorite theme. "With all those Reds there at Berkeley. Foreigners. God knows what all. But your Papa said you must go. It's all your fault, Mario. You've always spoiled her. Something like this was bound to happen." Then turning to me, "Helena, the Sunday you left for college, when I came back in the house fighting the tears away, here sat Julia and Gloria, in this very living room, crying their eyes out. Even poor little Nicoletta. You don't know what you're doing to your family! What have we done to deserve it?" Words got washed away in tears, and Papa was saying, "Now, now, Fran. You gotta pull yourself together, honey," as he took her in his arms.

Not to be consoled, Mama crossed herself; called on the saints and the Virgin Mary; alternately cajoled and cursed; made an end to rational talk, if there had been any to begin with; said things, provoked others to say things, that could not be unsaid; made impossible any reconciliation; made sure there would be sleepless nights ahead for all of us; ensured that the weeks that remained would drag on painfully.

The worst of it was knowing that Mama and Papa were right. In their own way. They had crowned me with encouragement and hope; laid sacrifices at my feet. And I had set them up with something they hadn't bargained for, something they weren't prepared to cope with, a surprise of the worst kind: I had asked them to let me go, 10,000 miles away, into the arms of a stranger. What would that day be like, I wondered, when they would have to do just that?

17

Events took a new turn in the Majra household with the beginning of spring. At first I was too busy being pregnant to notice the changes taking place around me, too preoccupied with my expanding middle and broadening waistline and the barely perceptible stirrings of life. I sat delighting in the one-with-nature feeling, finding fresh pleasure in basking in the sun. I walked barefoot through the new-mown grass as though I'd never made contact with the earth before. I took note of the woodpeckers on the lawn showing off their black-and-white topknots, seeing them for the first time. There were the bravely blooming roses of late January to admire, whose stalks Mali Chella Ram, the gardener, under Rano's instructions, had carefully nurtured through the hot summer. There were the sweet peas and nasturtiums to watch as they nodded giddily in the winter winds. Dahlias, amaryllis, and phlox ran riot, and scarlet canna lilies stood back-lit and on fire in the rising sun.

They all had a spurious air about them. What were these temperate dainties doing here? They sprang up out of the ground surprised to have found themselves in this rich, tropical soil and oblivious to the fight for their lives they had coming to them from termites, brightly-colored beetles, and ants that would make lace of their leaves in a day; from locusts that would reduce them to stubble in one afternoon's nibbling.

However, I was to discover the changes weren't all in the world of nature. There was a shift in family alliances going on, and the nature and intensity of the quarrels and reconciliations were changing. The fights amongst the women over protocol and little privileges went on, but with more aggres-

153

siveness. There were daily altercations between Rano and Goodi about clothes, jewelry, who got to go where, and when. When guests were present, the women had even more to get rankled about. There were lots of comparisons made, between girl-cousins, boy-cousins, sisters of a family, daughters-in-law. Someone always came out second best; sides were always taken.

The men, for their part, carped over farm work. Tej grumbled that Hari was irresponsible; Hari complained that he got little reward for all the work he did and was forever pressing for a larger share of the profits whenever a crop was sold. Pitaji made it plain that he regarded Tej's preoccupation with music a waste of time and his frequent forays to places as far away as Jullundur in pursuit of it, sheer self-indulgence.

A ride on a bullock cart was a good time to sort things out, come to grips, find out what was happening. I caught up on what had been going on within the family all those months I was napping. It was during a shopping trip to Ladopur.

Mataji, Rano, Goodi, Nikku, and I were on our way home. We sat at an angle on the slanting wooden cart that was hitched up to the bullock so that the front was higher than the back. The only sensible thing was to ride facing backwards while hanging onto the wooden poles at the sides to keep from slipping down. There was a dhurrie underneath us to make things less splintery, but it didn't do anything to make the road less choppy or the bumps easier to take. If I hadn't known better, I would have sworn the wheels were square instead of round. Yet the beauty of it was that we went along so slowly that everything by the side of the road was accessible and touchable, even, as we drove by. I got out and walked from time to time over the three miles to stretch my legs, and rest my aching bones.

The sun still went down early in late winter, and we were riding toward it. It filtered through the diaphanous dupatta that Goodi was wearing. Dust from the bullock's hooves was thrown up all around and created an enchanting haze through which the dying sun glimmered. As we plunged along on the dirt track, rutted and ground to a powder, I remembered the village shopkeeper's wife who only the week before had given birth to a baby on a bullock cart on the way to the Mission Hospital. Mataji perhaps recalled the same incident as we went over a particularly bad bump, for she put her arms around me to brace me against the shock and said, "Are you all right, *beti*?"

"Yes," I answered, glad for the support and at the same time wondering how it would feel to go into labor on a bullock cart.

Mataji shouted at Gian to slow down. He'd been called away from his work around the house to drive the cart that day. "*Hauli chalo. Hauli,*" she said in a voice louder than usual.

Rano, who was sitting solidly on the other side of me, prevented further jostlings. "I hope you're not finding it too bumpy a ride, Bhabi," she said.

Goodi had been pouting the entire way home, and sat to one side, not saying a word. Nikku had asked her a load of questions which she hadn't chosen to answer.

"What's the matter with you?" Mataji said to her. "The child's asking you something. Why are you ignoring the poor little fellow?"

"I don't feel like talking," Goodi said.

"Don't feel like talking!" Mataji repeated. "What about the child? What do you think *he* feels?"

"I don't know why you brought me along," Goodi said, flaring up. "I don't know why I was not left at home with Bhabiji. She was alone and had so much work to do. I could have helped. As it is, all I did was tag along after all of you, while you shopped and shopped and shopped. You bought Rano Didi cloth for a new salwar-kameez and Bhabi some new shoes, and Hari. . . ."

"Be quiet!" Mataji said in a tone that would have discouraged a lesser person than Goodi.

"Well, it's true," she went on. "You didn't buy me a single thing."

"Why do you have to keep accounts like that?" Rano said. "So what if you missed out today? Next time it will be your turn. You already have three more outfits than I do, and all made of more expensive material, just because you fussed with Mataji about it."

"You also be quiet, Rano!" Mataji said. "This is stupid talk. I don't want to hear any more." She called up a Punjabi saying to the effect that everyone gets a fair share in due time. It just takes patience. Thereafter, we rode along in silence. Mataji's arm still steadied me. The friction in the air subsided as fast as it had started, and before long Rano and Goodi were planning their next joint embroidery project, some floral design on a kameez of Goodi's, while Nikku turned to Mataji for the answers to his unending questions.

I got out once more to walk along beside the cart and think my own thoughts. The baby on the way certainly made a difference, I concluded. If Mataji had looked upon me earlier as a temporary and unreliable inhabitant of her world, the fact that I was now carrying on the family line had caused a change in her behavior toward me. Perhaps she believed I would stay. Perhaps the piece of paper from the District Commissioner's office in Ambala saying Tej and I were married was seen to be valid, after all. Whatever the case, Mataji was making sure that I ate for two. There were extras now: dried dates and preparations fortified with powdered ginger; large dollops of butter in the dal, and omelettes with breakfast parathas. Lots of buttermilk. Almonds. Coconut.

More than once I caught Dilraj Kaur's bitter scrutiny of my tray of food, loaded with these delicacies, when she thought no one was looking. If Mataji was around, she would drop an especially generous blob of butter on top of my bowl of dal. She had a way of making even this routine gesture disdainful, allowing the butter to fall from a height so that her hand would not come into contact with my eating utensils. More than once I caught her staring at me, willing me indigestion, or worse still, the drying up of the fetus inside.

That day she had stayed at home. Someone had to ensure that dinner was prepared properly, and of late, it had been Dilraj Kaur who was left behind to see to things; I was the one included on outings. It was no accident that Goodi had made a point of it. Even now I could hear the conversation in the bullock cart. It had to do with how Dilraj Kaur had begun fasting once a week.

156

"On Tuesdays Bhabiji doesn't eat a thing but fruit," Goodi declared, as if it were news to everyone. In fact, no one could have been unaware of the great ceremony that attended this weekly observance.

"And some milk with it," Rano put in. "Fasting's a good way to avoid getting fat, and also a good way to get out of work one day a week."

"That's enough!" Mataji said sternly.

"It's a pious thing to do," Goodi said. "She spends the time she would be working saying her prayers. She's doing it for Bhaji Tej's long life, she told me."

"She tells everybody that," Rano said.

Mataji gave Rano a hard look. "What does that remark mean?" she demanded.

"She also goes to see Veera Bai in the evenings sometimes," Goodi went on, unwilling to let go of the subject of Dilraj Kaur.

"She *what*?" Mataji exclaimed, turning to Goodi.

Goodi, sensing she had said something wrong, tried to back track "I mean . . . she went once to Veera Bai's, that's all."

"Why would she want to go to that sorceress?" Rano asked.

"How should I know?" Goodi replied, wanting desperately to retreat from the conversation she had carried on too long.

"When did she go?" Mataji asked.

"I don't know," Goodi said.

"Then how do you know she went?" Rano asked.

"She took me with her," Goodi said, blurting out the secret. "I mean, I asked if I could go with her, and she said yes."

"No place for a child to go," Mataji said.

"I'm not a child," Goodi declared.

"What business would you have there?" Mataji asked. "A place where love-potions are dispensed like medicines, magic chants are whispered, chants powerful enough to destroy enemies; charms to win favors from those who can give them. What would you want with those things?"

"Nothing."

"Foolish of you to go, then," Mataji declared.

Nikku asked what a sorceress was. Nobody paid any attention to him. Mataji looked angrily at Rano and Goodi. The girls had resumed their bickering over Dilraj Kaur's fasts and visits to Veera Bai.

"Be quiet, both of you," she said finally. "If you can't say anything sensible, don't talk."

"Tell us about Uncle," Rano said, changing to a subject more likely to appeal to Mataji's interest.

"What about him?" Mataji wanted to know. "You know as much as I do. Your Pitaji received a letter from him two days ago."

"What news did he have?" Goodi asked.

"Everything is fine," Mataji said without committing herself to anything further.

"What about that . . . girl. That young widow? The concubine?" Goodi asked.

"You don't expect him to write anything about her, do you?" Mataji said.

"What's a concubine?" Nikku wanted to know.

"I say, be quiet, all of you!" Mataji said, sharply this time. "You make my head eat circles with your arguing and crazy questions."

And so we reached home. The sun had dropped below the horizon, and the men were back from overseeing the sugarcane harvest. I walked into our room. Tej was already there, having a wash before dinner, tidying his beard, adjusting his turban, changing his kurta, all with the deft, precise movements that set him off from everyone else. I must have looked glad to see him.

"How are you two?" he asked, taking me in his arms as though I had been away for a month instead of an afternoon.

"We're fine," I said. "Great."

"I've got some news for you," he said. "We're going to Delhi."

"You've got that job!" I exclaimed. "The one at the Bhakra Directorate!"

18

I was wrong. We were, indeed, going to Delhi; but Tej hadn't got the Bhakra job. Instead he was going for an interview for another one.

A lectureship at a Delhi engineering college had been advertised, and Tej had applied for it. They'd called him to appear the following morning at eleven o'clock for an interview. He wanted me to go along so that he could show me Delhi. But the letter had taken so long to reach Majra (I thought of the boy on the bicycle pedaling at a leisurely pace and multiplied him by several more boys on bicycles between train stations and post offices here and in Delhi) that it gave Tej and me only a couple of hours to pack. We'd have to catch the train that stopped, for only five minutes, at Abdullapur station at 2. A.M. in order to reach Delhi on time. Some heady, anticipatory thoughts that surfaced as I stuffed my Rollei and some doubtful, aged rolls of film into my bag included a break from meals served to me by Dilraj Kaur. Would she, at the behest of the sorceress, include a toad wrapped up in the breakfast paratha one morning? The fights and wranglings and makings-up; the sudden, inexplicable alliances and eventual estrangements—there would be a couple of days to breathe free of these too. And a vision of myself opened up, as mistress of my own house, server of food I had cooked myself, nurturer of my own family, in a place I would not feel like moving away from. Ever. What had seemed like an eccentricity in the Ranikaran Babaji—his never leaving sight of the pool there once he had discovered it—was beginning to make sense. I thought of him that night as we set out for the station. His wild beard, his beatific smile, his wonder at the constancy of things that he tried,

159

but failed to communicate to the Aggarwals and others. His pleasure in giving us all some hot tea, a simple meal, clean beds, a warm pool to bathe in.

This was the first time out of Majra for the two of us since our wedding trip to the hot springs. The air was cold, the night black, and the sky overcast. No stars! We carried as little baggage as possible for the short stay; Tej was reluctant to keep Gian up all night to go to the station to see us off, and the cousins from Amritsar as well as Hari, who would have gladly done us the honor, had gone to attend a wedding in Dhariwal. Some relation on the cousins' mother's side was marrying a girl with a B.A. in economics.

We fought our way onto the crowded Delhi mail train at 2 A.M. and sat on our baggage the rest of the journey, all the two hundred miles to the city. Once we arrived, there was a hastily bolted-down breakfast at the station, a quick selection of a hotel nearby, and an even quicker bath and change. Tej put on a freshly-starched turban and his best summer suit for the occasion. I was to spend some time shopping while he attended the interview, and we planned to meet at the American Express in Connaught Place at two o'clock. We packed into that morning in Delhi a month's worth of action, Majra time.

"You've got to beware of bottom-pinchers," he warned as he left me to go to the college. "Don't look anyone in the eye, and don't loiter around. Just keep moving, if you want to window shop, and . . ."

". . . And good luck!" I called after him.

Then I was on my own, for the first time since I disembarked from the *Corfu*. It was like stepping off a cliff and having the good luck to discover you have wings. There was this feeling of lightness: dizzying, exhilarating, frightening. I wanted to laugh, cry, hang on. I had to get reacquainted with my old self, the one that had, now I realized it, been left behind on the ship that day.

Negotiating the sunny corridors of Connaught Circus, I kept seeing myself in shop window reflections: Helen. Very pregnant. A "Western" girl in a sari. Helen, with an old Rollei. It was slung over my shoulder, and a little leather handbag I had bought in San Francisco just before leaving

160

was tucked under one arm. Each new window offered a small shock: a familiar face? More than that; it was *me*. At the same time I needed to keep alert to my surroundings lest I stumble over a pavement hawker or unwittingly bump into a fellow pedestrian.

I don't suppose tourists feel like this, I thought. I met with a few striding purposefully along, wearing sun hats and carrying the latest cameras. On the lookout. For the exotic shot; the unrepeatable moment when the snake charmer's king cobra rises to his full height, spreads his hood and flicks his tongue, while the mongoose sizes him up. Or the one with the supercilious white cow lounging in the middle of the road, stray cars carefully steering around it. These tourist pursuers of souvenir photographs would not have left *their* old selves behind on the P. & O. liner to slip into new identities ashore. More than their pink complexions and pale blue eyes, their intact selves made them stand out from the crowd, and gave them the surefooted gait that got them through the busy, sun-filled verandas bordering the shops of Connaught Circus without stubbing their toes. I would not have been surprised to encounter Edith Ritchie on her return journey from visiting her brother in Penang.

By the time all the windows were shopped and presents bought for the family in Majra, it was nearing one o'clock. I had bought for myself and consumed two chocolate bars imported from England, and a cream puff from one of the pastry shops. I also bought two nineteenth century paperback novels to take back to Majra to read at my leisure and a Lucknowi kurta for Tej. There had been only one attempted bottom-pinch, and that failed because I happened to turn around at the right moment.

Only the travel section at the American Express was open by the time I got there. I found a chair to settle down in and some travel folders and international air timetables to peruse while I waited for Tej. I sank into the unfamiliar leather seat and rested my elbows on the leather-upholstered steel tube arms. The slick paper of the folders, the pure, glowing colors of the photographs made flight seem smart, easy, attractive, exciting. The names evoked visions of faraway, inaccessible places, like Los Angeles and San Francisco; Honolulu and

New York. Ten thousand miles and thousands of rupees in tickets away. I remembered the International House Hungarians who had sat out their youths in Shanghai waiting for U.S. visas. Once in the United States they had to play cards to keep a grip on things. They might wake up one morning and find themselves back in Shanghai, the time in between a dream they couldn't handle.

I wondered what if I, instead of being a seven-month pregnant, sari-clad young Western woman with hair pulled back in a bun, were like my compatriots at the counter. They were a couple of tanned girls in shorts and polo shirts and sunglasses who reminded me of Carol. Judging from the conversation they were having with the Indian clerk, they were trying to confirm their reservations back to Chicago. They spoke in loud, distinct tones, as if the unintelligibility of their American mid-western accents could be overcome the louder and slower they pronounced each word. From them getting to Chicago was a matter of confirming a previously made reservation. For me, an impossibility, even if I had wanted to go there.

The timetable was smooth and slick in my hand, the photograph on the cover unnaturally bright, to make the Golden Gate Bridge stand out against a sky of unreal, sapphire blue. A place I had been to countless times, a bridge I had crossed on all kinds of occasions without thinking about it, was now only a shiny picture on the cover of a timetable in my hands. It was as remote, for all practical purposes, as one of Saturn's rings. I folded the brochure and put it in my purse. After ten minutes, Tej was there.

"How was it?" I asked.

"Okay," he said. "Three interviewers on the panel. A waiting room full of applicants." His summer suit had become wrinkled during the hours of waiting.

I could see he was worn out, but I had to ask, "Any idea of what your chances are?"

"It looked like they already had somebody picked out and this was just a tamasha, a show, to go through the motions. To say they'd held interviews. Anyway, the whole charade has made me hungry. Let's get something to eat before I show you Delhi."

He tried to keep it light, but I sensed he was disappointed, disheartened, and not a little relieved at the same time: no boat would need to be rocked, no drastic change made in our lives.

The rest of the afternoon was given over to sightseeing. I took a picture of Tej sitting in a clumsy carriage mounted on an old Harley Davidson motorcycle chassis that ordinarily carries six passengers on seats facing each other. Tej is negotiating for the whole vehicle just for ourselves. My shot is in black and white, but I can remember the lemon yellow oil-cloth canopy of the "phut-phut."

The driver was an old man in dirty white cotton pajamas and kurta. Tej was laughing and saying something to him. They had just struck a deal. We were to be shown as much of Delhi as possible before dark, for ten rupees. And we swung off into the broad streets. Roundabouts. Bright white bungalows set amidst dark green lawns and tall jamun trees in which brilliant green parrots perched—all these rushed by as on a movie set, while we sat stationary. Or so it seemed. New Delhi was a broad, flat city, with no skyscrapers, and open, cloud-dotted skies. An occasional car nudged its way at fifteen mph around bicycles swimming the roads like schools of fish, weaving and swaying to some hidden law that governed their progress through the city. Bullock and camel carts, prime subjects for tourist snapshots, lent their own exotic touch, and I promised myself not to photograph them for just that reason.

Here's another shot of Tej. At India Gate, this time. A low angle to make both him and the Gate hold up the sky. Here's still another. Of us both. At an historic site on the outskirts of the city. Taken by a tourist from Bombay whom we recruited to hold the Rollei after I'd taken the light reading and focused it. He too had come to Delhi for a job interview and also to see and be seen by the family of a Maharashtrian girl with whom, he told us, his marriage might be arranged. Taking a photograph was tricky in that fading light. The setting sun filtered through the pillars of an ancient Hindu temple, highlighting in bas relief the curved festoons of bells suspended from long chains, the ecstatic riders on horseback flashing into eternity, and the occasional smashed nose of a

163

river goddess. Next to it the Qutub Minar rose like a pointed finger into the sky. Tej and I had to struggle to keep from squinting as we smiled into the sun.

"Let's keep going around on this merry-go-round!" I said to him when the picture taking was over. I was laughing, but I meant it.

"What?" He smiled uncomprehendingly.

"Let's stay here for always," I said. "Driving around Delhi in this 'phut-phut.' You and I."

"And baby," he reminded me.

"Yes. Baby too, of course," I said. "Wouldn't it be great? The three of us living here, with a little place of our own?"

"I'd need a job first," he said.

"You'll get one." I stopped still and put my hand on his arm. "Tej," I said, so serious now, it almost hurt, "I don't want to go back to Majra."

"We've got to," Tej said.

"I know. I don't mean right now. I mean we need to be on our own. Soon. Otherwise . . ."

"Otherwise what?" he said.

"I don't know what will happen to us. To you and me. And the baby."

The "phut-phut" driver was waiting for us to get back into the vehicle. Long stopovers were not part of the deal. But we sat down on the grass to have it out.

"It isn't that the family, almost everybody, has not been good to me, beyond what I expected, even," I went on. "But it's not working out, Dilraj Kaur and I under the same roof."

"What is there to work out?" Tej asked. "She lives her life. You live yours."

"That's not easy when we're thrown together all day, every-day," I said. "While you and Hari and Pitaji are off, busy in your own work, the women in this house make a battle-ground out of the kitchen."

Tej looked as if this were something puzzling, and best left that way. He didn't need to hear any more about it, but I went on anyway.

"All these fights take place off stage, as far as you men are concerned. When you're around, everything's made to look harmonious."

"And it isn't," he said simply.

"Not by any means," I said. "It's a rough game going on in there, and I don't seem to be able to get the hang of it. All that malice and pettiness. I'm no match for Dilraj Kaur. She's even begun going to Veera Bai, and . . ."

"Veera Bai? The sweeperess?" he asked before I had a chance to go on.

"She's the village sorceress by night," I explained.

"Is she?" he said. "That's news to me. Anyway, I don't see why that should bother *you.* Dilraj Kaur has always been superstitious. Used to go and see fortune-tellers and so on. I don't know what she goes there for. But it's nothing to get excited about."

The driver honked his horn, a manually operated device consisting of a rubber bulb attached to a brass instrument that could be heard city blocks away. Tej motioned to him to wait.

"You'll be okay when the baby comes," he said. "You won't have time to brood. Don't worry, *meri jaan.* Nothing's going to 'happen' to us."

"But say you'll find a job; say we'll move here to Delhi," I insisted.

"It may take time."

"And *my* time is running out," I said. But I don't think he heard me because he'd already got up and was walking back to the "phut-phut."

The afterglow turned the city into a soundstage as the driver delivered us to our hotel door and collected his ten rupees plus a tip. Behind the hotel, the silhouettes of the Jama Masjid and the Red Fort, those other architectural dreams of Emperor Shahjehan come true, loomed like a background set for a sad ending to what might have been a happy day. We'd be going back to Majra in a couple of days. I could feel my throat tighten and my eyes smart from unshed tears when I realized I couldn't even make a guess about when we'd see Delhi again.

19

Now that I look back on it, everything started building up as soon as Tej and I got back from Delhi, so the events of his birthday and after should not have come as a surprise. We had been gone from Majra only three days, yet there was so much tension in the air as we entered the compound of the house the noon of our return that it could have been cut with a kirpan. In spite of our unsatisfactory talk of the future and the slow train ride, we arrived flushed and cheery after our brief breath of Delhi air. Right away, an awkwardness set in as the changes sensed a few days earlier were thrown into bold relief by the short time and distance away from Majra.

Talk was unnatural; conversations died when I entered a room. Mataji was still solicitous, yet there was a watchfulness about it rather than concern. Dilraj Kaur looked lean and haunted. I was shocked to see how gaunt she had become. Goodi and Rano accepted with polite smiles and formal thank-you's the salwar-kameez cloth pieces we had brought them as presents from the big city. Even Pitaji had turned his attention and trust in some subtle way from Tej to Hari. Only Nikku was truly glad to see us and uninhibited in expressing it. He greeted Tej with hugs and questions about Delhi, a city he had never seen.

It could not have happened in only three days, this grand shift; still it took that much time away for me to sense what ominous permutations had been set in motion. Someone was making bold moves on the chessboard, but the hand of the player was hidden.

"What's happened to everyone?" I asked Rano several days after our return.

She and Goodi were alone in the courtyard sitting on a

166

charpoy shelling peas into a big, brass tray. Piles of empty pods collected on the ground on either side of them, awaiting removal by the sweeperess.

"I don't understand what you mean, Bhabi," Rano said guardedly.

"There's something queer in the air. Everyone is behaving as if they were in a play, or something, reciting their lines, but not sure of them."

Rano still looked puzzled.

"What I mean is, everyone is acting in a forced, unnatural way. Ever since we got back from Delhi," I explained.

"That's because you and Bhaji went off alone without taking any of us along," Goodi spoke up.

Rano gave her a hard look. "You keep quiet. That's not it. Not the whole of it, anyway," she said sharply.

"Go ahead, Goodi," I said, "say what you wanted to say."

"It's that we felt left out, Bhabi. You hardly said a word about going, and then you were off in the middle of the night."

It was easy enough to make Goodi understand our need to get to Delhi in time for Tej's interview; however, she was still hurting for not being invited to go along. "Bhabiji said it would have been proper to at least ask one of us if we wanted to go, instead of running away by yourselves without saying anything."

Later I discovered there had been talk in our absence of my having "cast a spell" over Tej to make him behave so coldly toward everyone. That I was slowly luring him away. Destroying the fabric of the close-knit family. Pulling out the threads one by one. I was, finally, a bringer of ill-luck, an avoider of duties, a spoiler of harmony. By the time we got back, we had already separated ourselves from others, in the minds of some.

Pitaji, who had always been deaf to Tej's urgings to give Hari more to do and more money to spend, was now turning over a larger share of the profits to Hari and depending on him more.

Meanwhile life in the kitchen had become quieter. Fewer rambling, gossipy conversations. More silent work going on, at least while I was around. One afternoon when Udmi Ram was down with fever, I made Mataji a cup of tea. She protested and at the same time allowed herself to bask in this small attention. I overheard her telling Dilraj Kaur two days later how pleased she was that I had done this, and Dilraj Kaur (unaware of how much Punjabi I had picked up, or not caring if I understood or not) said, "Yes. She looks after you very well. Makes you tea sometimes. Sees to your little comforts. Fetches your things from upstairs. Goes out of her way. All these duties she no doubt performs . . . ." Here she stopped to draw out a long sigh before continuing. "What a pity it is all done without love, without any affection whatsoever!"

After dinner every night, when the family had retired to their own rooms, I could see the light in Dilraj Kaur's room at the opposite end of the "L" and upstairs from ours. Her tall shadow loomed motionless and intent behind the curtain. I wondered if I too was for her a shadow staring back. One night I saw her come out on the veranda and go quickly down the stairs. Just as quickly, and keeping to the shadows of the house, she disappeared beyond the compound gate.

Meanwhile, the achingly short spring burnt itself out in a couple of weeks of riotously blooming flowers and fine, cirrus cloud-crossed skies. At the same time, our isolation, Tej's and mine, from the rest of the family became more pronounced. The subtle ways, perfected over centuries of joint family living, of forcing certain members into social ostracism, for one reason or another, were at work. Without knowing how or when it happened, Tej and I became onlookers rather than partakers of the life of the family, that entity without life of its own that a family creates for itself, out of itself, and off which each member feeds. Tej, true to his reluctance to define relationships, was either unaware of it, or unwilling to talk about it.

The formality continued. Was some grim announcement about to be made? Had some unspoken taboo been violated? Had I inadvertently committed an outrage on some religiously held custom or belief? If so, how had that involved Tej, who now appeared to share my lonely status?

April arrived all of a sudden one day, and the wheat crop ripened with it. Tej's birthday was on the tenth, and for a week I pored over a cookbook I had found in my big red steamer trunk. I was looking for a cake recipe that could be adapted to the materials at hand: coarse whole wheat flour for fine cake flour, an improvised contraption for an oven, a small tin of baking powder of doubtful age got with difficulty from Ladopur at a shop recommended by the Mission ladies. It was going to be a surprise.

I thought I had taken care of everything and got together all the necessary ingredients and utensils beforehand. But when I went into the kitchen that morning ready to get started, I could see at a glance that the services of Udmi Ram and Chotu were not going to be available to me. They were both busier than usual, trying to fulfill the instructions of two or three women at a time and getting little done in the process.

Giant cauldrons had been gotten out from the storeroom, and ladles to match. Mounds of wheat flour, raw rice, dal, and spices were being measured out by Dilraj Kaur (dressed at that early hour in red, bridal finery!) while Mataji was seeing to the lighting of fires in big stoves made of mud and cow dung that had sprung into being overnight. Outside, under a mango tree, the tandoor for baking six chapattis at a time was being got ready. It was a woman's show. Pitaji and Hari and the cousins from Amritsar had gone off to see to the harvesting, while in the kitchen, there was an inspired purposefulness—that and a kind of sober gaiety—to the proceedings. Something big was going on. For Tej's birthday? Nobody had bothered to tell me about it. Was I supposed, somehow, to know without being told? Was it one of those things so taken for granted that no one saw fit to enlighten me? Or was it, as it appeared, that everyone was too busy, and I was in the way? Rano in passing breathed something about the feast being given "for Bhaji's long life," and then hurried away to help Goodi supervise the readying of brass trays for serving a multitude, judging from the stacks being brought out of the storeroom and rinsed off by Ram Piari.

Onto this busy scene I made my cautious way, found a small mud stove in a corner, one which was for everyday use, and decided to manage the cake somehow on my own, no matter how long it took me to locate a big pan, hunt for some

169

sand to heat in it, find a lid that fitted and some hot coals to put on top, all to create oven-like conditions. Eventually I acquired all the material on my own and through my own exertions the singed fingers, blackened nails, smoke-reddened eyes, and sweaty forehead that testified to my industry. But it somehow seemed selfish, one-sided, lonely, diminished, taking place as it did in the shadow of the larger, communal effort led by Dilraj Kaur. Mataji and the girls and the entire battery of house servants, joined by others loaned for the occasion from other houses with whom the family had close relations, awaited her instructions like a disciplined army platoon.

They began arriving early that morning, Majra's poor, the birthday guests, as it slowly became clear to me. Children first, each carrying an aluminum plate; then their parents. Landless peasants. Not happy ones with cheery faces, but destitute and ill-clad and sullen in faded, earth-colored clothes. Drab dupattas, rags and hand-me-downs for turbans, frayed hems, lined faces, dirt-clogged fingernails; rough, gnarled hands; big, splay-toed, bare feet; burnt-out eyes in which curiosity and anticipation of the meal flickered. They lined up, sat down on the ground, smiled white-toothed, obsequious smiles. And waited.

Dilraj Kaur emerged from the kitchen to order them all in military tones to arrange themselves according to caste. She wanted the potters, the water carriers, the carpenters, and the leather workers, all to sit in separate groups and be counted. Children who had arrived together with their friends, split up to sit with their parents.

After that the food was plentifully if hastily served by Dilraj Kaur herself, aided by the girls and Mataji. Within minutes the whole of it was consumed. From somewhere someone produced a drum, and a desultory shuffling of feet began. Dust got kicked up. The rhythm got faster, and some of the girls and women started to dance. Caught up in the fun of it, they forgot momentarily who they were in the presence of. Giggled, laughed, shouted! Kicked up more dust. The words of the songs must have got too racy for the family's chaste ears, as Mataji told them to sing something else, and Dilraj Kaur abruptly ordered them all off. I glimpsed

170

Tej in the veranda in front of the door to the living room. He was acknowledging in an embarrassed, self-conscious way (so untypical of him) the salaams of the guests as they silently filed out of our compound, the children seeking out their friends, the castes getting all mixed up again in the process. Nobody in the family had said "happy birthday" to Tej. I supposed that was a Western thing to do, just as feasting the poor on a son's birthday was Punjabi.

When they had all gone, something made me look at Dilraj Kaur. She was about to faint. Her face was pale, and she was breathing hard. There was an odd, intense look in her eyes. By an act of will, she might make it to her room and lie down. In the excitement of family and servants ensuring that she did just that, a handkerchief soaked in cold water was applied to her head, tea was made, a doctor sent for. Exclamations were heard: "Poor thing. She is fasting to death!" "She's overworked!" "All for Bhaji." "His long life." "She saw to the whole thing today herself."

And I forgot the cake. When I went to take it out of the "oven," it was a charred block of dough on the outside, raw inside. I grabbed it up in a towel, and when no one was looking, went outside the courtyard into the area where the cattle were kept. I threw it as far as I could, ran after it and then gave it a fierce kick. Pieces of it landed in the shed where their unexpected appearance caused no show of alarm in the bemused expression of the cow standing there by the feed trough.

20

Word got out that night: Veera Bai *"khaid di hai."* Veera Bai was "playing." News like that got around, somehow, from kitchen to kitchen, via the servants. It spread, a quiet fire, through the village, never lighting a conflagration, but hurrying along from one place to another, like the fiery glow along a slow-burning fuse. Those in Majra who craved messages from the spirit world, hoarded love charms, relied on amulets to ward off disease or to ensure the long life of sons, who burned to do someone in, or were simply curious, would visit Veera Bai's hut that night. I had heard there would be big gatherings on some occasions, and only two or three people attending at other times. With the coming of summer, and on a night of the full moon like tonight, Veera Bai's clientele could be expected to pick up, Rano once told me.

I wondered what Veera Bai got out of it. Did she really have any control over when the fit would come on and the spirit of a dead person would enter her? Did the full moon have anything to do with it? It had risen in the early evening, all the more orange because of the dust haze and smoke from village fires. Now it was well overhead and white as I watched it from my window. Shadows in the yard were thrown into bold contrast against the rest of the surroundings on which where conferred the clarity of day.

Tej and Hari and the cousins from Amritsar had left for the fields right after an early dinner. The wheat crop was being harvested round the clock. Tonight the work would be made easier, lighted as it was by the white globe of the moon. The operation had to be completed as quickly as possible, and labor had been contracted on a twenty-four-hour basis. It was going to be a long shift for Tej, since he had to leave for Ambala early the next morning to take care of some affairs for Pitaji at the District Headquarters. There had been barely time before he left for the fields for me to present him with the knitted tie I had made for his birthday, surreptitiously over a period of months, from a kit I had brought with me from California.

A stillness enveloped the house. The dogs, untied from their daytime confinement, had exchanged their nocturnal greetings and growls and had fallen silent. The sound of the harvesters singing to their task, borne along on the night wind, came clear and strong from fields that were acres away. The light in Dilraj Kaur's room was on. Her shadow behind the drawn curtain. She had not come out of her room since her near collapse hours earlier. To ensure her a good night's rest, Mataji had suggested taking Nikku to her own room to sleep after seeing that Dilraj Kaur had had something to eat. As I watched Mataji leading Nikku off, I made a decision that took me less than half a minute to come to.

The night settled down into a moonlit, shadow-splashed calm. Work in the kitchen was finished. The servants had bedded down for the night, the women had retired to their rooms. Yet there was a busyness. It emanated from outside our compound and had to do not only with the singing from far away, but with the electric current in the air that began and ended with Veera Bai "playing." Her hut was on the village outskirts in the heart of the colony for sweepers and others who performed what was considered lowly tasks. It wouldn't be hard to find. All I had to do was get into costume and wait for my cue. It came before many minutes had passed.

The light in Dilraj Kaur's room went out, and I saw her door open. As on earlier occasions, she left the house, keeping to the shadows, walking briskly but lightly across the compound and disappearing through a barely visible gap in the hibiscus hedge beside the gate. I kept a certain distance behind her, hoping the dogs would not be alarmed by my unusual appearance in the yard at that time of night and give me away. Once outside the compound, I came to appreciate the institution of purdah. Covering my head, face, and shoulders and a shawl had rendered me anonymous, especially

173

since I'd thrown it over the dullest colored outfit I had. I could have been any woman, of any age.

Dilraj Kaur hurried off in the direction I knew she'd take. The way led through a mango grove that was adjacent to our house and along a path that skirted the village. She abruptly cut off into a side lane and then headed for the sweepers' colony where the light from a hut shone dimly in the distance, drawing the villagers on like a lamp attracting flying termites after a rain.

I was only a few yards away now and could hear the sound of cymbals being struck. Six or seven women hung back tentatively on the threshold of the hut, not knowing whether they wanted to go inside or not, while others pressed eagerly on. A few children stood about, expecting to be sent away any moment, and so kept out of the way of adults. When I got to the door a fat woman in a hurry jostled past, and I found myself pushed against the outside wall. A young girl pulled my shawl to get me to sit down. And so I sat—looking into that diorama of a scene, boxed in as it was. The foreground figures melted away into the hazy backdrop of Veera Bai's hut.

Villagers already inside were conferring with one another. I could scarcely see them, and, as far as I was concerned, they were mere voices speaking out of the darkness made murkier by the smoke rising from incense and from some burning coals that flickered in an earthen pot in front of the seated Veera Bai. "She won't go through with the session tonight," a woman said. "Of course she will," another contradicted her. Yet a third voice, this time a man's, said, "Whenever she starts playing, it never stops until the spirit has spoken."

Gradually my eyes got accustomed to the dim light, and I was able to make out some familiar faces: village women who had been present for the feast earlier that day; a young girl who occasionally came to help in our house when we had more than the usual number of guests to deal with. And there was Dilraj Kaur. She had walked in ahead of me without looking right or left, and was allowed to take her place in front of the others. In deference to her caste? Her status as a member of the most important family in the village and

174

the daughter-in-law of the Major-Sahib? Or just because she was Dilraj Kaur? Whatever the reason, she now sat directly in front of Veera Bai. A low stool had materialized especially for her to sit on. It appeared to be the only item of furniture in the room.

I was amazed at myself for being able to sit there and take in the scene without bolting, because I was on the far side of becoming overwhelmed by fear. It was a fear that went beyond my anxiety not to be recognized. It went beyond shaky legs and heart palpitations. Instead, hostile hands held me in their fierce control. They were hands that could neither be seen nor touched, and were all the more terrible because they could be felt. I couldn't free myself from their grip. The conviction that I couldn't move was altogether irrational and ran riot along the nerves like some message gone haywire. Besides, the place itself had a bad "feel," some madness to it older than the human race. Sitting there became an exercise in unmasking that madness and finding my own features behind the false face.

Here was our young sweeperess, Veera Bai, seated on a mat in the center of the room, with ten or fifteen women and men around her. The ground they met her on was not of the everyday world of Majra. Before losing contact with that world myself, I wanted to stand up and say, "Listen to me. That's just Veera Bai. Why are you all sitting around her as if she were a goddess? She keeps our yards swept clean. She has a smile for us in the morning. She's the one you shout at when you're not satisfied with her work. So why this now?" I wanted to say all this, but at the same time I was not sure whether it was the truth exactly. It was this dilemma that made me want to get out of there before I lost the sense of who I was. The purdah had already concealed my identity from others and given the lie to reality. At this moment, I was incognito, even to myself.

Meanwhile, the sweeperess was undergoing a startling change. She stared at the burning coals in the earthen pot in front of her and at some other paraphernalia before her which I couldn't see from where I sat, but could only guess at. There would be a conch shell, perhaps. Some colored beads or a peacock feather. The flames created a red, low-

175

angle glow that illuminated her deep-set eyes and high cheekbones and projected her shadow against the wall behind her, transforming the girl into a giantess.

Seated cross-legged on the floor, she closed her eyes and began to sway slowly. Not back and forth, but in a circular motion, describing a figure eight. Each configuration was wider than the previous one and was accomplished at a faster speed. Shortly thereafter she began to moan and, before long, Veera Bai's hair uncoiled from its knot and fell in a coarse, thick rope around her shoulders.

With each completion of the ever-widening, ever-faster circle, her hair flew about more wildly until it became a swirling, whipping mass of black about her head; the moan rose to a wail. The crowd ceased to breathe. This is what they had been waiting for. When it became clear that no flesh and blood could endure more ecstasy, Veera Bai slumped forward without warning and became perfectly still. All the while, Dilraj Kaur, like everyone else there, sat rigid with anticipation.

When the girl sat upright again, she was no longer Veera Bai, but a human vessel containing the spirit of a dead person and brimful of its messages. Her pupils were rolled back. The whites were laced with red. Drugs? Delirium? Rapture? Or the sheer exquisiteness of being possessed?

"The spirit has entered her," a woman mumbled.

"How will we know when it leaves?" a small girl beside her asked in a loud voice.

"Shsh!" an old woman sitting in front of them hissed.

From somewhere in the darkened room a voice came: "You will come to know, all right. The earthen pot on the shelf there will fall and break into pieces," it said.

Everyone looked around, but no one could tell who had spoken. No one moved for a full minute. The sorceress sat impassive, in a trance.

Then I overheard one of the women near me whisper, "I once saw a sorceress in another village take a lock of baby's hair that a woman had handed her. She tied it up in a scrap of red cloth and gave it back to the woman."

"Must have been a lock of a male child's hair. To do him

harm. To bring him bad luck. Death," her companion said in an undertone.

"The woman was told to leave the baby's hair wrapped up in the same cloth at a crossroads," the first woman whispered.

"Yes. Always at a crossroads," said the other. "And whoever picks it up will also be cursed with bad luck."

The sorceress continued to sit, her head thrown back, red-eyed, staring at nothing. When she finally opened her mouth to speak, the voice was not Veera Bai's nor anyone else's the Majra villagers had ever heard. They listened with their entire bodies, heads nodding, eyes intense, waiting to be called, to receive from her magic hands the charms sealed in metal lockets and strung on black threads that, tied around the loins of a male child, would ensure his survival into adulthood. There would be short mantras whispered into the ears of jealous wives, chants that would win back a wayward husband from his mistress; phials of love potions to start romances.

Dilraj Kaur signaled that she had a request. She drew closer to the sorceress and said something in a low voice. This time the spirit was heard only by Dilraj Kaur. She asked question after question, and the answers came pouring out of the mouth of the sorceress, in hoarse whispers. Dilraj Kaur's face was turned toward the door now, as she bent to hear the words from the spirit. I thought she had caught sight of me. Had recognized me. But she was only staring in the direction of the door, I decided, while concentrating on the message she had come to hear. It was almost possible for me to read the answers in Dilraj Kaur's expression. She was frowning, her eyes wild and bright with purpose. Once or twice she appeared to ask for further directions or explanations about whatever it was she was being advised to do. At length the sorceress, her bloodshot eyes still fixed on another world, held up an amulet on a black string, tied it ceremoniously in a piece of blood-red cloth, and handed it to Dilraj Kaur: literally pressed it into her palm and closed Dilraj Kaur's fingers over it.

Then everything happened at once. There was one last rough whisper from the spirit before the earthen pot on the shelf crashed to the mud floor. It was as if an alarm had gone off. Astonished cries went up from the crowd, followed by groans of disappointment. The spirit would speak no more that night. Meanwhile, Dilraj Kaur had gotten up hurriedly and made for the door of the hut. In my rush to get a head start on her, I dropped my shawl. It slipped from my head and fell around my shoulders. A small boy beside me looked up in surprise. "It's the Mem!" he cried. "The Memsahib from the big house!" His eyes danced with excitement, and a smile lit his face as he turned to get the attention of others he could share the news with. In an instant, a cluster of curious faces stared into mine, and exclamations of disbelief, shock, and amusement arose. I covered my face again as fast as I could, but not before Dilraj Kaur had shot me a startled look of recognition as she rushed past me without saying a word. Once home, I turned off the kerosene lantern and went to bed. But I couldn't sleep. I kept seeing Dilraj Kaur's bright glance as she took note of my unexpected presence at the door of Veera Bai's hut. I got up, and the full moon followed me as I paced back and forth. I went to draw the curtain and looked out of the window. Dilraj Kaur's light was on, and she was standing on the veranda outside her room. I watched her a long moment. She seemed to be beckoning to someone below. And then I saw Tej, back from the harvesting, crossing the yard. Instead of coming straight to our room on the ground floor, he climbed the stairway to her veranda, and the two of them went inside.

The act belonged to the oddness of the time, of the night itself. And I stood there, looking through the window, asking myself all the sensible reasons why Tej should go to Dilraj Kaur's room at half-past midnight. Everything about that night belonged to the irrational. It had achieved a kind of sense of its own during the past hour when time stopped meaning anything, and place was a matter of opinion.

Instead of wringing my mind dry with further conjecture, I flung the shawl over my head again, let myself out of our room, and headed for the stairs leading to the upper floor. Before I could reach the top, the light in Dilraj Kaur's room went out. The window opening onto the upstairs veranda was ajar; the door to her room closed. I stopped for a moment and grasped the banister. Their voices, disembodied and unreal, floated on the night air like smoke arising from incense through the open window. I strained to listen to those voices that were all too familiar, but now strangely new. Locked in speech. Heard in low tones, in words and phrases; the masculine and feminine sounds, Punjabi sounds, the timbres of the two complementing each other, like well-matched instruments, the utterances still unintelligible.

Meanwhile, something had happened to me. Physically. I wanted to climb the stairs the rest of the way. Yet I couldn't trust my legs to take me up to the door, my hand to fling it open, my voice to say, "What the hell are you doing here, Tej?"

Instead, I became a fanatical eavesdropper, a lurker in shadows, an onlooker with nothing to witness but the surrealistic visions inside my own head.

"You never used to call me that," Dilraj Kaur responded to something Tej had said.

"What do you mean?" he asked.

"You never used to call me Bhabiji after we were married. You called me Dilraj. Remember?"

"But you are my Bhabiji now. Again." His voice grew faint on the last word. It was an explanation of sorts, but she chose not to be tutored.

"What's the difference now?" she asked.

"You know as well as I," he said.

She said something I could not understand and followed it up with a low laugh. I couldn't recall ever having heard Dilraj Kaur laugh before.

"Well, it's true," he went on from where he'd left off.

"It doesn't need to be," she said. "I'm not the wife of your older brother anymore; I'm *your* wife." If words could caress, hers were doing just that.

Tej mumbled something inaudible.

"How can you say that I'm not?" she asked.

Again, I could not hear what Tej replied. But she said, "Why should that make any difference?"

"It does," he said.

Then I could hear them both move; getting up from somewhere? Coming toward the door? Walking away from it?

"Come," I heard her say. "I have something for you. The

least you can do is accept it. It will ensure your long life. Do this for me?" She lingered on the last words.

They were clearly walking away from the direction of the door now. Their voices were harder to hear, and their footsteps fainter. There was a short, unamused laugh. I recognized it as Tej's. I knew what the expression on his face would be: raised eyebrows, an ironic look in his eyes. He laughed like that when he was embarrassed by something unexpected, when he sensed something was required of him, but he didn't know what.

My frozen arms and legs and hands suddenly grew hot. Blood shot into my cheeks and raced along, filling the arteries and veins to the point of bursting. In two steps I was at the door and throwing it open.

21

Some moments in time stretch and snap like rubber bands. The door took a century to swing back on its hinges, and Tej a decade to react to my entering the room. The moonlight slashed in through the open door like a spotlight. Dilraj Kaur looked up without surprise. She took an age to take her hands away from Tej's shoulders and to release the smile that her face continued to hold captive for too long. It took her even longer to try and cover her femaleness that threatened to overflow the boundaries of the room and spill out into the night. She was all breasts and belly and thighs; loosened hair and naked eyes.

Tej floated up and away from the charpoy on which he had been sitting, his back to the door. Was he levitating or merely unsteady when he got to his feet? At the same time, Dilraj Kaur sank down on the charpoy with a leisurely, languid gesture of resignation and made a slow, token attempt to cover herself with her dupatta.

Then everything snapped. "What's going on?" I said, the sound of my own voice reverberating in my head. Tej stood looking at me; he was confused and mad and surprised all at once, and he made a move to hurry me out the door again. Dilraj Kaur sat silent and self-possessed as on a slow-moving carousel, amidst clothes, cast off and left where they fell; sheets and pillows creating a muddle on the unmade bed. She looked first at Tej and then at me, a spectator instead of a participant.

"We'll talk when you come to your senses again," Tej said. "Right now, you're not ready to hear anything I have to say."

"I'm as ready as I'll ever be. Besides, it's not up to you to decide when I'll be 'ready'. It's just a way you have of getting out of answering my questions."

181

Dilraj Kaur muttered something.

"This is her room," Tej said. "Let's go where we can talk, if you want to."

"I want to talk, all right. But it will be right here. In her presence. We need to have it out one way or the other."

"Come with me," he said.

"No. All three of us have got to talk this out. Now," I said.

"You can do your talking, then," Tej said. "Without me." And he went out the door, slamming it behind him.

Dilraj Kaur stood up, about to say something to stop him. It was too late. There were just the two of us left, and half a language between us to communicate with. We stood staring each other down. Her grey eyes had lost all color. It gave her the look of some wild thing at night caught in the beam of a car's headlights. She pushed her hair away from her face.

"So now you talk," she said in heavily accented English, groping for words. The sound of my own language on her lips came as a shock. "First, you tell me. What you were doing tonight? Tell me. At the hut of Veera Bai. I saw you there, covered up like a thief, sitting in the doorway."

"Why don't you leave Tej and me alone?" I said, ignoring her question because I had no reply ready. "You've spent all the time I have been here trying to wreck things."

"Who's wrecking?" she said. Then, lapsing into Punjabi, she went on. "You are the one who has ruined everything. Made everything rotten. Brought down the whole house, the whole family."

After that, she started talking too fast for me to understand anything more than the fact that she hated me. I allowed her to run down like Pitaji's old manual phonograph when it needed re-cranking. When she finally exhausted her store of abuses I began again, in what I thought was a reasonable tone of voice. "I haven't done anything intentionally to hurt you. I mean, I have not wanted to hurt you. I haven't . . ."

"What you are saying?" she interrupted, in English again. "Everything is okay? You come here. Take my husband. Act like a memsahib. Sit around all day, getting waited on. Don't work. Not talking, even."

"I . . . ."

She interrupted me again. "Why you don't leave? Why?

182

You and that child in your belly. You are not wanted here. My husband and me, we were okay till you come. Like a concubine. Into the house itself. You take him away from the family. You take him away from me. My husband. My son's uncle." She punctuated her words with signs and gestures that made any misunderstanding impossible.

"Look, what you're saying isn't true. I haven't taken anyone or anything away from you," I said firmly, drawing on an argument Tej had often relied on. "Your position in the family is secure. Nikku's is secure. Nobody's threatening you. So why blame me? If Tej has not treated you properly, blame him."

"There!" she said triumphantly. I had inadvertently proven one of her points. "That is what I mean," she said in Punjabi again. "You don't care for him. You have no respect for him, calling him by his first name itself. Saying I should blame him, and all. When it's no fault of his. You have cast a spell on him. That's the kind of woman you are."

"That's just nonsense," I said. "I only want to be left in peace without all your tricks. Don't think because I've been silent I haven't noticed all the things you've done. You've tried to turn Mataji and Goodi against me. And you've worked on Rano too. All the filthy insinuations about me and Pitaji. And now *this*. You don't stop at anything, do you?" I delivered this half in Punjabi and half in English, and I had no idea how much of it she understood. She got perfectly well my gesture that indicated her current state of undress, however, and pulled her dupatta over herself in a belated show of modesty.

"He is my husband," she said. "How you dare come into my room like that?"

"Your husband, under the *chadhar*," I said. "You know very well that widows never really remarry," I couldn't help adding. She understood my insinuation; it made her furious.

"You are a witch," she cried in Punjabi. "You have tried to turn him away from all of us. He's a different person now. Not the man who left for California two years ago. You have changed him. Still I understand him better than you do." Then switching to English again, "All the time he is worried about what the memsahib will think. About your comfort. About this and that. He sits playing the sitar for you instead

183

of attending to the farm properly. You have turned our lives upside down." She paused for breath. Getting up from the charpoy, then, Dilraj Kaur stood confronting me, so that our faces were bare inches apart. "Where have you come from? Why don't you go back there?"

It was more than a question. It was a plea. She had used up her store of strength and energy. Even the fund of anger and hatred that fueled her words seemed exhausted. Now there were tears in her eyes, and I didn't wait to find out whether they were because of anger or distress, fury or despair. Whatever it was, I had no answer to her question. I left the room as quickly as I had entered. The shaft of moonlight lighted my way out.

"Well, that was a short talk," Tej said when I got back to our room.

"It's your turn now," I said. "I'm waiting to hear all the reasons why you're doing this to me. To us."

"Doing what, for heaven's sake?"

"Betraying me; betraying our relationship," I said, trying to blink back tears and not succeeding.

"You come barging into a room. Rush to judgments and decide I'm betraying you," he countered. "You were really acting crazy with your craving for drama. I don't know what you thought you were doing."

"Don't try to put *me* on the spot. I don't have to defend anything I've done. You're the one who has got us both to answer to. Dilraj Kaur and me. I never knew her until tonight. But I think I do now. She's fighting for her life and for her son's. She mistakenly thinks I'm out to ruin her, and she's trying to get me first. she's tried everything. To isolate me from others in the family; to keep me away from family events—like your birthday today; to make me out to be some kind of concubine, with no status. She'd like to relegate me to the position of a whore and our kids, when we have them, to bastards. That way they'll have no claim. And now . . ."

"What rot are you talking?" he shouted. He seized me by the shoulders. Shook me. Stared into my eyes as one would stare into the eyes of a madwoman. Trying to fathom depths that the pupils refused access to.

184

"And now," I went on, "she's got me where it hurts the most. . . ."

"What do you mean?"

"Do you think I didn't see her, half-naked, leaning over you and you sitting on her bed? What was I supposed to make of that?"

"Anything you like. But I will tell you. I saw her there on the veranda when I got back from the fields and thought I'd see if she was okay. She seemed to want to talk to me. I thought I ought to see what about, especially since she was unwell after feeding those villagers on my birthday and all."

"Go on," I said.

"She was just putting this around my neck when you came in. It's for my long life, she says. She brought it from a place of pilgrimage she visited with her brother. I humored her and . . ."

"It's nothing of the sort," I exclaimed, lifting the amulet on its thread. "She got this from the sorceress, Veera Bai, tonight. I saw her with my own eyes. It's a love charm like Veera Bai hands out at these séances of hers," I said, yanking it off the thread and throwing it across the room as hard as I could.

"What the . . . !" he exclaimed, grabbing my wrist. "What's the matter with you? Why don't you listen to me? Have I ever lied to you? Have I?" he cried, still holding me, willing me physically to say *no*.

But I couldn't say it. "How can I tell?" I said weakly. "After tonight."

He let go of me then. "To hell with it," he shouted. "To hell with you. I just want to get out of this madhouse. I thought you were someone special. Above stupid pettiness. Beyond kitchen feuds. Someone different from the general run. I thought *we* were special. Our relationship like no one else's." He turned away from me and started toward the door. I put my hand on his arm to stop him.

"Why don't you level with me," I said.

"Just leave me alone, will you? I was wrong about you. About us. There's nothing great about us. Never was. We were just ordinary people pretending not to be. You've never

185

understood how I felt about you. Now it's gone. The feeling. Dead. I just want to get out of here."

"It doesn't have to be like this, if you'd be honest with me," I said again.

"We're going to be parents in another month or so. And you haven't even grown up yet!" he shouted.

"How about you? Resuming a relationship with that witch. While I'm pregnant and clumsy and unattractive. Or did you never break off with her?"

"What did you say!"

"Did you never break . . ."

"Break off? I'll show you what breaking off is," he said in such a quiet voice now that I lost my breath waiting for what he was going to do next. "Nothing can get into your thick head," he said, striding in silent fury over to the corner of our room where the sitar sat wrapped in its cloth cover beneath a photograph of Panditji. I can still see myself putting out my hands to stop him, saying "No! Don't do it! Don't . . ."

It all happened so fast, there was nothing to be done. Before I understood what was happening, he had pulled the instrument out of its cloth cover and had hurled it against the wall. It fell into bits on the floor.

What happened after that remains a muddle in my mind. To reconstruct the shattered moment of his leaving is impossible. Perhaps he pushed past me on his way to the door. It may have been that he grabbed some papers lying on the red steamer trunk and stuffed them into his briefcase before he went out. There was a brisk madness about his striding to the door, flinging it open, and rushing out. I didn't watch him go. I only heard the door slam shut. I sat down to think about how I was going to spend the next fifty years.

Not like *this*, anyway. I was sure of that. I could see myself heading out. Pregnant and all. Tonight. This morning. Before dawn. Before Tej got back from Ambala; before the others woke up. Heading out for *where*, I wondered. I observed myself busy about the room, keeping pace in physical acts with the speed of my racing mind, as it picked up and discarded alternative after alternative. I collected bits of the sitar off the floor by the wall where Tej had smashed it. Looking down at my hands, I was surprised to find pieces

186

of gourd clutched in them. There was no putting the instrument back together again. But I collected all the pieces I could find and set them aside for I don't know what. The amulet, too, lay on the floor where I'd thrown it. I picked it up and tossed it into the old shortening tin I had turned into a wastebasket.

I got out the travel brochure I had picked up that day in Delhi. It was still in the little leather purse where I'd put it. The Golden Gate Bridge still hung suspended over the entrance to the Bay against a brilliant blue sky where it sat waiting to be crossed again by me. My mind was riding a whirligig of an idea: All it would take would be a telegram to Papa to send me the fare home. I wondered for a moment if that was the word to describe my parents' house anymore. If it was the place for a child of mine and Tej's to grow up in. A house without a father.

When I thought about it, the only place for our child to grow up in would be *our* house. Tej's and mine. But that didn't even exist as something I could picture. It certainly wasn't Majra. The powerful craziness of Dilraj Kaur had swept up everyone along with it; no one remained untouched. Everyone collaborated in this madness, driven by the fuel of her mania, misinterpreting it as religious fervor, superhuman loyalty to Tej, or simply indispensable usefulness. She had made it her house. Now she wanted to reclaim Tej as hers too. There was no space for me to breathe. I decided this was no place for our child.

I wished I had Aunt Teresa to talk to about all this. She could be depended upon to see everything straight. She had a way of knowing exactly what was going on.

I always thought it was because so much had happened to her in life. She had married early; lost every child she conceived; supported Uncle Oreste after his last accident on the job by taking in sewing to do. She over-ate, grew huge on polenta and cheap, red wine; shuffled around in bedroom slippers all day and stitched sacklike cotton dresses for herself that were more like tents than anything else. Coarse, curly, iron grey hair that had once been black. Soft, wrinkled cheeks. Varicose veins. High blood pressure. Aunt Teresa. She was ten thousand miles away. Writing to her wouldn't help. She was never too good at writing and never answered letters.

Finally, it would have to be Carol. One last letter to Carol before I took a blind leap into an uncertain future on my own. After this, there wouldn't be anything more to say, one way or another. Setting down my thoughts might help me decide between the possible and the impossible, and prove to be a remedy for the pain of indecision that nagged me.

As things were at that moment—only half an hour had gone by since Tej left—I had no idea which way to go. But go I had to.

Carol, Again

22

I suppose the most unsatisfactory part of remembering Helen Graziani is not knowing what eventually happened to her. Did she succeed in life, finally? Did she find what she was looking for? All I have to rely upon is this last letter of hers, which I've just found amongst the pile of papers I've been sorting through before moving to the new place. It's unlike any she had written before, full of self-doubt and indecision. And more than that: There's an urgency and desperation. With what or with whom is unclear. What was I supposed to do with what she wrote me? When I remember myself at that time, I'm struck with how unable I was to put myself in her place, to understand her predicament, what little she revealed of it. She wanted advice. But who was I to give it? I was in as much need as she was of direction, of guidance at that time. How was I supposed to respond? What action could I have taken? I've often been plagued with these questions because it seems to me there should have been something appropriate for me to do, besides replying to the letter. Which I did. But she never followed it up, and I never heard from her again.

Years ago, one or two friends from the Berkeley days, back from postwar reconstruction jobs with agencies in Europe, claimed they'd seen Helen during *Fasching* in Munich or in a Left Bank bookstore near Notre Dame, but that she'd disappeared from sight almost before their very eyes. If, indeed, it had been Helen.

I used to fancy we'd encounter one another somewhere, quite by surprise, in some unlikely place, she entering on a summer afternoon the Chartres Cathedral or Westminster Abbey or the Sistine Chapel by one door; I leaving it. Eschew-

191

ing the tour groups, we'd each be alone, coming to individual grips with these architectural wonders. We'd laugh and talk and have an aperitif, perhaps a meal together somewhere. We'd recall the old days, promise to keep in touch.

Once I'd imagined both of us visiting our hometown together. I'd go off again with her on one of her bizarre excursions, to the outer limits of Los Angeles, to hear an Indian patriot give a speech or a dancer from Calcutta perform to the accompaniment of drums and cymbals and burning incense. To Helen, places far away always beckoned like lighted windows of home. She was forever heading out, even if it were only across town. If in San Francisco, we'd again try to find that Basque restaurant in North Beach we had once spent a whole Saturday in our freshman year trying to locate. I would then finally learn what exactly she went to India to find and whether, indeed, she found it.

Comparisons are almost impossible to avoid. And I admit one reason, the main reason, I was so obsessed with finding out the answer to this insistent question all along was to satisfy myself that I had gotten a better deal in life. I hasten to say that jealousy or envy has nothing to do with it. I thought too much of Helen for that; wished her too much good fortune. It's simply that what she did was altogether provocative. It turned upside down all our notions about ourselves, our values, our culture, our "progress," our sheer power. Things we took for granted. She put them in question. With her sudden flight to an unfamiliar world she'd raised doubts that a lifetime could not put to rest. She ought not to have succeeded; she ought not to have gotten away with it. Otherwise, what did my own life prove? What did it add up to? A professorship, achieved at last after the males on the staff had been accommodated? An award or two? An honorary citation? An entry in the *Who's Who of American Scholars*? A couple of exchange professorships? An intended compliment once overheard, that I had a *masculine* mind; that no woman could *think* like I did?

My analyst has said I have particular difficulty in forming lasting relationships. I must say I have survived rather well without them. I have, in fact, found that when you lose a lover—through a quarrel, estrangement, or separation—

your grief is anyway not so much at the loss of the other person as at the loss of your Self as "Lover." This is especially so, if becoming a lover has long seemed a desire impossible of attainment and *being* a lover at last an unbelievably euphoric experience. The loss of the lover, then, is like a reaffirmation of your essentially love-less, lover-less state. Because it begins and ends with me, it's something I've always been able to handle, the Dante scholar notwithstanding.

As long as I'm taking the occasion to reflect, I could ask myself if I miss the man I might have married or the three children I aborted, those faceless, sexless fetuses who would now be individuals in their own right—twenty-eight, thirty-five, and forty years old? I've never stopped and allowed myself to ask. And now those questions belong to the "what-might-have-beens" of life.

Helen's child would be middle-aged by now. It's an idea difficult for me to conceive of. This is because Helen, and all things and all persons surrounding her (including myself at the time I knew her) have been encased in a memory capsule for more than forty years. I can see myself locked in that capsule and I search in vain for some connection between that over-made-up, boy-crazy young woman that I was and the one who stares back at me now from the mirror across the room. Helen and Tej and the child (I never found out whether it was a boy or a girl) remain unchanged, there being no photographs, no further word to testify to their having grown older. I have wondered from time to time whether Helen and Tej grew older together. What did Helen mean by "the intolerable situation" she refers to in this last letter? What did she do about it? She says it has not so much to do with Tej as with someone else. Who was that "someone?" "Issues are at stake," she writes, "touching on the very integrity of the relationship between Tej and me as a couple, and of both of us as parents of the child expected in six weeks' time." In another place she says she hesitates to take any "irreversible action" (a chilling expression) because of the baby she's expecting. Yet, she says, she's being "driven to the wall." By whom? By what?

She goes on to say everyone (presumably Tej's family) has been good to her, except for one person who "wishes her evil." A way of putting it with gothic overtones. So overstated, and yet I know Helen was not given to exaggeration.

And so I felt—still feel—I should have done something: taken the first plane out; rushed to her aid; saved her somehow, from whatever it was, or whoever it was that prompted this letter; sent her wise counsel, at least. With so little to go on, it is difficult to say what that counsel could have been.

"I don't know if I'm doing the right thing," she writes. "Or even if I have the courage to do what I must. I remember how you mentioned 'courage' at least on one occasion before I left. I guess I dismissed the idea out of hand so that we never really talked about it. I pretended to take it on literal, physical terms to avoid getting into the 'moral' or 'psychological' courage you no doubt had in mind. At the time, it seemed all too grim: Now I'm having to come to grips. Wish me well."

After that, just her signature, "As ever, Helen."

And so, regretfully, I have to consign all that remains of my dear friend to the flames; regretfully, because there's so much unaccounted for. I will have to burn her letters along with all the other mementos, papers, and obsolete documents I've carried around like baggage all my life. From now on I have to travel light. Where I'm going, there will be no space for further doubts or unresolved issues or even memories, perhaps.

At the same time, I realize that it hasn't really been Helen that I've been saving for later all this time, but myself.

Summer, Again

23

It had helped to write to Carol. I finished my letter to her, then wrote and rewrote several times a tortured, brief note to Tej to tell him that I was okay, not to try to find me, and that I'd let him know later to what address to send my belongings, if he felt like sending them. I wrapped my camera, some film, and a few other possessions in a piece of cloth, put my passport and other important papers in the leather handbag along with the travel brochure, covered myself with my *chadhar,* and like any poor village woman, took off toward town before sunrise. I might have been on my way to sell milk or eggs.

Once in Ladopur, I wasted no time boarding a bus out of town, one that would take me far away from Majra. Not necessarily in the direction I intended finally to go. There would be time and opportunity later to change buses and destinations.

I was not the first woman eight months pregnant and loaded with baggage to take a breathless climb up the steep steps onto a bus. This was new to me, however, and I felt exhilarated at being able to do it. I found a corner seat near the back where I'd attract the least attention, and settled in to take stock of things and to rediscover during the ride that self I'd briefly resumed the acquaintance of in Delhi a few weeks earlier.

The California self. A single self. That self, I soon decided, had been a deceptive ghost that did not exist anymore. I had to let it go. At the same time, I wondered if I would always be setting out for somewhere. Would all the departures start feeling alike? Would it become easier, each new time, heading out? Would I become a constant performer on the tightrope?

A perennial walker from here to there? Would there come a time when I wouldn't make it to the other side?

Up to this moment, leaving Mama and Papa and my sisters had been as hard a thing as I'd yet dared myself to do. The time after New Year's the previous year had oozed on until I finally boarded the train for New York six long weeks later. It was Aunt Teresa who made everything all right the very day I was to leave.

"Give the kid a chance," she told Mama and Papa as we all sat at breakfast that morning before leaving for the station.

Nicoletta, Gloria, and Julia sat at table stiffly, aware that something solemn was going on, but innocent of what it was. I was going away. Ten thousand miles held no meaning for them; nor did the fact that I had no return ticket. The rest of us, trying to forget these details, applied ourselves to the task of swallowing bites of cold toast on which the butter had hardened and drinking tasteless black coffee. Mama had bought a dozen doughnuts and some Danish pastries she knew I liked. It was one last turn of the screw, those Danish pastries, and I dutifully ate one in spite of the frosting sticking like paste to the roof of my mouth and the heated dough all gummy and tasting of stale shortening.

Mama said, as I knew she would, "This is Helena's last breakfast with us for God-knows-how-long."

The last breakfast. Everything had been the last *something* for the past six weeks.

"Give the kid a chance," Aunt Teresa said again. "She's in love. That's not so bad. Everything's gonna be okay. She'll be back here along with her husband before we know it. We gotta send her off with hugs and kisses, Fran, wishes and prayers, like we all needed when we started out. Nobody's gonna cry, okay? Nobody's gonna make her feel bad today. When she gets on that train, she needs to remember happy faces all the way to New York and then some. She needs some laughs. She's gotta long trip ahead of her." She turned and looked at me then, through her bifocals. "Haven't you, sweetheart?" she said, giving me a hug.

I nodded and looked across at Mama. She was about to say something. Her eyes said it for her. And then she managed a smile. "Come back home soon, Helena," she said, having trouble getting the words out.

Nicoletta looked with China-doll eyes from one to the other of us, while Gloria and Julia stabbed their Danish pastries with listless forks.

"Mario, watta you say?" Aunt Teresa nudged Papa. "Watta you say?"

He looked at Aunt Teresa and then at me, and then tried out his old way of talking in the new and dreadful situation. "Win, lose, or draw, kid, I'm always for you. You know that," he said, attempting a smile.

And so he had been. His letters came regularly, if infrequently, and were my only link with the family on that side. He would be surprised to receive the cable I was mentally composing as I rode along in the bus through the morning that was becoming progressively hotter and dustier. The wording was important. I should not be going back defeated. I should, at the same time, give him room to say *no* if he couldn't afford the money for my return ticket. I could not even contemplate the slow torture of a return by sea. I had to go by air, and if I had known of some other way to buy the fare, I would have explored it. As it was, Papa was my only recourse. I knew he would help me if it were in his power; if his paycheck weren't already all taken up in installments to some finance company that kept him a constant captive.

By noon, I had made one change of bus and of direction and was heading northwest. Another change would see me due north by evening, if I remembered the details correctly. I'd save the cable-sending task for a large town, where the service could be relied upon, the boys on the bicycles more energetic, business transacted with more urgency. I remembered the rest house where bus passengers spent the night. I'd probably be sharing a room there with one or two other women passengers whose questions would have to be answered before we'd get any sleep, and so I gave over half an hour to anticipating what those questions might be and to inventing replies, since I wasn't good at on-the-spot fabrications.

By the time we reached Ghuntor the following morning,

I had still not sent off the cable to Papa. Fear of missing the bus, or missing connections along the way, not knowing where to find the telegraph office in a particular town, and a dozen other concerns prevented me from getting it sent. The previous day I had picked up a blank form somewhere along the way, at some town whose name I couldn't even remember. But I had kept it in my purse without filling in the message I'd prepared so carefully. I hadn't even made an attempt to do so.

There would be a long stop at Ghuntor. Last time, I recalled, we had waited for hours for the connecting bus. The memory from the recent past threatened to multiply into others and I willed it away. I had, instead, to apply myself to the present and find a post office. This was my last chance. I searched around for a quarter of an hour and found it housed in a shed clinging to the side of a mountain and manned by a village youth whose Hindi was uncertain and who knew no English at all. I waved the cable form in front of him, and he nodded an enthusiastic *yes*.

Outside the post office I sat down on a stone bench that seemed to have been made for a giant. When I began to fill in the message, the lines on the form went all queer. There was no way I could hold them still; besides, the directions were first printed in Hindi, with the English translation printed below; neither was legible because of the poor printing job. Even the familiar California address looked odd, once I had written it down. I had to assure myself that *Mr. Mario Graziani* was Papa. I began to wonder what the message would look like when it reached the other side, with white printed strips pasted on pink paper. Mama always got excited by the arrival of a telegram, taking it to mean bad news. She would cross herself before opening it.

I was ready to hand the form over to the youthful postmaster when I was interrupted by the sound of the wheels of a bus crunching over the gravel on the road above the post office. The insistent honk of its horn bounced off the opposite mountain side, returning as an echo. Past experience told me I had to be fast on my feet if I was to make it; there would be numberless villagers and pilgrims from the plains fighting for the seats. I grabbed the uncompleted cable form, stuffed it into my purse, picked up the rest of my things, and made for the bus that had just arrived from Ranikaran and would return there as soon as the driver had turned it around. It could be anywhere from two hours to two days before it appeared again.

It wasn't a very unique thing to think of doing, I said to myself when I'd settled in for the last lap of the journey. Not very original. Sending home to Papa for money. Going off in the first place. Then getting stuck. Thinking of running home to Mama and Papa when events piled up crazily. When people didn't do what you thought they were going to do, or what you considered they ought to do. Took strange stands. Became unpredictable. Finally, I thought about the possibility that every failure in life begins with a telegram home (literal or figurative) asking to be bailed out. Sending mine off would be the sign of a mediocre kind of defeat, I decided at last. It wasn't for me.

The two weeks in Ranikaran remained a period in time altogether apart. The place was small, hemmed in by mountain and river, so there was no place else to go. More days than I can say passed without anything happening but the predictable rhythm of the place beating gently away while I caught up on lost sleep and slowly came to myself again after days of traveling.

It was only after emerging from this cocoon that I woke up to the metamorphosis. I was *alone.* The sounds I awoke to were all different from the everyday sounds of Majra: strangers' voices speaking strange languages. Only occasionally did I pick up the brisk, nasal lilt of Punjabi. No voice of the sitar sang me to sleep at night or woke me in the morning like the echo of a dream. The river thrashed against boulders in its way; steam hissed from the hot springs.

The sights were unfamiliar too. New pilgrim faces appeared each afternoon after the arrival of the bus two miles below Ranikaran ashram and disappeared again, the following noon. None of them looked like anyone I knew.

The Ranikaran villagers who helped the Babaji serve the meals were rendered faceless by the similarity of their dress and speech and behavior. Only the Babaji and the old Sikh in the pink turban who distributed bedding and collected it again were reassuringly familiar. However, they carried on with their routine without reference to me. I joined the villagers when help was needed in serving food or washing utensils and spent long hours in contemplation by the side of the pool. I took warm baths in the womblike covered area which, illuminated by a single candle, was especially reserved for women. In there I duplicated in another dimension and on an amplified scale the slow, floating life of the child inside.

At night no warm body slept next to me in the bed, no arm was flung in sleep across my stomach, no legs were entwined in mine, no soft breath reached my ear, no muscular back was there to curl around. I spent the dark hours swallowing back panic with wide-open eyes, replaying that last night in Majra and reigning in, with doubtful assurances, my galloping thoughts of an uncertain future. The frightening certainty that I had, indeed, made a successful getaway left me suspended over a void with nothing holding me up but the tenuous thread of my own self-awareness. If I let go of it, I would be lost.

A week passed and each night became easier to get through. The days were more manageable. Meanwhile I had not taken any sort of action. I hadn't sent the cable to Papa and I knew I wouldn't now. There were other possibilities to be considered, and Ranikaran provided me the time and the place to think. Each day I found more ways to make myself useful to the ashram to compensate in labor for the expense of my meals and my room. I watched what others did, and in time came to discriminate between one village child and another, one face from another, and finally the names that distinguished one individual from another.

I stopped waiting for the "rescue" I had imagined during the first few days. The scene where the hero, like Charles Boyer in *Love Affair,* after a reel or two of anguished searching, finds his way at last to his lost love, to the accompaniment of a chorus and full orchestra on the soundtrack. Tej would come in breathless after the climb from the bus stop, discover me in the ashram kitchen rolling out chapatti dough, lift me up and crush me—still shaking flour from my hands—in his strong arms. "I'll do whatever you want, *meri jaan.* Whatever you say, forever and ever," he would promise. "I've been blind to your troubles in the past, but never again. This has taught me a lesson I'll never forget. Only come back. Never go away again." In real life, things didn't happen that way, and I had come to know it.

The Babaji appeared loath to be drawn into conversations that did not concern the hot springs, their constancy, the inevitability of rice and dal being cooked in half an hour. He did not ask me why I had not gone back with the same group of pilgrims I came up with nor how long I intended to stay. He accepted my presence as a matter of not-very-interesting fact and in return gave me peace.

"Would you like some tea, *beti*?" he would ask in the mornings on my coming down from the cubicle I occupied to where he sat on the veranda by the pool. "Or would you like to have your bath first?"

Later, he would recite to the pilgrims who gathered around him the same speech he had delivered to Tej and me. The occasion for unburdening my heart never came, while the need to do so gradually disappeared as one day flowed into the next.

The version of my immediate future that finally came out of all the thought I applied to it was, I hoped, workable. A great deal depended on me. I sat figuring out the details, picturing the scene against which my life and the baby's would unfold in the next few months. The baby would be born in Ranikaran. The village could be depended upon to have a midwife who would make up in skill what she lacked in hygiene. *That* could be taught in six easy lessons beforehand. I would go to Delhi when I was strong enough and find a job, a little flat, an ayah to take care of the baby.

I'd have to do all this in two months because that's when my money would in all probability run out. Once I got a job, everything would be all right. At least money would be coming in every month. Then, when I'd earned enough . . .

It was always at this point where the film broke. And that too was all right. One couldn't work out each and every detail of one's life for the next fifty years.

"The baby will be born here, if it's all right with you," I said to the Babaji one early afternoon. A group of pilgrims

203

had left just before another was to arrive. He was sitting in his usual place, outside the entrance to his cave-room. I sat down on the stone bench in front of him to have a talk before he retired for his afternoon nap.

"As you wish, *beti*," he said. "And if God wills it. Yes. But have you thought about your own comfort and the baby's? You're a foreigner, and . . ."

"I'm comfortable here, Babaji," I broke in. "But I need to know the name of the midwife in this village so that I can talk to her beforehand and call her when the time comes. I'd like to . . ."

I paused. Something had caught the Babaji's attention, because he wasn't listening or even looking at me; he was looking behind me, over my left shoulder. The same instant, I felt a kind of electrical charge zing up my spine. I turned around.

"Hari!" I cried, getting up and hurrying toward him as he crossed the bridge over the pool. "How did you know I was here?"

24

Our reunion, Tej's and mine, was not what might have been imagined. Not even by the standards I had recently come to acknowledge as true to life. The picture show was over. Hari arrived first. An advance party of one. I don't think I had really looked at him so closely since that day almost a year ago when he was there to meet Tej and me when we got down from the train at Abdullapur station. He was a man now. More confident. Less puzzled about me. Through all the family rifts and misunderstandings at Majra he'd remained a well-wisher. That was plain to see as he greeted me with obvious relief and affection that afternoon in the unlikely locale of the Ranikaran ashram.

"*Sat Sri Akal,* Bhabi," he said. And then asked "Are you all right? Is everything okay with you?"

"I'm fine, Hari," I said. "Really very well. The Babaji has looked after me like a father. He . . ." I turned around to introduce the two, but the old man had already left for his nap, and Hari and I found ourselves sitting alone on the ashram veranda. It soon became evident that he was there to plead on behalf of the whole family that I come back home.

"Majra is not the same without you, Bhabi," he began. "Mataji is sick with worry, and Pitaji beside himself. The girls can't understand, none of us can understand, why you ran away; what made you do a desperate thing like that?" He paused for breath in what was taking on the sound of a prepared speech. "Tej Bhaji hasn't eaten or slept for days. He hasn't been himself, but like some mad person, with only one idea in his head—to find you. He's been to the police, for them to try to trace you. But they were too slow. They said there was too little to go on. An old woman from Ladopur said she saw you get on a bus. It was the same morning we discovered you were gone. But she couldn't remember which bus. She wasn't even sure it was you. Tej Bhaji and I have even been to Delhi. To find out if you had been there, to the American Embassy or to the hotel you stayed at, that time in February."

He described to me how my going away had plunged the household into gloom. The details came out, not as I have put them down here, but in half-sentences, false starts, repetitions, and falterings because he wanted to get it all said, because of the oddness of our surroundings, and because of what he felt to be the urgency of the moment and the seriousness of his mission. All the while I half listened to Hari and half watched for the sight of Tej.

"How did you think of looking for me here?" I asked. "And where's your brother? Why hasn't he come?"

"He *has* come," Hari said. "He sent me ahead. He'll be here before long. He got the idea day before yesterday. It was when we got back after looking for you in Delhi. He thought you might have come up here."

Hari went on to say they had been sure they'd find me when the tea-stall owner back at the bus stop told them he had seen a foreign woman arrive with a group of pilgrims from the plains two weeks earlier.

Hari made no mention of Dilraj Kaur. How had she reacted to my flight, I wondered. Had she held a private ceremony to celebrate her victory? Waved a candle thrice over some cowrie shells? Sacrificed a toad? Stuck a doll that had my name on it with pins? It was impossible for me to put myself in her place, to experience the kind of insecurity and helplessness she must have felt all along. Nothing could assuage it. It festered on its own fears and swelled to include anxiety for her son's future, for his place, even more than for her own place, in the family and the claim to his share of its fortunes.

Tej arrived half an hour later. He came toward us in just his particular way of walking, like nobody else's in the world. I stood up, and while each of us waited for the other to speak first, Hari went off for a round of the ashram. We hesitated for a moment longer amidst the gaudy presences of Lord

Krishna, Shiva, and Parvati, and the stoic Sikh martyrs watching us from their calendar pictures on the wall.

"How are you two?" he asked finally, taking a step toward me.

"We're fine," I said, unable to restrain myself from touching his arm. "But you've lost weight."

"I haven't felt like eating," he said. "Even your cheeks have become hollow." He put his hand to my face. The palm was warm. Familiar.

"Ashram food," I said steadily, looking into his eyes. "Wholesome and plentiful, but no variation and not very tasty."

Even before I got the last words out we were in each others' arms, reaching across the expanse of my middle to achieve an embrace.

"Why did you do this to us?" he whispered against my hair. "I tried to explain what happened that night, and you wouldn't listen. Just ran away like a crazy person. Eight months pregnant. Do you know what could have happened to you? To our baby? How did you think we would've lived without each other?"

His words brought me suddenly to myself. "Tej, you want to put me on the defensive with questions like that," I said, holding him at arm's length. "But it won't work. I've had a lot of time to think in the past two weeks. I've reached a measure of peace here. I've come to decisions about the future, the baby's and mine. . . ."

"What do you mean, the baby's and yours?" he said angrily. "It's my baby too; don't forget that. Its future is as important to me as it is to you." He paused for a moment and added in a quiet voice, "As a matter of fact, your future is as important to me as my own is."

"Life in Majra is impossible for me," I went on, slowly picking my way through words, and hoping by the very saying of them that some magic might be wrought to make everything all right again, to turn back the clock; wipe out the time between then and now. "You and I and Dilraj Kaur locked in that impossible relationship. I was never able to get you to understand what was happening. You never listened

207

to me. And now, even if the things that happened the other night were as you say, I still couldn't go on like I have."

"Talk about not listening, you refused to hear me out then," he said. "The least you can do is hear me out now."

I waited for him to go on.

"When I came back from the harvesting, I stopped by her room because she called me. I wanted to see if she was okay."

"And . . .?"

"I didn't know what to make of her. She was getting ready for bed; she was half-undressed. I'll tell you frankly it wasn't the first time I had seen her like that. We did play at being 'married' for a little while before I left for the States. But she soon discovered that neither I nor anyone else could ever take Hardev Bhaji's place."

"And what did *you* discover?" I asked.

"I was put off. It was like making love to an older sister. We couldn't get used to each other as husband and wife. I thought going to California solved everything."

"But then you were in her room that night, and . . ."

"She wanted to put this charm around my neck. I thought, okay; let her do it, and let me get out of here."

"And then I came 'bursting in'; that's how you described it. As if I had no business there, and you did."

"Well, you know the rest," he said.

"Yes."

"And Hari has told you what things have been like at home ever since?" he asked, willing me, with his eyes, to understand.

"I still can't come back, Tej. Not to *that*," I said.

"Why not?"

"Don't you see? It's that whole Dilraj Kaur scene," I said, looking him straight in the eye. "I don't know how I could make my meaning clearer: I've quit the place."

"But . . ."

"I've quit the place, that's how strongly I feel. She's taken over. First it was the kitchen. And that's okay. Then she turned the family against me, or tried to. Now she'd like to shove me out of my own bed. Yours and mine. Of course, she probably still thinks of it as *hers* and yours. When does a marriage between two people cease to be? Does it ever? She'd like to reclaim the place she feels I usurped."

208

"You make the bedroom into a political arena with this talk," he said. "Every word you say makes our life together nothing compared to the maneuvres of a desperate woman. I wish you'd shut up."

"Have I said anything that's not true?"

"Maybe not. But you have left out a whole world in your thinking. Our world. Yours and mine. And you've left me out!"

"Have I?"

"If you don't know it now, you never will. Do I have to nail a declaration on the wall every time you have a row with Bhabiji that I love *you,* want to be with *you,* can't imagine life without *you?*"

We needed time to breathe, back away for a minute. Tej turned away to study the calendar pictures. Krishna was still playing the flute, as he had eight months ago, for an adoring Radha, and Shiva sat in meditation while the Ganges poured out of his hair.

"You didn't give me a chance to tell you," he said, breaking the silence. "Bhabiji will be going away soon. I've talked to Mataji and Pitaji, and I've written to her brother Arjun Singh in Faridkot. I've told him she needs a rest, a long one, and a change of scene."

"She'd have to come back some day. And the whole thing would begin all over again," I said. "We need to start a life of our own, Tej. Just you and I and the baby. In our own house. Or flat. Or whatever. If we continue to stay on in Majra with Mataji and Pitaji we'll always be irresponsible children. Depending on them for everything. We'd never have a chance to grow up."

"Are you making your return conditional on our moving out?" he asked.

"If you want to look at it that way, yes. Job or no job; money or no money. We can't wait. We've got to give ourselves a chance on our own."

"You feel that strongly then?" he said. He looked surprised, a little bewildered. "I never realized how you felt until you ran off like that."

"But you know now," I said.

209

"All the same, Helen, you can't have it all your way. You have to give a little, take a little. Trust me. We'll work things out."

What the compromises were had to be thrashed out later, because Hari was back from his rounds, the Babaji had got up from his nap, and a fresh batch of pilgrims was due any time now.

25

The idea of keeping my reentry into Majra low-key didn't work out. I went into labor the very night of our return, an event that threw the already excited household into top gear. Since no one wanted the baby to be born on a bullock cart on the way to the Ladopur Mission Hospital, Ina Mae Scott was called in. She arrived by jeep half an hour after she received Pitaji's urgent message, her medicine bag and her driver-helper in tow.

That night a few splatterings of hot raindrops sent up the great pungent earth-odor I remembered from the previous year. They settled the dust that whirled through the sky as the winds relentlessly transferred the Rajasthan desert, grain by grain, to East Punjab. Through the long hours of the night and early morning I counted these drops of the first premonsoon shower one by one.

Dilraj Kaur was there when I came out of labor at day-break. She entered the room as if nothing had happened between us and played out her role as a woman in the house with diligence and detachment. I wondered if anybody other than me noticed her thinness and the feverish look in her eyes as some fanatical fire consumed her from within.

We called our son "Bawa" until the time we'd have the leisure to choose a name for him from the *Guru Granth Sahib,* and hold a proper namegiving ceremony.

During the next few days Pitaji sent off telegrams to relatives in far-flung villages in Punjab and Rajasthan and distributed baskets of sweets to local friends and acquaintances who arrived by the score to congratulate the family and have a look at Bawa. The Tehsildar and his wife were the first to arrive, in their horsedrawn carriage, at ten o'clock, the morn-

ing after Bawa's birth. Mataji saw to it that I drank lots of
ginger tea and ate plenty of butter, dried dates, and sweets
rolled in sesame seeds and almonds. She also regaled the
women, each fresh arrival, with the story of what a difficult
birth it had been.

"*Choti bahu* was in labor all night. The whole night," she
said, exaggerating things slightly. "The Mission Miss-Sahib
herself came from Ladopur to deliver the child."

Rano and Goodi took turns dressing and undressing Bawa,
giving him oil rubs and combing with a little blue comb the
tuft of black hair on the top of his head. Nikku spent long
moments watching Bawa sleep, waiting impatiently for this
fat infant to grow up so that he would have a permanent
playmate. In a letter to Mama and Papa I wrote that Bawa
was so appropriated by everyone that Tej and I scarcely got
any time with him. "We're mere custodians," I wrote.

On the third day relatives started arriving from out of
town: the Uncle and Aunt from Amritsar, aged parents of
Prem, Sukhdev, and Jeet; a second cousin from Ludhiana
who owned a factory which manufactured men's underwear;
and the sister-in-law of Mataji's real cousin-brother from
Bhatinda (the sister-in-law was from Bhatinda, not the
cousin-brother) who had been a famous beauty and at
seventy-three still dressed in the height of fashion to the delight of some and the disapproval of others.

Two young boys had to be brought in from the village as
added help in the kitchen, and they settled down with Udmi
Ram and Chotu peeling potatoes and exchanging gossip.
Gian and Ram Piari handed out rolls of bedding that had
been packed away for just such an occasion in Mataji's big
quilt boxes in the storeroom. Ten charpoys were borrowed
from neighbors to put up guests for the several nights they
were expected to stay.

On the fourth day after Bawa's arrival I was brought out
ceremoniously and seated on the downstairs veranda outside
our room. An upholstered chair from the sitting room had
been brought out for the purpose. For a brief moment I felt
a chill run through me that could have originated from a
Himalayan peak; instead it was Dilraj Kaur watching me from
the upstairs balcony outside her room. The next moment,
Mataji was seeing to it that I sat straight in my chair, the

better to set off the new gold necklace and six bangles she and Pitaji had presented me with, and the new suit she had had stitched for the occasion. It was stiff with gold embroidery and still had the smell of the tailor's shop—a combination of stale marijuana smoke and sewing machine oil.

"Sit here," she said to me as a parade of village women entered the compound. Each of them carried a spray of paddy and laid it at my feet.

"What am I supposed to do?" I asked Rano.

"Just sit. Smile. They've come to sing and dance for you, Bhabi," she said, "and to see Bawa." She placed him, wiggly and red-faced and dressed in his finest, on my lap. It was a scene that could not have been possible without Bawa in it, nor me, his mother. It was dismaying to realize I had achieved status at last, not by dint of mastering some exotic skill, but by doing one of the most ordinary things in the world: having a baby.

Uncle Gurnam Singh had the farthest to come and so arrived last, in a swirl of dust, in his jeep, with his retinue. By then I was up and about and was there with the rest of the family to greet them.

I watched the baggage being unloaded from the jeep and passengers piling out, laughing and talking and shouting *Sat Sri Akal*. Instead of Shiv Kanwar Singh, Brother John, and Santji, there were other people accompanying Uncle Gurnam Singh this time. Two women and a little girl called "Baby" alighted along with Surinder, Uncle's youngest son. One of the women had to be Aunt Gursharan Kaur, the other perhaps a younger sister or cousin of Aunt's. The latter stepped down from the jeep and looked circumspectly around. I guessed this was her first visit to Majra. Tej and Hari and Pitaji formed a group in the yard with the other men surrounding the laughing Uncle Gurnam Singh who had just had something witty to say and was appreciating his own joke.

The women were all herded into our room to have a look at Bawa. Aunt Gursharan Kaur, a greying, comfortable woman with heavy-lidded brown eyes and a cheerful smile, stood half a head taller than the others around the cradle. Their talk and laughter woke up Bawa, and he began to cry.

"*Na, na, beta,*" Aunt Gursharan Kaur said. She picked him

up and held him against her ample bosom until he quietened down again. She continued to pat his back long after he stopped crying.

"He looks just like Tej did as a baby," she declared to the company at large.

"But he has Helen's eyes," Mataji said. "Everyone says so."

Every woman in the room, including Bibi Harminder, as the young woman along with Aunt Gursharan Kaur was called, had her own idea about who Bawa looked like.

"He's just like Mataji," the young woman declared. She was short and sturdy, with strong arms, hands used to hard work, a cautious expression, and a discreet sense of rank. It was plain to see from the start that she knew how to make herself useful and accommodating to elders.

Aunt Gursharan was soon at the heart of things. She had a way of busying herself with various small undertakings which consumed time marvelously and provided unending interest to the other women and girls. When she embarked on a cooking project it would take hours, perhaps half a day, and watching Aunt prepare halwa, everybody's favorite dessert, offered a minor spectacle. She sat in the middle of the kitchen on a squat, brightly painted stool, giving orders to Udmi Ram in her soft, persuasive voice, while Bibi Harminder hulled almonds, ground spices, and stirred concoctions bubbling on two or three fires at a time. Aunt went on unperturbed when the wheat, parching in melted butter, got too brown. As I watched her, I kept thinking she couldn't possibly be as happy and contented as she appeared to be, given the circumstances of her life with Uncle. And his concubine.

And then, of course, the plain truth bubbled up and boiled over like a pan of milk forgotten on the stove. Bibi Harminder was the concubine! I wanted to laugh. At my own dull-wittedness for not recognizing her in the first place, her and her little girl. At Uncle's audacity in bringing them along. At the two women themselves, neatly complementing each other, dividing up the work and the responsibilities in the kitchen; sharing the man between them, whatever little time he had for them. They had more to do with each other than either of them had to do with Uncle, preoccupied as he was

214

with his farm, his political career, and his tours around the countryside. Bibi Harminder must have come as a welcome pair of extra hands in the running of his overburdened household.

And it had worked. They succeeded where Dilraj Kaur and I had failed. They shared the same values, had the same expectations, were propped up by the same underlying beliefs. Dilraj Kaur and I were like bits of matter spun off stars from different galaxies. Neither of us knew where the other was coming from as we whizzed toward each other on a calamitous course. I knew in that instant that, much as she had tried to force the comparison between me and Uncle's concubine, she could not make me out to be Tej's concubine. It had been foolish of me to fear that she could.

But here in this kitchen, watching this world of women in whose orbit I myself was spinning, I wanted to sing out in celebration. To cheer Mataji most of all! I remembered her earlier expressions of disapproval and outrage at Uncle bringing his concubine into the house. Now she accepted Bibi Harminder and her daughter "Baby" as a matter of fact. Uncle had seen fit to bring them along, and so they were guests, welcome, but with not quite the same fervor, perhaps, as the others were. Mataji's about-face had to do with something indefinable, with the way each person's thread is woven into the complex fabric of life, once that fabric is on the weaving frame and the shuttle in motion. No questions asked. No more than one would "question" the pattern of a particular shawl on a loom.

The halwa for tea was ready now. Aunt Gursharan Kaur had lifted the big cooking vessel off the stove and handed it over to Bibi Harminder, who ladled out the sweet. No one remarked about Dilraj Kaur's absence from an activity she'd normally be part of until Goodi ran breathlessly into the kitchen, swinging wide the screen door and allowing it to bang shut.

"Bawa's hair's been cut!" she exclaimed. "Rano Didi and I were going to comb his hair, and the little bit on top is missing!"

"Just snipped off!" Rano said, hurrying in after Goodi.

215

Epilogue

There's talk of Tej and me moving to Delhi with Bawa. To start a new life on our own, just the three of us. Tej says Majra will always be home, and he's right, in a sense. But then again it may be that Delhi will be home. Or somewhere else. It may be that home is a state of mind where repose holds sway, where the series of stills we perceive as motion ceases, where wonder at the constancy of things lies at the heart of a sure feeling of having arrived finally.

Mataji and Pitaji have become reconciled to the idea of our going, and they're already talking about finding a bride for Hari. Majra continues to be a place where only deaths occasionally occur suddenly. Everything else takes time. Dilraj Kaur left for Faridkot a week ago, a full fortnight after Bawa's lock of hair, tied up in a red cloth, was discovered in her room. She took Nikku with her. Her brother Arjun Singh came to escort her to his village. She took a lot of baggage—almost all her belongings—as her stay there is to be indefinite. Nikku cried when he said good-bye to Tej. As they passed through the gate that Gian swung open for them and started out onto the road to Abdullapur, Nikku cast me a look over his shoulder that was half appeal, half apology. For what? On whose behalf? Mataji called him back for one final hug. She wiped the tears from her eyes with her dupatta as she sent him hurrying after his mother and uncle.

Each day Pitaji scans the skies for signs of rain clouds. The air is heavy and laden with moisture, the white heat clamped down under a lid of dust haze. It is that time of year again. The leaves on the trees and in the hedges have turned crisp in the hot winds of summer and wear a layer of fine dust. The fields have become dry, cracked tracts of land covered

216

with stubble left after the wheat harvest. The hours from dawn to dusk are spent indoors, listening to the wind and breathing in dust particles that find their way through the smallest cracks in the doorjambs and window frames. Inside the thick walls of the house, we try to keep cool as we wait for the monsoon.

If Tej and I and Bawa go to live in Delhi, it will be like this: We will leave some hot night, in the middle of the night, to catch the 2 A.M. train from Abdullapur station. My red steamer trunk, boxes of kitchen utensils and crockery from Mataji's storeroom, suitcases of clothes, thermoses, and bedrolls will be piled high onto the bullock cart. Hari and the Amritsar cousins will walk with us the four miles, taking turns carrying Bawa and stopping to lift the cart out of a rut when its wheels get stuck in the mud.

Good-byes will have to be quick, because the train to Delhi stops for only five minutes.